# "This is a rather evening for a bu I must admit I am quite curious as to why you're here."

Paine leaned back in his chair, steepling his hands and trying to look as if he weren't aroused by the sight of her magnificent figure or the sound of her voice.

He saw the long column of her neck work briefly as she swallowed. For the first time since she'd entered the establishment, he felt her resolve waver.

"I need you to ruin me." The words came out in a rush, and a light blush colored her flawless alabaster cheeks.

"Ruin?" Paine quirked an eyebrow. "What do you mean by 'ruin'? Shall I ruin you at the gaming tables? I can arrange to have you lose any amount of your choosing."

Her gaze met his evenly, in all seriousness, her courage having returned in full force now that she'd begun talking. "I don't wish to lose any money. I wish to lose my virginity. I want you to ruin me in bed."

\* \* \*

***Notorious Rake, Innocent Lady***
**Harlequin® Historical #896—May 2008**

# UNDONE!

Loosening the laces.

Scandalizing the Ton!

Delicious stories to seduce your senses...

This month

Willful debutante Julia Prentiss seeks out the Ton's legendary Black Rake, Paine Ramsden, for one night of passion that will free her from an unsavory marriage in

*Notorious Rake, Innocent Lady*
by Bronwyn Scott

Look for more sizzling tales of seduction from Harlequin Historical

Coming soon!

# BRONWYN SCOTT

## NOTORIOUS RAKE, INNOCENT LADY

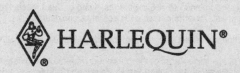

TORONTO • NEW YORK • LONDON
AMSTERDAM • PARIS • SYDNEY • HAMBURG
STOCKHOLM • ATHENS • TOKYO • MILAN • MADRID
PRAGUE • WARSAW • BUDAPEST • AUCKLAND

ISBN-13: 978-0-373-29496-1
ISBN-10:    0-373-29496-4

NOTORIOUS RAKE, INNOCENT LADY

Copyright © 2008 by Nikki Poppen

This edition published by arrangement with Harlequin Books S.A.

www.eHarlequin.com

**Printed in U.S.A.**

## Acknowledgments:

Books aren't simply the product of one person's writing but that of countless others who make the writing process successful. Thanks to all of you who support my work.

Thanks to Michele Ann Young and her research assistance on Regency-era bankruptcy practices.

Thanks to Ellen Holt, my personal speed-reader, who is happy to be a sounding board for early drafts.

Thanks to my kids, Rowan and Catie, for playing outside every afternoon so I could write.

And to Baby Bronwyn, who took extra-long naps when I needed them most.

Thanks to my whole family, who support each of my projects unstintingly with their interest.

Thanks to my PEO chapter for their support and publicity.

Thanks to my husband for being the best there ever was.

Thanks to my great coworkers at the college:
Leon, Ann, Connie and the rest, who celebrate each cover with me and listen to me ramble about new plots.

Special thanks to my agent Scott Eagan,
who knew exactly where I belonged.

Extra special thanks to my editor, Joanne Carr, for all her attention to detail and her unique brand of polish, which gives each book the sheen of perfection.

## Dedication:

For Scott and Joanne, my agent and editor respectively, who made my goal of being a Harlequin author before my 40th birthday come true!

And for the kids: Rowan, Catie and Bronwyn. Remember you can have your (birthday) cake and eat it too. Someday when you're old enough, that will make sense.

# Chapter One

*London, early May 1829*

She would not be sold like a prized mare at Tattersalls! Julia Prentiss's elegantly coiffed head swivelled in disbelief between Uncle Barnaby and Mortimer Oswalt, the lecherous old cit who had come to offer for her. She could hardly countenance the conversation that flowed around her as if she were not standing in the centre of her uncle's study listening, nor had a mind of her own and was quite capable of speaking for herself.

'I would, of course, provide a handsome bride price for your niece. Say, fifteen thousand pounds.' Mortimer Oswalt spread his hands confidently over the purple expanse of his waistcoat, which gave him the appearance of an overripe grape. He leaned back in his chair, perusing Julia with his dissipated blue eyes, still bloodshot from a night on the town.

Fifteen thousand pounds! Julia fought back a surge of inappropriate comments. How dare he offer for her in the same manner one might offer for goods on the dock or at an auction house. The force of his vile gaze made her skin clammy. She could not bear to imagine how his hands would feel against her skin. But surely there was no sense conjuring nightmares that would not come to pass.

Julia turned her frantic gaze on Uncle Barnaby. Uncle Barnaby would certainly refuse the offer in spite of how advanced the talks had become. After all, Mortimer Oswalt was not from their circles. Her uncle was Viscount Lockhart, a noted politician in the House of Lords. Oswalt was merely a London merchant. A *wealthy* London merchant, to be sure, but still a merchant, regardless of the fact that his annual income was at least triple theirs. The Lockhart title might not be possessed of a fortune, but they were peers and peers did not marry cits.

'Fifteen thousand pounds, you say? That is quite generous, a very respectful offer. I am sure we can come to an agreeable accord.' Uncle Barnaby gave a resigned smile, carefully looking anywhere but at her.

Julia was dumbfounded. What had possessed him to *sell* her to this old man? She would have dug her toes into the carpet she stood upon if it had had any pile left on it with which to do so. It was time to speak up. This ridiculous notion—nay, this repulsive notion—had gone much too far for her liking. Julia summoned her best manners.

'I respectfully decline.'

Her voice was sufficiently loud to be heard. It cut across the two men's conversation. Incredulously, both men shot her quelling glances and continued their discussion.

'Five thousand pounds now and ten thousand after she is certified by my physician. I will have a draft drawn and deposited for you this afternoon. My physician will return to town in five days. We can do the necessary examinations then and I will write a second draft to you immediately upon his surety of her condition.' Oswalt was all brusque business in spite of the intimacies of his contract.

Julia blanched at his coarse requirements. She stared directly at her uncle and was gratified to see that he wavered over such terms, but only slightly.

'I can vouch for my niece's chastity. I assure you that such indelicate proceedings are not needed.' Uncle Barnaby coughed with embarrassment at such frank discussion.

Mortimer Oswalt shook his bald pate. 'I must insist. I have not made a fortune in business dealings without making absolutely sure of the quality of my investment. Let me remind you, I will be sixty in November. My first two wives were unable to give me the heir I required. My medical advisers confirm that whatever prior difficulties have occurred in that area, a virgin wife would overcome those concerns. I must have an heir quickly. My bride must be of virgin stock and must be quite capable of conceiving and birthing a child in short order.' He fixed Uncle Barnaby with an intimidating eye. 'I will pay the family an extra five thousand pounds upon the birth of my child.'

Julia watched in horrified fascination as her uncle capitulated to the bribe. Well, she was not dazzled so easily.

'I will not consider it!' She stamped her foot for emphasis, making sure the men could not ignore her a second time. 'Uncle, I cannot be married under duress. There are new laws. The Betrothal Act of 1823 allows people to marry out of free will.' It was a weak appeal and she knew it. Legislation was only enforced when one had an advocate or the means to acquire one. She had neither.

Uncle Barnaby opened his mouth to scold, but Oswalt raised a hand to stall his reprimand. 'Lockhart, allow me to explain it to her. She is to be my wife soon enough and must learn to take direction from her husband. Young women are a sheltered lot and must be tutored in the ways of the world.'

Julia fought the urge to cringe. It would be a cold day in hell before she took 'direction' or anything else from the lecherous likes of Mortimer Oswalt. She struck a defiant pose, disgusted that Uncle Barnaby demurred.

Oswalt continued. 'Miss Prentiss, the subtleties of this arrangement may have escaped your notice. Young ladies like yourself are often not aware of the rigours associated with maintaining the lifestyle you take for granted—the horses, the country home, the gowns, the entertainments and all the fal-lals a young woman expects as her right.

'It is especially difficult to raise a beautiful girl like yourself since it is much more expensive to accommodate her needs. A lovely girl stands out. She cannot afford to be seen in the same gowns as a wallflower who isn't noticed. A pretty girl must always be shown to her best advantage. In short, a lovely daughter or, in your case, a lovely niece, can become an asset to the family.

'Your uncle has fallen into need of such an asset. His coffers are empty. There is no one who will advance him any further loans. He has mortgaged all he can simply to lease this *borrowed* town house and to give you *one* Season. You are the last pearl left to the Lockhart title. Failure to make a financially advantageous match on your part will land your aunt and uncle and cousins in dun territory, to say nothing of yourself. You will suffer the deprivations with them.' Oswalt finished his lecture and began picking his nails. 'They have given you this Season not merely for your personal enrichment, but in hopes of getting a return on their years of investment.'

'Tell me it's not true, Uncle?' Julia demanded, whirling on the poor man. Oswalt's disclosures had discomfited him and he seemed to shrink in the leather chair he occupied behind the desk. Julia's throat constricted in terror at the morbid truth.

'It is true. I cannot deny any scrap of it. Our pockets are to let. We need Oswalt's offer.'

'There must be another way! I do not love him. I will *not* grow to love him. He is a despicable old man to buy a bride in this way.' Julia gave her tongue free rein, not caring that Oswalt sat feet away, absorbed in his nail picking.

'Julia! Hush. This outburst is most unladylike,' her uncle admonished. He craned his neck to speak around her and she could see the fear in his eyes that Oswalt would retract his offer at the display of her temper.

Julia put her hands on her hips, ready to do battle. 'What about Cousin Gray's ship? Surely the payoff from that cargo will see our problems resolved.'

'Gray's venture is fraught with risk. It is a gamble. I would rather bet on a sure thing.' Uncle Barnaby gave her a terse scolding. 'Remember your manners, Julia. It is not good *ton* to speak of money in company.'

'You don't seem to mind. You and Oswalt have divided me up like so many stock dividends on the exchange.' The comment went beyond the pale, but if a temper tantrum got her out of this unholy arrangement, then so be it.

Oswalt was not fazed. He gave Julia all his attention. 'Ah, I've got myself a cinnamon-haired virago, have I? Perhaps all that hot blood is what I need to warm myself. My dear, I welcome your passion and I care not a whit if you love me. I certainly don't love you, nor do I intend to cultivate affection for you. I merely need a well-bred virgin in my bed from a family who will accept my offer. All that aside, it will be exciting to tame you to my hand. Should all go well with my physician, I'll have a special licence in hand by week's end and we'll be wed by Sunday.'

'My wife will want to give the wedding breakfast,' Uncle Barnaby put in, relaxing again now that the deal had not been retracted.

Oswalt gave a gracious nod. 'My new bride will enjoy a last chance to associate with family and friends before we depart.' He fixed Julia with a crawling stare filled with a wealth of meaning. 'I will have no desire to stay in London, where the pleasures of the Season might detract from our marriage. We will journey promptly to my country home in the Lake District. It's very remote and well supplied. We won't be bothered by outside interruptions. Once we have good news to share, I will return to town.'

Julia swallowed hard. His libidinous intent was clear. She was to be locked away in the country. Her only task in life would be to service his base needs and produce an heir for his cit's fortune. She was nineteen and her life was about to be over.

She gave them each a curt nod of her head. 'I give you good day', then she turned hard on her heel and exited the room before either of them could see the fright they'd wrought in her with their thoughtless negotiations.

Once in her room, Julia locked the door and leaned against its solid oak panelling, taking comfort from the thickness of the wood. The little ormolu clock on the table beneath the window suggested the whole reprehensible interview had taken a short twenty minutes. It was barely eleven o'clock in the morning and her life was nearly ruined. The good news was that her life was only 'nearly' ruined.

It could have been worse, she supposed. Oswalt and her uncle could have signed the contracts already. Oswalt could have arrived with a licence and vicar in tow and married her in the study.

Julia shuddered and thought uncharitably that the

scenario was unlikely since his coveted physician wouldn't have been on hand to certify her virginal status. Five days. That was all the time left to her, barring the unforeseen circumstance that the physician return to town earlier or that Mortimer Oswalt's need for haste caused him to engage another physician who wasn't on holiday.

This was a time for action unless she reconciled herself to a life under Oswalt's rule and hoped he didn't live very long. It was clear from events in the study that neither protests nor legislation would avail her now. It was true, a law had been passed that allowed people to marry without parental consent, but it didn't *prevent* parental arrangement of her marriage to another.

Her uncle's financial situation had been made painfully clear as well as the reason for her Season in London. She was the one thing her uncle had left to pawn. He'd used her on the Marriage Mart to garner an offer that would save the family from penury.

Not for the first time, Julia cursed her unusual beauty. Ever since she'd turned fourteen and started to come into her womanly form, her looks had held an appeal for men that she could not understand. When she looked in the mirror, she saw a normal girl with green eyes that tilted up slightly at the corners, a mouth that might be described as wide, and a heap of red-brown curls her cousins often teased looked like the hue of autumn leaves. But there'd been local callers aplenty at the Grange where they lived when she started receiving last Christmas and her dance card had been full at the local assemblies. It had been the same in London after her presentation at court.

She knew, although it was difficult to admit, that this proposal from Oswalt wasn't the first time her uncle had used her looks to ward off a financial situation. It had never been as dire as it was now, but he'd sent her to the village on several occasions, telling her to talk to the merchants to whom he owed money, to see if they'd extend his credit a little longer.

Julia paced the chamber, her fright giving way to anger. She would not allow herself be used again in such a shameless manner. They would have to tie her up and drag her from this house in order to see her wed to Oswalt. She stopped pacing. It would come to exactly that, she was sure of it. Dragging her to the altar, literally, would be just one of the many indignities she would be put through this week if she remained.

Her options hit her with startling clarity. If she stayed at her uncle's rented town house as a virginal débutante, she would have no way to fight her wedding to Oswalt. There was nothing for it. She would have to find a way on her own to break the contract. There would be severe consequences, but she would suffer them.

Immediately, her mind raced over her options. The most obvious option was to run away. Where could she go? Who could help her? She sat down on the bed and sighed. She had no answers to any of those questions, but it hardly mattered. She was far too bright to ignore the reality. If she was discovered at any point, she would be brought back to London and forced to fulfil her uncle's contract.

No, running away wasn't a valid choice. Julia prided herself on being practical. If she was honest now, she had to admit that the prospect of successfully eluding Oswalt, who would most likely hire professionals to hunt her down, was a slim one indeed. She had learned much during her short time in London, but she had not learned enough to hide herself indefinitely, or at least until her twenty-fourth birthday, which marked the end of her uncle's guardianship. Even then, she wasn't certain being four and twenty would nullify her uncle's contract with Oswalt.

She stood up and started pacing again. 'Think, Julia, think. How do you get out of the contract?' She mumbled to herself. She could use the 1823 legislation and marry another. Her uncle couldn't stop her. She discarded that notion immediately. Where would she find a husband in five days who would be willing to risk marriage against a pre-existing contract?

A husband might be too ambitious on short notice, but one didn't need a husband to be ruined. She could cast aspersions on her suitability. That option might work. A plan began to form.

There was a rout tonight at Lady Moffat's. It would be well attended and many of the beaus who made up her court would be there. She would lure one of them out on to the terrace, coax a walk in the garden, flirt with him a bit and make sure they were found in a compromising situation.

Yes.

No.

Julia shook her head. The only way that would work would be if Oswalt cried off in the heat of his anger over being cuckolded before the ink dried on the contract. He might not care. He might not believe her and insist on the examination anyway and the physician would discover her hoax. The idea left too much to chance. Besides, even in her dire straits, she couldn't lower herself to be like her uncle and use an innocent pawn in a deceitful game. She couldn't countenance one of her swains being used so poorly at her whim.

She must be thoroughly ruined in order to ensure the contract would be void. She must be ruined tonight and back in the morning to prove it. Then Oswalt would be thwarted in a very final manner. Julia tapped a finger on her chin. How did one get ruined quickly?

There was prostitution, of course. She could saunter into Covent Garden and offer herself to the first man who came along. But that wasn't much of an option. She knew from a stern lecture she'd accidentally overheard Cousin Gray give his younger brothers about the importance of being selective in 'satisfying their urges' that people could get infected with sexually related diseases. Unfortunately, Gray had seen her before she could learn much more. But while all the nuances of catching such a disease were beyond her realm of knowledge, she didn't think it was much of a trade to risk infection and what Gray had termed as 'certain lingering death' for being Oswalt's enslaved wife. At least with Oswalt, there was the chance he would die soon. With the other, there was no chance of any redemption on the horizon.

Common prostitution might be out of the question, but the direction was correct. Julia turned at the wall and paced another length of the room, veering around the bed to the window. She'd also heard vague, scandalous references from her male cousins regarding brothels that held virgin auctions. That was a distinct possibility. She didn't know precisely what such an event entailed, but she would *definitely* be compromised.

Julia's stomach clenched and she experienced a wave of nausea at the import of what she meant to do. Could she go through with it? Could she give herself to an unknown man? Would that be any better than the indignities Oswalt's proposal forced upon her?

The truth was, she found her options as abhorrent as marriage to Oswalt. It was positively terrifying to imagine the consequences of her choices. If she chose to run away, she'd be running away from a lot more than Oswalt. She'd be shut out of society for ever. No one would dare countenance a friendship with a woman who had done what she was contemplating. There would be no husband or children of her own in the future. Such action could not be erased. Her family would have nothing to do with her. After this, she would be irrevocably on her own.

She would be free. Entirely left to her own devices.

Julia sat down hard on the bed, momentarily stunned by the revelation. Freedom had suddenly become quite expensive. It was clear now that freedom would cost her more than embarrassment at a brothel and an uncomfortable confrontation with her uncle. Those things would be over in a week. But she would keep paying for the rest of her life, and life, the way she knew it, would be over for good.

Her life would be over for good with Oswalt, too. No matter what she chose to do, it was a certainty that everything was going to change irrevocably this week. She was at a crossroads whether she wanted this to be so or not. She wished Cousin Gray was here to talk things through with her. But Julia supposed she'd better get used to being alone and relying on no one but herself. It was going to be her lot in life. Today might be the last day she had to decide her fate. Would she put her faith in her own capabilities to make her way in the world or would she put herself into Oswalt's hands?

Better the devil you know? Not this time. She would summon her courage and take matters into her own hands.

Resigned and more than a little bit frightened, Julia bit her lip and began to think through the only choice open to her. It would have to be the auction. In her mind's eye, she could see her strategy unfolding.

She would convince her aunt and uncle that she was accepting, even glad of the decision they'd made on her behalf. She would call for the carriage and tell her aunt and uncle that she wanted to share the good news of her betrothal with her friend, Elise Farraday. Hmm. She'd better make sure of the weather first.

Julia drew aside the curtains at the window and peered outside. Good. The morning fog was clearing away to reveal a blue sky of late spring. The driver would believe her if she asked to be dropped a few streets from Elise's home in order to walk and enjoy the lovely day. Then she would make her escape and wend her way through the streets to Covent Garden and from there to the finer brothels of London where she'd make her plea. By morning she would be ruined.

By a stranger.

In humiliating circumstances.

From which there would be no turning back.

It was a plan.

It was her only choice.

*Only?*

The word gave Julia pause. As a rule, she did not believe in dichotomous thinking. Life was far too complicated to narrow the world's complexities into a mere two categories of black and white, yes and no, true or false, do or do not.

Was there another way? A more private way? Julia felt cowardly to even consider it, but perhaps there was a way to be ruined and to preserve discovery unless forced to reveal her fate beyond the confines of her uncle's contract? If so, she'd much prefer it to the public exposure of an auction and the risk of someone recognising her, the risk of being revealed before the deed could be accomplished. The spark of a counter-plan flickered to life in the back of her mind and gathered impetus.

Another way.

Another man.

None of the young bucks that peopled her débutante's court would qualify. Unbidden, there came to mind a blurred image of a man she had encountered once—she couldn't use the word 'met' for she'd only seen him from a distance at a crowded rout one of her first nights out in London. But whispers about his presence had made the rounds of the ballroom readily enough and for once no one thought about editing their words in front of débutantes. Indeed, the opposite was nearly true. Mothers apparently felt their pristine daughters needed to know about the dangers this man posed.

He was Paine Ramsden, third son of an earl, known in less charitable circles as a dark rake with a reputation so black he could not be countenanced in polite society. Julia had learned quickly that he attended the rout solely as a favour to his aunt, the Dowager Marchioness of Bridgerton, Lily Branbourne, who insisted he was her favourite nephew, regardless of the public outcry against his morals.

Julia smiled to herself. By repute, Paine Ramsden was an irresponsible charmer who was loose with his affections and his finances. There were other reports, too, circling the ballroom that night—darker rumours that went beyond the usual complaints of womanising and wastrel tendencies—rumours of time abroad in foreign lands as penance for his involvement in a duel over a woman. The rumours didn't end there. It was quietly reported that since his return he'd been living hedonistically on the shadowy fringes of the *demi-monde,* having bought a tumbledown gambling hell of his own to support himself.

Julia didn't care two figs for his proclivities. The more debauched he was, the less likely he would be smitten with a case of misplaced honour in the morning. Paine Ramsden it would be. She was sure of her course now. She had only to find him and convince him to ruin her. For the latter, she had her pearl earbobs tucked in a small bag to provide any additional financial inducement he would need to see the deed done. A gambler like him would know where to pawn them. Yes, the latter would be easy. Based on his poor social standing, it would be harder to do the former.

She might not know where he'd be, but she had a good idea of where he wouldn't be. He wouldn't be at any of the soirées or *musicales* scheduled for the evening. He wouldn't be at any of the fancy gentleman's clubs or gaming establishments on St James's. The gossip she'd heard maintained that he took rooms on Jermyn Street. There was little chance he'd be there at the time she planned to seek him out, but that was where she would start. A landlady or a neighbour might know his direction for the evening or be able to guide her to one of his favorite haunts. True, she didn't know which of the bachelor establishments he lived at, but if she had to go door to door asking landlords, then that's what she'd do. That time of night, the bachelor tenants would most likely all be out carousing and there would be few home to note her presence.

Julia cast another glance at the clock. Eight hours until dark. Eight hours to convince her aunt and uncle of her acceptance of their decision and that she wanted to stay home that evening to work on her trousseau. No. That sounded too suspicious, given that she despised needlework. Better to go with them and give them the slip at the rout tonight. Lady Moffat's entertainment was bound to be a crush and her aunt and uncle were not vigilant chaperons once her dance card was full.

It should be easy to clandestinely slip away through a back-garden gate without being missed for some time. Her uncle would be in the card room, oblivious to what was happening in the ballroom, and her aunt would be caught up in conversation with her friends. Her aunt would assume she was with the Farradays, who often acted as her stand-in chaperons at such events.

Determined to follow through with her decisions, Julia gave her attention to the massive oak wardrobe standing in the corner. She strode to it and threw open the door, revealing dozens of gowns made of the finest silks and fabrics. She eyed the gowns with a new cynicism. Her uncle had not spared any expense when it came to outfitting his niece for her Season. The reasons for such extravagance were horribly clear.

Now, for the last decision. Julia tapped a long finger against her chin, considering the array of finery spread before her. What did a girl wear to her ruination?

# *Chapter Two*

'I never guessed you held aces!' Gaylord Beaton, the young man seated across the card table from Paine Ramsden, threw down his cards in disgust. 'You've the luck of the devil tonight, Ram.'

The others at the table in the dimly lit gambling hell laughed and threw in their hands. 'What do you mean "tonight"? Ram has the devil's luck every night!' another exclaimed.

'Have you considered I might have something more than luck?' Paine Ramsden gathered his winnings with a swift, practised move of his arm.

'What would that be? A fifth ace?' The table broke into guffaws at Gaylord's bold jest.

'Skill,' Paine replied drily, giving them each a piercing stare before he began to deal. He'd heard the underlying anger in young Beaton's jest.

This was the second night these bucks had been in to play and the second night they'd lost heavily. In his experience, an angry gambler was a dangerous gambler. He'd have to keep his eye on the young man. He'd hoped Beaton had learned his lesson last night and taken steps to preserve the remainder of his quarterly allowance. But apparently Beaton thought those steps involved trying to win back his losses, a common enough mistake and one Paine had made during his own misguided youth.

The five of them were playing high-stakes Commerce. He was winning thoroughly, having won a hundred pounds from each of the four young bucks at the table. Paine should have been enjoying it. Instead, he was bored. No, he was beyond bored. He had been bored three nights ago. Now, he was apathetic.

Paine discarded one of his three cards and drew the queen of hearts. With the addition of the queen, he held three of a kind. They were all going to lose again. He waited to feel the elation of victory. He felt nothing—not the excitement of winning, not the pleasant blurring of the edges of the world from the cheap brandy in his glass, not the spark of arousal from the sassy promises of the lightskirt who hovered near his shoulder. He was numb.

How had that happened? When had the usual thrills lost their abilities to sate him? There had been a time earlier in his return from abroad when simply being in a seedy place like this, several streets away from the well-lit halls of St James's, had been thrill enough to send his adrenalin racing at the prospect of needing to draw the knife secreted in his boot. He'd liked the prospect so much, he'd bought this place from the owner, who was looking to retire.

These days, he was the king of the roost. He'd made the seamy gaming hall his private kingdom. Young bloods looking for racy diversions came to try their hand against him at cards. Hardened gamblers appealed to him for loans when their luck was down. The whores offered themselves to him willingly. He had gone looking for the underworld and now it came looking for him.

He hardly left except to make a rare appearance in the *ton*, as he had done several weeks ago to escort his Aunt Lily to an early Season ball. He genuinely liked his Aunt Lily and her forthright manner. But as for the *ton*, Paine much preferred life outside high society's restrictions and expectations. His time in India had taught him that. The fact that he had grown tired of his current arrangement merely indicated he needed to find a new excitement.

Paine set down his cards to a chorus of groans from the table and began unrolling his shirtsleeves.

'You're not thinking of leaving before we have a chance to win back our losses?' one dandy cried in dismay. 'It is only midnight.'

'Exactly so—' Paine replied, breaking off in midsentence. He narrowed his gaze and looked into the smoky gloom beyond the table towards the entrance. There was a commotion at the front. 'Gentleman, if you'll excuse me, there seems to be a problem that needs my attention.'

Paine strode towards the door, aware for the first time that evening of a prick of anticipation growing within him. This was what he needed, something unknown and unpredictable, to spark his enthusiasm again.

'John, is there anything wrong?' Paine asked the doorman.

'Doorman' was a polite word for John's occupation. The hulking man with the crooked nose was charged with the duty of keeping people in who didn't pay their debts and keeping out those who didn't belong to the murky depths of the hell. It was a duty he did well. There was seldom an occasion John couldn't manage. Tonight seemed to be a rare exception. John appeared relieved to see him, although Paine was having difficulty noticing what the trouble might be.

'It's this 'ere chit. She's asking for you.' John stepped aside, revealing what his girth had hidden from Paine's approach.

Paine's breath caught and his member stirred violently. The girl was stunning. One look at her generous invitation of a mouth and his mind was awash with images of bedding her, of stripping her out of the turquoise silk that hugged her curves exquisitely and kissing her until she cried out for all of him. In his veins, his blood began to heat at the prospect. He was alive again.

'It's all right, John. I'll speak with her.' Paine clapped the big man on the shoulder. Was that relief he saw on the girl's face? He was certain he didn't know her. She looked far too fine to be familiar with the places he frequented. And too innocent, he amended. There were no chandeliers or crystal goblets here, but the woman beside him had the carriage and clothing of a woman who was familiar with such trappings.

He gave her one of his rare smiles and offered his

arm, drawing her inside. He felt her gloved hand tense where it lay on the sleeve of his linen shirt as she took in the surroundings and he saw the place through her eyes while they wended through the tables; the smell of stale smoke mingled with alcohol and unwashed sweat; the worn garb of the patrons, the faded upholstered chairs and scarred tables.

Belatedly, he recalled he had left his own jacket at the table and that he wore no extra adornments as was his wont when gambling. No diamond pin twinkled in the folds of a nonexistent cravat, no gems sparkled at the cuffs of his sleeves. By *ton* standards he was in extreme dishabille, garbed only in a plain white shirt and tan breeches—a far cry from the expected dark evening wear.

Paine turned down a narrow hallway and opened the first door on his left. It was a small room that served as his office of sorts for when he discussed loans or other private issues. He ushered her inside and motioned that she should sit.

'Can I get you a drink? I have ratafia or sherry.' She shook her head and Paine shrugged, fixing a brandy to give himself something to do. Once he had his glass, he took his customary place behind the plain wooden desk and studied her, waiting for her to state her business.

Beautiful and nervous, he concluded, although she was hiding it bravely. She didn't fidget with her pristine white-gloved hands, but held them clasped tightly in her lap. Her posture was rigid. Despite the control she held over the rest of her body, her eyes gave her away completely. Her eyes were bold, challenging orbs of jade.

He'd seen the exact shade in the gem markets of Calcutta, transported from the mines of the Kashmir Vale, an exotic green polished to an emerald sheen. She wanted something.

He could not imagine what he had to offer a stranger such as herself. But whatever she thought he had, she wanted it desperately. The challenge in her eyes said as much.

She did not speak and Paine felt obliged to fill the lengthening silence. 'Since we have not met, let me introduce myself. I am Paine Ramsden. However, you already know that. I feel distinctly at a disadvantage, for I have no idea who you might be.'

'I am Julia Prentiss. I thank you for agreeing to see me.' She spoke matter of factly, giving Paine the unlikely impression it might have been daylight outside and this meeting nothing more than a standard interview.

'This is a rather unusual time of evening for a business appointment. I must admit I am quite curious as to why you're here.' Paine leaned back in his chair, steepling his hands and trying to look as if he weren't fully aroused from the sight of her magnificent figure or the sound of her voice.

He saw the long column of her neck work briefly as she swallowed. For the first time since she'd entered the establishment, he felt her resolve waver. When she did not speak immediately, Paine offered a lifeline. 'Do you need money?' Perhaps she had a gambling debt. It was not unusual for women to wager beyond their capabilities at cards at a ball or house party.

She shook her head, causing the aquamarine earbobs to dance lightly. Too late, Paine realized his faulty reasoning. The earbobs alone could have been discreetly pawned to cover a small debt. Good lord, he'd only known her for a handful of minutes and she'd addled his wits. His manhood strained against his trousers. He hoped she'd get to the point soon so he could begin his own manoeuvres.

'I need you to ruin me.' The words came out in a rush; a light blush coloured her flawless alabaster cheeks.

'Ruin?' Paine quirked an eyebrow. 'What do you mean by "ruin"? Shall I ruin you at the gaming tables? I can arrange to have you lose any amount of your choosing.'

Her gaze met his evenly in all seriousness, her courage having returned in full force now that she'd begun talking. 'I don't wish to lose any money. I wish to lose my virginity. I want you to ruin me in bed.'

His mind warned of danger while his member fairly exploded at the anticipated pleasure being handed to it. Dangerous pleasure—his favourite kind of diversion. 'I am not opposed to such an arrangement, but I would know more,' Paine said coolly.

'I am to marry a man I find completely unsuitable in five days. He will not have me if I've been…' She paused, casting about for a word she could utter. 'If I've been touched by another.'

Paine felt a surge of disappointment. Partnering her in this request had any number of obvious drawbacks, not the least of which was the odds of facing a duel. Danger was one thing, illegal proceedings like duels were another. Still, it needn't end so drastically. It wasn't as if he had a reputation to protect and the chit wasn't looking for him to do the honourable thing afterwards.

'This is a rather rash course of action, one that is irrevocable, Julia.'

He spoke her name, liking the sound of it and the familiarity it implied. He rose and came around to the front of the desk, determined to teach her a lesson about the nature of men. He half-sat, half stood at the corner, his arms crossed, his lower body exposed so that there was no mistaking his maleness or his arousal, which pressed unmistakably full and hard against the fall of his breeches. Let her see what such a request involved. He would give her one chance to back out.

'Have you thought this through? Is there no chance of resigning yourself to the marriage? Perhaps you will come to rub along quite well with your betrothed in a year or two. Many women find once they marry, have a home and a family to look after, that all else settles itself with time.' Good lord, he sounded like a finishing-school marm.

Fire lit her eyes and she replied, 'I am not a silly chit rebelling against her parents' choice for a husband because I fancy myself infatuated with another. I assure you, I have no desire to "rub along well" with this man. Mortimer Oswalt is a lecher of the worst sort and I refuse to be reduced to nothing more than his legal brood mare! Even if it means I shall not stand a chance of ever marrying.'

Paine felt his heated blood chill at the name. Mortimer

Oswalt was well known to him. There was old animosity between them and a vengeance to be repaid over a woman. It would be fitting to ruin the man's betrothed. He was no longer a stripling. This time, Mortimer Oswalt would not be able to manipulate him so easily. This time, an innocent would escape Oswalt's clutches.

He studied the girl before him. Bedding her would be no act of charity. She was a divine beauty and his body clearly wanted her. She was more than beautiful, though. He wasn't so fickle as to be aroused by appearance alone. Julia Prentiss had spirit and courage. Not every girl in England had the power to rebel against a chosen match and to take action on her own. Such passion boded well for what they could share in the bedroom. First, he would ascertain with actions the willingness she professed with her words.

'Stand up, Julia, so that I may see what I am getting myself into.' He held her eyes, noting that her gaze did not flinch from his scrutiny.

She rose, her skirts brushing his legs. The lemon scent of her soap filled his nostrils, conjuring up images of sunlit days in faraway places where trees grew exotic-scented fruits. Paine let his eyes roam the length of her, stopping to rest intently on her firm breasts shown to advantage beneath the aquamarine bodice. He stared long enough to know her cheeks were heating.

Paine stood up from his lounging position against the desk and closed the half-step gap between them. He fitted his hands at her slender waist appreciably. Still, she did not move. He ran a hand up her ribs to cup the underside of a full breast. 'Very nice, very firm. I like that,' he said huskily.

Without warning, a hand slapped him hard across the face. He took a step back, releasing his grip on her. 'What the hell was that for?' He massaged the stung cheek.

'For trying to scare me off. I see your game and I won't scare.' The coldness of her words matched the coldness Paine saw in her eyes. He'd expected her to be stunned by his vulgar assessment.

Julia delivered a scathing set-down. 'You can't do anything more humiliating to me than what awaits me with Oswalt. At least when I am done here, I'll have my freedom. However, I would still ask that you not treat me like prized cattle.'

Paine gave a sardonic laugh. 'Who's treating whom like prized cattle? You are the one who has marched in here and demanded I play the stud.' He was gratified when she coloured a bit at that.

'Enough. Will you do it?'

She was magnificent in her scolding, her colour rising, her eyes starting to thaw with her temper. He liked that better. He had no use for ice maidens. A wicked grin lit his face. He advanced again, his stung cheek forgotten. There was one final test. 'Darling, have you heard the bedtime story about the princess and the pea?' He whispered, catching her chin between his forefinger and thumb so that her lovely face was turned up to meet his.

'Wh-what does that have to do with anything?' she asked, startled, her eyes widening.

For an answer, Paine bent his head to capture her luscious mouth with his. He coaxed her mouth open with a light pressure from his lips, letting his tongue probe her mouth, running across the smooth surfaces of her teeth, tasting the fruity sweetness of evening champagne, feeling her compliance.

He opened his mouth wider and pulled back his tongue to offer her an opportunity to reciprocate. She did, tentatively letting her tongue explore him. Paine groaned as her teeth nipped at his bottom lip and she giggled at his response. Paine moved his hands to her waist and pulled her against him, letting her feel his hard member, letting her feel the power she had to summon such a response.

Paine grabbed her hand and held it between them, against the straining length of him. 'Do you feel what you do to me?' he murmured, tearing himself away from the kiss. This was meant to be his test. When had he lost control?

Instead of being embarrassed by the intimate nature of her touch, Julia looked exultant, her face flushed with more victory than apprehension. If she looked this beautiful now, Paine could hardly imagine how glorious it would be to see her after a thorough bedding and know he was the one responsible for such a satisfied glow. There were countless positions and tricks he could show a willing participant.

'Does this mean you will do it?' she pressed, breaking into his thoughts before they could start to vividly itemise the lessons he wanted to give her.

Paine gave her one last assessing glance, not wanting to appear too easily conquered for pride's sake. Whatever rumour might say about him, whatever rumour might have led her here under the premise he was not discerning about his bed partners, Paine knew otherwise. He considered his bedmates carefully and with utmost discretion.

'Yes. Yes, I will do it.'

Paine visibly saw the breath she'd been holding go out of her, so great was her relief. Looking past him, her eyes evaluated the room. He followed her gaze to where it rested on the narrow cot with its drab blanket shoved against the wall. She pursed her lips into a resolute line and nodded towards the bed with dogged determination. 'Then we'd best get on with it.'

Paine thought he heard a note of sadness in her voice, perhaps regret, and he moved to eradicate it. She might be forced to surrender her virginity, but it didn't have to be a degrading experience. His own considerable pride as a lover bristled at the notion. No woman should ever leave his bed feeling demeaned by the experience of his lovemaking. He made a quick decision.

'I think you'll find my rooms better suited for our needs.' He nodded towards the cot. 'I've spent enough nights on that to know it is not even passably comfortable for one, let alone two people engaged in intimacy.'

She blushed and Paine was struck afresh by her innocence. For all her forthright behaviour, she was young and pretty and apparently alone. The last resonated with him strongly. He knew what it was like to be alone and he felt a kinship with her that he had not felt for another person in ages. Something that slept deep within him was waking up.

'My carriage is in the back. We should leave before someone comes poking around,' Paine suggested, moving the interaction forwards. Now that the deal had been struck, Julia had fallen silent, her gaze pointedly fixed on her gloved hands.

He held out his hand. 'It's time to go unless you are rethinking your choices. Once you leave here, there's no turning back.' He gave a small chuckle meant to reassure her. 'I am sure it has come to your attention that I want you.'

Her head shot up at the comment, her eyes blazing with fire. 'First of all, how could you want me? You know nothing about me beyond my name and even that could be a fabrication on my part. Secondly, I haven't had any choices to "rethink" since eleven o'clock this morning, when my uncle sealed my fate with his greed. Thirdly, there's been no turning back since the moment I left the Moffat rout tonight. I don't need your pity. I know exactly what I am doing, but I don't have to like it.'

Paine tossed back his head and laughed, partly out of relief that his vixen had returned and partly at the pert speech. 'You're right. You don't have to like it, but if your performance a few minutes ago is any indication, I bet you will.' He would make sure of it.

# Chapter Three

The carriage ride was accomplished in silence. On her side of the carriage Julia seethed inwardly over letting Ramsden goad her. Like it, indeed! She might be an innocent, but she was not utterly naïve. She knew quite well 'it' referred to the sex act. Paine Ramsden was as handsome as purported with his midnight hair and riveting blue eyes and twice as conceited if he thought she'd find pleasure in what she was about to do. In his male arrogance, he'd quickly forgotten she'd been forced to these measures.

She hadn't picked him for his skill. She had picked him for his willingness and she'd been right. He had acquiesced with very little persuasion. She had been prepared to beg, even pay for his services.

The carriage rolled to a halt. Julia sucked in her breath and steadied herself. Paine leaped down and turned back to hand her out. She'd expected to see

Jermyn Street with its bachelor residences. Instead, she found herself in unfamiliar territory.

'Where are we?' she asked, casting her glance up and down the street, looking for a marker. A *frisson* of doubt travelled through her. It was the height of foolishness to go with a stranger in a closed carriage without telling anyone of her whereabouts. Should he will it, Paine Ramsden had her entirely at his mercy.

'Brook Street. I just acquired a house here. I have hopes of turning the place into a luxury hotel that will appeal to an elite calibre of clientele.' Paine gestured to the rest of the street where other hotels had recently sprung up. 'The location seems ideal.' Then he winked conspiratorially, 'It's ideal for us as well. We will be less likely to be disturbed here.'

Paine produced a key and proceeded to unlock the door. 'You will have to excuse the absence of furniture. The place is quite bare except for the bedroom upstairs and a little office I cobbled together in the back. I imagine I'll be making good use of the rooms once renovations begin and my presence will be required around the clock.'

Julia gave a forced smile, appreciating his effort to put her at ease. Now that she'd had the space of the carriage ride to review what she was doing, her nerves were doubly on edge. Still, she *must* go forwards, she'd come too far to back out now.

Julia stepped inside, unprepared for the opulence that met her gaze. As he'd warned, the place was empty of furnishings. But it was not devoid of decoration. The richness of the marbled tiled entry with its gilded mirrors did not resonate with her image of Paine Ramsden's financial status. He was a gambler by trade, a man who ran a seedy gaming hell. Those were not the traits of a man with money to spare. Yet, this was a house only a wealthy man could afford to purchase. And it would take a large sum of money to renovate it as well.

They reached a curved staircase and halted.

'Would you like to go straight upstairs or would you prefer to sit and talk in my office, makeshift as it is?' Paine offered, gesturing to a room farther down the hall.

Julia lifted her skirts with resolution. 'Straight upstairs, if you please. I am eager to see this business concluded.'

'Do not be too eager, my sweet. There is much you might discover to be enjoyed if you take time and savour our interlude,' he said in low tones at her elbow.

'You are quite sure of yourself,' Julia responded with disdain. 'I am interested only in seeing the deed accomplished in an expedient manner.'

Paine laughed, a throaty, intimate chuckle that sent an unlooked-for thrill through Julia. She spared him a sidelong glance that lasted long enough to see that his blue eyes danced with smug merriment, giving her the distinct impression that he knew something beyond her comprehension.

She didn't like being so far out of her depth. She was not fool enough to believe that she'd ever held the upper hand in their dealings. He held all the knowledge and all the power. Should he decide not to go through with her request, she had no way to coerce him back into compliance.

They ascended the stairs and she reflected wryly on her earlier thoughts to offer her earbobs as financial compensation, thinking they would appeal to him in his lowly circumstances if she needed leverage. In light of this elegant house, her earbobs seemed laughable. But her powerlessness was not. She had no leverage now if he suddenly found his long-forgotten conscience and backed out. Then again, he was a rogue of the first water. Gossip had it that he seldom slept alone and the line of women parading through his bedroom was endless. He was a man of intense physical appetites. He wouldn't back out. He *needed* sex.

Paine stopped before a panelled oak door and opened it wide, allowing her to enter ahead of him. 'My chambers,' he said without flourish, but she could feel his hot eyes on her, watching her reaction.

She hid nothing in her response to the room. Indeed, she didn't know how she could have schooled her features to remain impassive when faced with the seductive opulence that spread before her. The room was exotic and utterly unlike anything she'd seen before—not that she made a habit of frequenting male bedchambers. In reality, seeing one or a hundred bedchambers was immaterial. She knew instinctively she could view every bedroom in England and not find one like this.

Candlelight from candelabras placed about the room lit the place in a soft glow, casting shadows on gold

damask-hung walls. Beneath the soles of her dancing
slippers, Julia could feel the plushness of the carpet, the
thick pile a marked contrast to the threadbare Axmin-
ster rugs that dotted the floors of her uncle's home. This
carpet was of soft wool dyed in rich crimson hues and
accented with gold to match the walls. Julia doubted
anyone else in England would have been so bold as to
decorate a bedroom in deep crimson and burnished
gold, but the differences didn't stop there.

Her eye was drawn to the furniture; an ornate cabinet
of ebony stood against one wall, inlaid with gold and
ivory to create a design, perhaps a symbol of some sort.
Low-slung chairs filled with pillows sat at angles to a
low teak table, but what garnered her gaze unequivo-
cally was the bed.

Unlike the high, pillared beds she was accustomed
to seeing, this bed was framed low to the ground, piled
with pillows and silken coverlets. Blankets seemed too
ordinary of a word to describe the lush swathes of fabric
that lay strewn about the bed, vibrant in their shades of
scarlet, saffron and jade. Julia could not resist the temptation to touch the fabrics. She walked to the bed and
ran her fingers across the surface of the closest covering,
revelling in the smoothness of the silk as it shushed
through her hands.

For a moment, she'd forgotten where she was and
why she was there. The heat of his gaze on her back
served as a searing reminder. She dropped the blanket
self-consciously and stiffened.

'It's a magnificent bed,' Paine said from across the

room in a slow drawl that indicated he'd watched her every move.

'It's very interesting. I've never seen one like it,' Julia replied stiffly, turning away from the bed.

'Are you sure you wouldn't like a drink before we get started?' Paine offered, opening the inlaid doors of the ebony cabinet to reveal assorted sizes of crystal glassware and an impressive collection of decanters.

Julia was tempted to say no. As a rule, she didn't drink beyond an occasional glass of champagne. But tonight, the thought-numbing properties of alcohol, which she had been warned against as a débutante, might be just the addition she needed to get through the evening. 'Yes, sherry, please.'

Before she could rethink her decision, Paine had the glass in her hand and was gesturing to one of the cushioned chairs. 'Let's sit and talk. It makes these encounters less formal.'

His coolness spoke volumes about his character, Julia thought. While she was fighting back nerves, he was entirely at ease, as if this were something he did regularly—which, in fact, it was, according to the rumours. He lounged casually in his chair, looking devastatingly handsome and comfortable. The only sign he was in any way affected by the presence of a female in his chambers was the burning intensity of his eyes—eyes that followed her every gesture, every move. She was supremely conscious she was fiddling overmuch with the folds of her skirts as she sat.

Julia sipped from her glass, giving herself a moment

to savour the warmth of the sweet liquor as it slid down to her belly. 'You must like to travel.' There. That was a safe topic.

Paine nodded briefly. 'I have found places in the world where I feel at home.'

'Are these pieces of furniture from any of those places?' Julia asked, her eyes sliding to the lacquered cabinet, looking desperately for a safe direction of conversation. She'd hoped he would have said more about his travels than the meagre offering of a single sentence. But the talkativeness he'd exhibited upon arrival seemed to have disappeared. 'Do you know anything about the design on the cabinet? It appears to be a symbol. Do you know what it is?'

'Yes. I know.' Paine followed her gaze to the inlaid panels of the cabinet doors, a smile quirking at his sensual lips.

The dratted man was a rotten conversationalist with his minimal answers. Julia put down her glass and rose. She went to the panels, tracing a portion of the symbol with a slow finger. 'Mr Ramsden, talking to you is virtually impossible since you are not the least bit forthcoming with any information. I feel obliged to tell you that a gentleman is able to make conversation on a diverse array of subjects.' She hazarded a sideways glance at Ramsden to see the effect of her veiled barb.

It had hit the mark, perhaps too effectively. Ramsden rose and came towards her with all the feral stealth of a jungle panther. He paced behind her, giving Julia the distinct impression she was being stalked. She had not meant to strike so deeply.

'Miss Prentiss,' he began in low tones, 'your very comment is a trap from which neither of the answers available shall save me. My dilemma, you see, is that while proving my worth as a gentleman I am at the same time besmirching that title by the same means. If I confess that I am no gentleman, I shall save myself from answering what the symbol is, but at the expense of my honour, which I hold dearer than you might have been led to believe. On the other hand, if I confess what the symbol is and provide an erudite exposition of my conversational skills, I shall vouch for my ability to perform the gentlemanly arts. However, discussing that symbol with any well-bred girl is a conversational topic that no true gentleman would broach. So I ask you—do you want to know what the symbol stands for?'

Julia bit her lip and fought the desire to step back, away from his masculine onslaught. He stood with hands on his hips hardly inches from her, his blue eyes penetrating and challenging as he threw down his gauntlet. She saw his ploy and the detection gave her strength. He still thought to scare her with his dares and the promise of blatant sin.

The man was positively aggravating. She was supposed to be the one baiting the hook and yet he'd neatly turned the conversation to his advantage. 'So you cleverly choose neither option. Instead, you lure me with temptation, betting that my curiosity will cause me to permit you to speak freely, thus absolving you of any gentlemanly obligation on the subject.'

'*Touché*. You see my ploy too clearly.' Ramsden covered his heart with a hand in mock hurt.

'You might as well tell me about the symbol,' Julia prompted. 'After all, I am about to grant you far more liberties than that of questionable speech.' It was as close as she would get to admitting her curiosity had won out. Since he'd made such a to-do over discussing the panel, she had to know what it was about.

Ramsden's hands came down on her shoulders, his fingers kneading gently through the thin material of her dancing gown. He turned her away from him to face the cabinet, his voice low and soft at her ear. In that moment, her senses were utterly encircled by his presence; the scent of him in her nostrils, the warm strength of his body against her back, the press of his fingers to her shoulders. He was the centre of her universe, the only person she could see, smell, touch or hear. Julia could scarcely concentrate on the tale he laid out in tones designed to seduce even the most resolute spinster.

'The symbol is known throughout the eastern world as yin and yang, two opposite but yet complementary forces that make up all aspects of life.' His voice dropped a notch lower, speaking now just to her. 'Yin, the dark portion of the symbol, is female. It represents valleys and streams. It is passive and absorbing.' At this, Ramsden ran a hand languorously down her arm, took her fingers between his and led them over the bottom part of the inlay, the ebony smooth and cool to her touch. He guided her hand over the top portion done in ivory.

'This is yang, her male counterpart, representing

light and heaven. Yang is penetrating and active.' He pressed his hips against the round swell of her buttocks, letting her feel the possibilities of penetration between her thighs, between them. Julia inhaled sharply at the suggestive display. He whispered huskily, 'Yin and yang express the interdependence of opposites. Without the other, neither is complete. Feel the need you arouse in me, Julia, a need only you can slake. '

Julia felt weak. Heaven help her, she was a wanton to react in such a base manner with a stranger she didn't know beyond a name. Her business proposition was quickly turning to unnamable pleasure. She wanted to sink back against his chest, let his arms close about her and take her weight. She wanted him to fulfil the ancient, earthy promises of his voice. She'd never guessed a simple cabinet could inspire this depth of longing.

One of his hands slid about her waist, drawing her against his hardness, the other was in her hair, slipping through the pins and pearls of her elegant coiffure until her hair hung loose and free. This time when his hardness jutted against her back, she could not even feign shock over his intimate proposal. This time, her inhalation was from pure desire that would not be put off any longer.

She turned in his arms, pressing her body against his, instinctively rubbing her nipples against his chest in a desperate attempt to quell the tempest brewing at her core. She looked up into his face. His blue eyes no longer reminded her of the colour of the sky on a deep summer day, but bore shades of midnight, darkened as they were by his arousal.

Something thrilled deep within her at the knowledge she had done this to him. But her own rising need left little time for contemplation or even a celebration of victory. She was drowning in heretofore unknown sensations and she clung to him for support. Intuition told her only he could provide an antidote to what coursed through her veins.

'Steady now,' Paine whispered to her, his hands on the buttons of her gown, expertly freeing her body from its satin casing. Through the thin linen of her chemise, he traced the silhouette of her body against the candles' flames. His thumbs teased her nipples through the cloth until Julia panted for release. She reached to pull the chemise over her head, suddenly in a hurry to be completely naked, as if by being so she could assuage the pressure growing within her, demanding emancipation.

To her frustration, Paine pushed her hands away. 'Not yet, my eager one.' He bent and swept her into his arms. Julia gasped at the sudden movement, but she hadn't the wherewithal or desire to protest when he laid her on the low bed amidst the silken covers. She made no move to cover herself. She could do nothing but hold Paine's intense stare. She reached for him to pull him down to her, but he stepped back.

'Watch me, Julia.'

Did she have a choice? Julia could not muster the fortitude to look away. Paine's eyes did not leave hers as he lifted his shirt over his head and stood magnificently bare-chested before her, his torso bronzed from years beneath a tropical sun, the strength of the arms that had lifted her evident in the obvious musculature of his shoulders and biceps. Julia groped for a word to describe him. Beautiful came to mind—sublime, masculine beauty, the kind of beauty sculptors carved in stone and for the night it was hers.

His hands dropped to the waistband of his trousers, reminding Julia that he was not done. He was not wearing small clothes underneath and the core of his manhood sprang free of the trousers, straining upright towards his belly in unabashed glory. Artfully, he bent to pull his legs free of the trousers, supplying Julia with an unadulterated glimpse of his backside.

He must be a fabulous horseman, Julia concluded, eyeing the muscled power of his long legs and firm buttocks. The thought was so errant and ridiculous, Julia choked back a giggle.

'What is it?'

'I was just thinking you must be a great horseman,' Julia confessed.

Paine smiled wickedly. 'I know how to ride.'

The cryptic remark puzzled her. She sensed there was a double meaning, but she could not fathom what it was, too enamoured of the sight before her to do anything else.

Seeing her consternation, his smile softened and he knelt on the floor beside her, the knuckles of his hand grazing her cheek in a caress. 'Ah, Julia, my innocent.' He reached for a trifle box on a low table and withdrew an unfamiliar item. Julia watched, amazed, as he fitted it on to his sex.

'It's a sheath to prevent us from making a child,' Paine explained softly. 'Now, we're ready for our true pleasure.'

Julia could not imagine more beyond what she'd already felt but Paine knelt at her stockinged feet and convinced her otherwise. Skilful hands rolled down the stockings and discarded them. Lips kissed the sensitive space behind her knees until she thought she would scream aloud from the sensation of it. Heat built inside her, a heat that was damp and scorching all at once as Paine's hands spread her thighs and his mouth nipped seductively at the tender flesh near her woman's core, his breath hot against the triangle of her curls.

Then he was over her, covering her with the length of his form, his sex strong against her leg. Without leaving her, he reached again for the trifle box and retrieved a small vial of oil that smelled of lavender when he removed the stopper and poured some into his hand. Julia watched, entranced as Paine moved his hand between her legs and gently inserted his oil-slick fingers inside her

'You're ready for me,' Paine whispered, covering her again and this time it was his sex that found purchase at her entrance. Julia felt him thrust in, just a little at first, and then, to her dismay, withdraw. She cried out her disappointment. Paine smothered the cry with a kiss and entered again, further this time, and withdrew, then again until Julia realised his rhythm and intention.

Secure now that she was not being teased, Julia fitted her hips against his and joined in the rhythm. She felt him plunge deep, felt a sharp stab of pain. He stilled inside her as she breathed a cry into his mouth and waited until she urged him onwards.

Deep inside her now, their rhythm increased, the pressure grew, spiralled to new levels. Not even his kiss could silence her moans of delight. In this new pleasure, she was free. She was not bound to the earth or to anything on it; beneath Paine Ramsden, she was flying, soaring. When she felt she could not soar any higher, she felt her core fracture into countless pieces, the pressure that had built in her since his first touch finally assuaged. She was boneless and drifting in a new satisfied world, aware only that Paine, too, had seemed to reach a level of fulfilment, contentment. He, too, had cried out at the last and now rested against her, his weight a warm reminder of their intimacy as sleep took her.

# Chapter Four

Paine awoke to the scent of lemons mingled with the musk of sex and the warmth of another body cradled against his own, his arm draped over the lush curve of a breast. It was a heady awakening.

Images of the evening came back to him with striking clarity: Julia Prentiss in her delectable aquamarine gown begging him to ruin her, her green eyes shrewdly assessing him as she made her plea; Julia naked on his bed, weeping for his caress as he initiated her to the pleasures of lovemaking; Julia crying out as the final moment of their joining took her to untold heights, her hips arched high into him, her head thrown back on the pillow as she gave way to unabashed ecstasy.

At that moment, all pretence of doing a duty, of thwarting her fate with her madcap scheme, had fled from her thoughts. He'd seen her eyes darken the moment she'd submitted fully to the pleasure between them, when business had ceased. She'd been utterly his, and utterly without artifice.

Everything in that instant had been truth. Not just for her, for him, too. He'd cried out at his pinnacle, feeling his own climax completely, devoid of the usual restraint he practised. It was his wont to give pleasure, not to take his own, not to give in to anything beyond the physical fulfilment of the act.

Last night had been disturbingly different. He'd found he could not hold back the emotional tide that surged at the sounds of Julia's bliss beneath him. He had given into temptation—a temptation that he rarely felt, if ever—and joined her at the height of her rapture.

The act of doing so was somewhat alarming, perhaps a sign of vulnerability in himself that he had thought long suppressed. Perhaps he wasn't as changed by his years abroad, his studies of the human condition, his adventures in far-off lands, as he had believed. There was danger in that. He'd been exiled once before for behaving rashly on behalf of a woman. He'd promised himself not to let such foolishness take him again.

Julia stirred beside him, nesting her buttocks against his groin provocatively in her sleep. He flared to life, his body responding immediately to the inadvertent invitation. He tamped it down. He'd taken her twice more after their first joining. She'd be sore this morning. He should refrain until she'd had a hot bath and soaked away the initial soreness. But neither could he lay by her side, playing the neutral eunuch. If he was to grant her a respite, he had to keep himself occupied.

Paine rolled over and out of the bed in a single, quick motion before his body could persuade his conscience to act otherwise. He would see about some breakfast. His new piece of property might be ideal for a quiet assignation—indeed, he'd only picked up the key two days ago—but as such, it was without staff or supplies. Paine pulled on trousers and shirt. He cast a last glance at Julia, sleeping peacefully, oblivious to the arousal he was fighting on her behalf. He would hurry so that Julia wouldn't awake alone.

Outside, the sun was up, its brightness something Paine realised he hadn't seen in quite some time. The streets were strangely quiet as well, something Paine noticed immediately, so at odds was the deserted scene with the crowded bustle he usually contended with. Of course it was London and the streets were never truly deserted. Even now, vendors and workers straggled down the streets to work.

Paine spied a milkmaid turning at the corner, no doubt seeking out the alleyway leading to the back entrance of a neighbouring mansion. He followed her. Milk would be a good start to breakfast. If the milkmaids were just coming out, he judged the time to be a little past six o'clock. Six o'clock! Hell's bells, it was early! The stark realisation hit him with a feeling of disbelief. It had been ages since he'd seen the city through morning eyes. Early it might be, yet he felt refreshed and ready to take on the day.

Three-quarters of an hour later, Paine stood in the doorway of his bedchamber, carrying a tray laden with the breakfast treasures he'd culled from the early-morning vendors. He indulged in the sight of Julia dozing. He smiled as she turned over, starting to wake. Paine set the tray on the low table near the bed and eased on to the bed at her side, waving an orange beneath her nose.

'Mmm.' Julia gave a breathy sigh, her eyes opening at the citrusy scent.

'Good morning, darling.' Paine reached out to push a tangle of hair back from her face.

Julia stretched, her movements drawing the loose covering sheet down to reveal a tantalising glimpse of a breast, reminding Paine that his hand had lain against the creamy flesh only an hour ago. The erection he'd subdued with his breakfast errand rose in defiance. She turned her green gaze on him, already sharp, not the least bit dreamy from sleep. 'What time is it?'

'It's a bit past seven o'clock,' Paine said, taken aback by the question. It was not what he'd expected. Most women didn't ask him what time it was when they awoke and saw him kneeling at their bedside.

But Julia had proven last night that she was not most women and he'd do well to remember it. Most women didn't invoke the depth of feeling that had accompanied his climax. He'd been tutored in the arts of the sexual sutras, learning the mastery of yin over yang in the arms of India's exotic concubines. Most women didn't have the ability to unman him as Julia had last night.

'Seven o'clock!' Julia sat upright, the sheet sliding to her waist in her agitation.

'I know it's early, but…' Paine said boyishly, tempted to reach for her and put off breakfast a while longer.

She didn't let him finish. 'Early? How can you say that? It's late. I never meant to stay this long! How could you have let me sleep the entire night away? I thought you understood.'

She was scolding him? She never meant to stay the whole night? She'd meant to slip away after their coupling? Wasn't that his line? This was all backwards. *He* was supposed to be the one leaving in the dark of night. *He* never actually *slept* when he bedded a woman. *He* left as soon as he could. Paine stared at her in utter confusion.

'Julia, whatever are you talking about?'

'I have to leave. I have to get back to my aunt and uncle's. With luck, they won't have checked my room yet.' She threw an accusing glare at him as if this was all somehow his fault. 'I meant to be home by two o'clock, long before they came traipsing back.' With luck, she'd even held hopes of returning to the ball before it was over. The Moffat rout had a reputation for running until dawn.

Her tone pricked Paine's temper. He rose from the bed, hands on hips. 'Dancing, deflowering and back by two. That was an ambitious agenda, Julia,' he drawled.

'It's what had to be done and, now that it is done, I have to go and finish what I have put in motion. Ruination isn't much good unless I go back and prove it.' Julia gave a belated blush and reached for the sheet, making an effort to rise modestly from the bed with the sheet draped about her. 'I will just dress and go, if you don't mind.'

Her haughty tone didn't sit well with Paine. He advanced towards her. 'I find I do mind, Julia, quite a lot. This is my home and my chamber. I will not be dismissed from it like a common servant.' With luck, she'd step backwards and run into the bed. Then he'd have her where he wanted her.

No such luck. Julia stood her ground, even though they stood only inches from each other. 'You can't stop me.' She stared him down, giving no quarter with her challenge.

Paine's eye caught the glimmer of aqua silk heaped in the corner. A wicked smile took his lips. He let his gaze linger on the heap long enough to draw Julia's attention.

She instantly divined the plan that had spawned his devil's smile. 'No, you wouldn't dare.' She barely got the words out and the race for the dress was on.

It was not an easy race. Julia didn't play fair.

Julia shrieked and shoved a chair in his path to slow him down. Paine shoved it aside and reached for her, laughing at her nerve. 'Vixen!'

He succeeded only in grabbing a handful of sheeting as she spun out of the linen and darted to put a table between them.

She was fully naked and panting, her auburn tresses falling over the heaving globes of her breasts as she stared at him across the table top. Paine was gloriously aroused. 'Temptress! Godiva!'

'Call me what you like, but I've got you now!' she crowed, her anger forgotten in the thrill of the race. Near-triumph coaxed a laugh from her throat as she gave over to the exhilaration of victory.

Paine saw the reason she gloated. The dress was on her side of the table. She simply had to make a dash for it and the gown would be hers. He feinted left, then right, keeping her attention while he made his decision. He would not stand a chance if he wasted a precious second going around the small table. He would have to go over it.

Paine lunged, coming over the table and taking Julia to the ground with him. She wriggled against him, struggling, tantalising with every movement.

'That's not fair!' she protested, obviously wanting to be put out by his audacity, but not quite able to void the laughter from her voice.

'You gloated too soon,' Paine teased, enjoying the friction of her naïve movements against the fabric of his trousers where she lay beneath him. He inched forwards and grasped at the hem of the gown. 'I win. I have the dress and I have you right where I want you, right where you belong.' He ground his hips meaningfully against her pelvis, his member in an overt state of readiness that could not be overlooked.

Julia angled her head back to see her discarded gown clutched in Paine's hand. She stretched to reach and take it from him. Paine pinned her gently with the power of his body. 'Do you think I would relinquish your gown so soon after winning it?' Paine tut-tutted.

'Please, give it back to me.' The earlier playfulness was replaced with a plea. He was alert to it at once.

'All right.' Paine sat up, straddling her between his thighs. He needed to be careful not to push Julia too far.

Such games of love-play could easily be misconstrued as something more sinister. He didn't want her frightened. That was never his intention.

'You may pay a forfeit.' He kept the tone light to remind her his intentions were not motivated by evil.

'What?' She was all wariness. She wanted to play the game, wanted to trust him, but knew better than to do so. Damn Mortimer Oswalt and her uncle for teaching her such cynicism already. It turned his insides to think of what a month of marriage, let alone a lifetime of marriage to Oswalt, would to do her.

Paine reached out a gentle hand to stroke her cheek. 'The forfeit is simple. Have breakfast with me.' He gestured to the tray waiting on the low bedside table. 'I went to a lot of trouble to put it together. I went out for it.'

'Just breakfast?' Julia queried.

'Just breakfast.'

'I can go after breakfast?'

'If that is what you wish,' Paine answered solemnly. He meant it. He would keep his word, although he hoped it wouldn't be necessary. This would be a breakfast Julia Prentiss would not soon forget.

Julia sat cross-legged on a pile of colorful pillows in the middle of the floor, securely garbed in a satin robe Paine had generously loaned her from his wardrobe. Paine lounged next to her, propped on an elbow, and dressed only in a pair of thin silk Indian-styled trousers, having forgone the wool trousers he'd worn out to find breakfast. He peeled a section of orange and offered it up to her, creating the effect that he was a loyal squire serving his queen. Having such a handsome man staring at her in overt adoration, serving her every need, was highly intoxicating.

It was also highly hazardous. She almost believed she was a queen when he stared at her thus, almost believed a host of other things, too: that last night had been more than a discharge of a duty, a fulfilment of a contract between them; that he'd felt what she'd felt at the end; that he'd stolen her dress and conjured up the forfeit because he didn't want her to go. Most dangerous of all, that there was something real between them, that their night together didn't have to end. That was the biggest folly of all.

'I love oranges. We seldom have them in the country except at Christmas,' Julia confessed, using a finger to wipe an errant dribble of juice from her chin.

'They taste better when someone else feeds them to you.' Paine hoisted himself up to take her head in his lap. He looked down at her with a soft expression in his blue eyes that did strange things to her stomach. He could feed her worms for all she'd care when he looked at her like that—as if she was a divine goddess and he a devout worshipper. This man was far more rakish, far more seductive than any rumour had suggested. He was a consummate master at his trade.

'Is it always like this?' She arched her neck back to see all of his handsome visage staring down at her.

'No, hardly.' He held a succulent orange slice over her mouth and made a show of gently squeezing sweet drops of juice on her lips. Julia felt her breasts tighten in analogy, remembering the way he'd manipulated her nipples with soft pressure until they'd been erect with need.

'I can see why,' Julia said softly. 'If such pleasure was so readily available, I doubt anyone would get much of anything done.' She blushed at her own frankness and Paine laughed again, popping another slice of orange in her mouth.

'How is it that you are privy to such carnal knowledge?' Julia asked between bites.

'I shouldn't tell you. A master never shares his secrets,' Paine flirted. 'But I can hardly have you walking around London thinking just anyone can do this.' He dribbled juice on her lips. She flicked her tongue across her lips to gather the juice and heard him groan at the action, a low throaty groan that had nothing to do with pain and everything to do with pleasure. It was a small, thrilling piece of power to think such a simple motion could affect a man of his experience.

He offered her a slice of orange dipped in ground sugar, sliding it into her open mouth and letting her suck the juice from it. She closed her eyes and sucked hard, wholly unaware at how the sight of her savouring the rare treat with abject delight was pushing the limits of Paine's restraint. His hand clenched in her hair.

She opened her eyes and looked up at him, recognising the intensity of the need mirrored in his gaze. He wanted her. His eyes said it. His body said it. She was sharply alert to the intimacy of his lap, the thinness of the silk fabric. She had only to turn her head slightly to encounter the full dimension of his rock-hard manhood. Julia thought of the orange slice, of its slightly phallus-like shape, of sucking the juice from it. Would Paine like that? The look in his eyes suggested he would. Hesitantly, Julia turned her head. She parted her lips and mouthed him through his trousers.

Paine gave a sharp gasp at the contact. She drew back, worried the idea wasn't to his liking after all. 'Don't stop, Julia, don't stop,' he pleaded, a gentle hand urging her head back to his straining member.

Julia was giddy with power. She sucked hard until Paine made no effort to confine his satisfaction to groans, but gave full vent to his enjoyment with loud cries.

'Julia, pull it out, let me be in you.' He panted, close to his end.

Julia found the hidden slit in his trousers and pulled free the swollen member, slick with its own juices. Her hand clenched about its tip, revelling in what she had wrought. She reached over his head for the trifle box he'd used last night and rummaged quickly for a sheath.

'Now, straddle me, Julia.' Paine instructed, helping her to roll the thin sheath over his sex. 'Take me inside you and ride.'

Julia lowered herself on to him, exhaling in wonderment as she slid on him. He was so large, much larger than she'd thought last night. Yet he fit perfectly, filling up the space inside her. She began her motions and he joined her in a seamless rocking rhythm that teased her, then ultimately fulfilled her as she found the place she'd found last night, soaring in Paine's arms. He drew her down to him as he shuddered his own release, muffling his cries in her shoulder.

They lay together, their breathing slowing in unison as the initial power of climaxing ebbed. Julia wanted to stay clasped against him, warm and sated in his arms, for ever. Reality intruded. If she moved, breakfast would be over. She would have to go. But she no longer wanted to.

She wanted to stay. She wanted to feel this pleasure he'd awoken in her again and again. She didn't imagine such pleasure could be found with Oswalt. She fought a shudder. The horror of doing such intimate things with him escalated against the backdrop of what she'd shared with Paine Ramsden.

'Are you cold?' Paine reached for a throw to wrap about them, misinterpreting the reason for her shudder.

Julia searched for a way to prolong the moment, the minutes of their time together. 'You have not answered my question yet.'

'Mmm.' Paine breathed into her hair sounding like a well contented man. 'There are studies, sutras, in India that teach men and women about sexual congress. Each person has a different task, a different function in the act. There are such teachings in China as well. Remember my cabinet with the yin and yang symbol?' He shifted Julia to the side and wrapped an arm about her, warming to his subject. She waited for him to continue, her curiosity getting the better of her at the idea of such studies.

'In China, the man is the yin and the woman is the yang. It's the man's task, through lovemaking, to make the woman give up her essence, her yang, without losing his own yin to attain it. When a woman climaxes, her essence is surrendered.'

Julia punched him in the shoulder. 'That sounds completely arrogant and not so enjoyable for the man if he can't—what did you call it? Climax?' She tried out the new word.

'That's the whole point,' Paine instructed. 'Attaining a woman's yang without climaxing yourself makes you strong and it increases your life. It's the mark of a skilled male to be able to claim such discipline. There's tales of men being able to have congress with up to fourteen women before releasing their yin.'

Julia levered up on one arm and searched his face quizzically. 'Last night, and just now, did you, uh, steal my yang, as it were?' She'd felt that he'd held back nothing, as had she. It would be a private disappointment to learn she'd been cheated in a fashion.

Paine smiled. 'No, my enchantress. I gave up as much as I took.' Paine folded his arms behind his head.

'So you've taken my virginity and I've taken your immortality,' Julia said drily.

Paine chuckled. 'I suppose so, but chances are I was mortal already. Those are old teachings. Some say they go back to the third century before Christ. Since then, the Chinese have shifted their focus. They discovered that denying women the yin denied men their heirs. Now, the sexual teachings have been adapted to be more cooperative in their outcome, much more similar to India.'

'Oh, no stealing of essences there, then?' Julia probed, utterly enthralled by such talk.

'No stealing, only giving. In Hinduism—that's the primary religion in India—sexual intercourse is seen as a metaphor for a relationship with the gods. Sex is spiritual and sacred.'

'I think I prefer the Indian way.' The words were out of her mouth before she could rethink the wisdom of them. She regretted it immediately.

Paine would think she meant something by them, something altogether much more personal than she intended their dealings to be. To cover her silliness, she sat up, letting her hair fall over her shoulders. She made no move to shove it back from her face. Its curtain obscured her face, which was just as well. She had what she came for—she was thoroughly ruined by now and fully instructed in more than she'd bargained for. Such knowledge made it hard to leave, knowing that she'd find no outlet for it in the English world.

It was past time to go and Paine Ramsden did not strike her as a man who responded well to womanly whines. Even in her naïvety, she knew he would be a hard man to hold. He did nothing for the sake of tradition and protocol. He operated by an entirely different standard of rules. The rumours about him had been right in that respect, although much else she'd heard did not ring true with what she'd experienced. She should put on her dress and be gone with all the dignity she could find.

# Chapter Five

Julia crossed the room to the forgotten gown they'd tussled over in the early morning. She hazarded a covert glance at Paine while she slipped into her undergarments. He had levered himself up on one arm, his shirt open, his dark hair dishevelled. The sight of such blatant, post-coital masculinity studying her every move as she dressed was potent. Julia felt her blood fire at the sight.

'What are you doing, Julia?' he drawled.

'Dressing.'

'I can see that. But to what purpose? I will simply undress you again.'

'Paine, I am leaving.' A rush of anxiety filled her. Would he let her leave? Would he renege on their agreement? 'You promised me I could go.'

'I promised you could go if you wanted to. Do you want to?' Paine replied with apparent nonchalance.

'The world often demands we act beyond our selfish wants,' Julia parried, pulling on her stockings, recalling with clarity how they'd come to be off her legs. Would she remember that every time she pulled on stockings for the rest of her life?

'Does it, Julia? What do you hope to gain by going back that you haven't already gained?' Paine gained his feet and strode to her side, his deft hands taking over the working of the buttons at the back of her gown.

'I have to go back and tell them the betrothal is off,' Julia stammered. The heat of his hands provided a very real distraction as they skimmed her back.

'I would think that would be obvious to them by your absence.' Paine chuckled, finishing the buttons. His hands rode at her waist, easing her back against his chest so that she was fitted along his length and his arms encircled her. 'Nothing but sorrow awaits you there. For a woman who seemed to have thought everything through so thoroughly, I am surprised you haven't realised that yet. Even if you break the betrothal with your announcement, they will not let you go again. They'll punish you, pack you off to the country at best. At worst, they will cast you out without a penny or force you into marriage with an unsuspecting dolt from the country just to get you off their hands. They'll have to find a way to countenance your dishonour.'

'I know. I have resigned myself to that,' Julia said stoically, although accepting those consequences was going to be far more difficult now after Paine's education than it was in her imaginings yesterday when she'd concocted her mad scheme. 'Regardless, they'll be worried about me. I owe them the courtesy of letting them know I am well.'

'Worried about themselves is more likely,' Paine drawled with cynicism. 'Don't delude yourself. You cannot simply waltz back home and put paid to the contract.'

His scepticism fired her temper. She didn't like to be laughed at. 'How dare you speak of them like that! You don't know them at all. You've never even met them.' To her embarrassment, her lip quivered and she fought back the urge to cry in her despair.

Her aunt and uncle weren't cruel, only desperate, and, in their desperation, they'd made some poor choices. But surely they would forgive her and see reason. When Gray's ship docked, everything would be put to rights without Oswalt's money.

The thought encouraged her. She shook her head and straightened her shoulders resolutely. 'My aunt and uncle aren't ogres, Paine. They're merely misguided. Whatever they do to me, it'll be better than marriage to Oswalt. I made my choices and I'll abide by them.'

'And the choices you made for them with your actions? Will they forgive you for driving them to the poor house?' Paine queried.

'What do you mean?' She looked baffled.

'I mean, will they get by without whatever Oswalt has promised them in exchange for you?'

'How did you know about that? I didn't tell you.'

Paine shrugged. 'If Oswalt is involved, money is involved.'

Julia looked guilty. 'Money is at the root of the contract. He's promised fifteen thousand pounds to my uncle. But my cousin Gray has a ship he's invested in. The cargo will cover our debts when it arrives and my uncle won't need Oswalt's money any more.'

'Wait, Julia,' Paine spoke slowly, putting his thoughts together as he talked. 'Has Oswalt given your uncle any money yet? An advance, perhaps?'

Her answer was just as slow. 'I don't know.' But then, there was so much she hadn't known just twenty-four hours ago. 'I suppose it could be possible.' The implications hit her full force. She twisted in Paine's arms to face him, hands clutching at his shoulders. 'Oh, no, if he has there's no way my uncle could pay him back. Any funds would already have been spent.' She thought with alarm of the wardrobe for her Season, that no expense had been spared for her gowns.

How had she ever thought her uncle and aunt could have suddenly afforded such expenditures when they'd sent her begging to the butcher to delay the meat bill back home on the estate? 'Now that I think about it, I am sure funds must have been given in advance.'

Paine nodded. 'Oswalt is known for his shrewd business dealings. If he's given someone money, there's bound to be a contract behind it, something legal done in writing to secure his investment.'

'There is a betrothal contract.' Julia looked frantically into Paine's face. What he said made sense, horrible sense. She couldn't decide which was worse: the cold reality that her actions would create a potential financial crisis for her family or that she had been bought and sold long before yesterday morning. What she'd thought was a prelude to her demise was in reality the finale. She swayed, relying on Paine's arms to keep her upright. 'Then this was all for nothing. My virginity was not a deal-breaker. He meant to have me regardless, just at a better bargain.'

'It is most likely the truth. Your uncle didn't think you'd run. Mortimer Oswalt doesn't care if you run—perhaps he even counted on the fact that you would.'

'Except he's lost his money. Granted, he's not out the whole sum but he's out a few thousand pounds,' Julia said, feeling a bit more herself now that the initial shock had passed.

Paine shook his head. Julia felt his grip about her waist tighten. 'Oswalt isn't a man who loses money with grace. He loses face with even less grace. He won't care if you run, Julia, because he'll find you. He'll count on your inexperience and lack of connections in the city, then will hunt you down and drag you back home in disgrace.'

Julia shook free of Paine's embrace and sank on to the bed. 'I have to go back and bargain with Oswalt. I have to fix this. I can't let my family suffer because of me.' She saw that Paine would protest that 'nice' people didn't sell their nieces.

'Really, they are good people. They've raised me since I was a little girl and I have repaid them with financial ruin.' She'd had her night of passion and got much more than she'd bargained for, a reward of sorts to act as a bulwark against the years to come. Perhaps for her family's sake she could stand it. In the morning light, it seemed to be the only solution in the wake of her transgressions the night before.

Her bravado received no support from Paine. Paine's eyes narrowed. 'I will not hear of it. Your solution is no solution at all. Oswalt is a lecher, but a keen student of human nature. He probably knew you'd run just as assuredly as your dolt of an uncle didn't think you would. This is just another perverse game he's invented for the entertainment of his sick mind. There's no disgrace in eluding him. Oswalt has probably engineered all this like a puppet show, knowing that eventually your sense of honour will bring you back, begging on your knees, and in the meanwhile, he can financially blackmail your uncle.'

Despair rocketed through her. There had never been a chance for her to win. She was playing a game that was far deeper than her abilities, a game that had been well under way, if Paine was to be believed, long before she'd joined it. She prided herself on her sharp mind, but she could not divine the layers laid out by Oswalt. She had no experience when it came to understanding the thought processes of the depraved.

What would she do now? She took quick stock of the inventory at her disposal. She still had a small opportunity and her earbobs. By now, Oswalt and her uncle knew she was gone, but they didn't know where. It was unlikely even Oswalt would deduce she'd gone out seeking someone to ruin her. They would think she'd act like a girl fresh from the country—perhaps seek a way back home or take refuge with girlfriends. They would check the houses of her acquaintances and the posting inns. That would keep them busy. But for how long? Long enough to catch a ship? They would check the docks next when the posting inns turned up empty, but maybe she could beat them.

Julia raised her head and drew a deep breath. She could not save her uncle; perhaps she never could have, even with her marriage. But she could save herself and pray that Gray's ship returned safely for the family's sake.

Her decision made, she could not impose on Paine Ramsden any longer. That was a shame. He seemed to know quite a bit about her betrothed and he made her feel unaccountably safe. 'If I could ask for one last favour, I would ask that you take me to the docks so that I may find passage on a ship. I have some money and I have my earbobs. I am certain it would be enough to get me a berth of some sort.'

God, the girl had courage. The news he'd imparted to her was dire, but here she was, already rebounding from it and planning her escape. The chivalrous fires she'd stoked in him last night roared to life at her suggestion. There was no way he would deliver her to the docks and leave her to set sail alone. There was no telling what kind of harm could befall a girl of such beauty, travelling without a chaperone on the high seas. No crew he'd ever sailed with would have let her go untouched. It was no credit to the scurrilous company he'd kept over the years, but the truth all the same.

Paine shook his head. 'Where would you go?'

'Anywhere. Whatever ship leaves first is the one I want. I haven't much time. They'll check the houses of my friends and the posting inns first. But they'll check the docks next.' Paine heard the frantic undertones in her voice. Courageous, but still frightened, then.

She took his reticence for refusal. 'I will go on my own if you will not assist me. It is not your responsibility anyway. You've done what I asked of you and that is the end of our association.' Julia rose from the bed, head held high and stuck out her hand. 'I thank you.'

Paine fairly exploded. Courageous, frightened *and* stubborn. The list of adjectives that described Julia Prentiss was growing rapidly. 'That's ridiculous, Julia. Sit down, you're going nowhere. When you do, it will be with me. You cannot face Mortimer Oswalt alone and you can't go wandering around out there on your own, resourceful as you are.'

He began pacing away his agitation, gratified to see that Julia obeyed. He'd fully expected she wouldn't. It was good to know she could do as she was told. She would need that skill in the days to come if they were to effectively deal with Mortimer Oswalt.

'They.' 'We.' His conscience warned him he was running headlong into all kinds of foolishness on behalf of Julia Prentiss, whom he had known less than a day; the foolishness of entangling with Oswalt again, and another kind of foolishness he couldn't name yet, but had everything to do with why the ancient Chinese warned against a man surrendering his yin.

Julia was peering at him through her thoughtful jade

eyes; a cool calculation crept into them, assessing him. 'Why?' she said.

'Why what?' Paine stopped his pacing.

'It has suddenly occurred to me that I know very little about you. *Why* should I trust you? Who's to say that you aren't just as sly or as debauched as he is?'

'You trusted me enough last night,' Paine shot back, angry that she had the gall to categorise him with the likes of Oswalt, although he knew she didn't know better—couldn't know better.

Julia skewered with him a stare, refusing to back down from her inquiry. 'Last night was about a temporary arrangement. It seems the stakes have changed a bit since then. Last night I didn't need to know. Today I do.'

Good lord, the woman was exasperating. Now was the time for plans, not for some parlour game of twenty questions. Paine sighed. Conceding this small victory seemed the quickest way to overcome the obstacle of her obstinacy and move forwards. 'All right, what do you want to know?'

'Only two things. Really, you'd think I was the Spanish Inquisition.' Julia gave a sigh of her own. 'First, let me ask my question again. Why should I trust you? Second, how is it that you know so much about my betrothed when you've only been back in England for less than a year?'

The questions brought Paine's hand to a halt, frozen in his hair where he'd been riffling through it. How had a simple bedding turned into something so complicated? He gave her the only answer he was prepared to give. 'You have two questions and I'll give you one answer that suffices for them both. Mortimer Oswalt is the reason for my exile.'

Julia looked ready to ask a thousand questions. He shot her a sharp glance that suggested she reconsider that angle of conversation. The answer he had given her was by no means a complete one, but it was the truth and it was all he was going to say on the matter.

He watched Julia draw a deep breath, her eyes never leaving his as her mind sifted through his latest revelation, weighing the facts he'd presented like a judge hearing a trial. And he did feel quite like a defendant, waiting to hear the sentence.

He tried to tell himself the verdict didn't matter to him. If she chose to leave, he'd be better off, able to return to his daily routine. If she stayed, upheaval was guaranteed. There would be a past to revisit and old wounds to reopen. Still, he could hear his own breath exhale with relief when Julia said in her firm, resolute tone, 'All right, all things considered, it seems best that I stay for now. But let's get one thing clear, Paine Ramsden, I will not be the subordinate in this. It's my fate and I will have a say in it.'

'Absolutely.' Paine knew that was a promise he couldn't keep the moment the words were out of his mouth, but he would have agreed to anything just to keep her safe. One woman had already fallen to Oswalt's evil wiles because of his failure. He'd make damn sure another one didn't suffer the same consequences.

Late that afternoon, Paine concluded Fate couldn't have sent a more obvious sign than Julia Prentiss than if that wily muse had sent him a letter. It was time to take back his life. The moment he'd decided to return to England, he'd known the day would come. Now it was here. It was time to finish his business with Oswalt and reclaim his place in society.

Not far from where he sat behind the wide, scarred cherrywood desk in the room he'd appointed as his makeshift office, Julia dozed on a clean but old sofa, a book haphazardly in her lap, still open to the page she'd been reading before nodding off. No doubt the activities of the last twenty-four hours were catching up with her. She slept like someone who knew she was safe. Her breathing was deep and even. She slept, knowing she would not be disturbed or rudely awakened by an unpleasant surprise. He envied her. It had been ages since he'd been able to sleep like that.

Paine pushed back from the desk, putting aside the pile of letters he'd been going through and propped his feet up on the desk's surface. Most of it was business correspondence. The grande dames of London had ceased issuing him invitations to their social events months ago. The only invitations he received were through his aunt's connections. London society had as much use for him as he did for it—very little. Until last night, it had been an amicable arrangement. That would have to change.

He couldn't protect Julia and effectively deal with Oswalt without the *ton*'s support. That had been his mistake last time. He'd been rash and overbold. Even though there had been those who had applauded his efforts, he'd done it in such a way and over such a thing that no one could openly champion his interference. He had not understood then that there were boundaries to what people would acknowledge, no matter the motivations.

He would be more careful this time, laying his foundations, establishing his credibility, before going after Oswalt. Paine recognised this was about himself as much as it was about Julia. Oswalt had once attempted to ruin him altogether for his sense of misguided honour. It was time to pay him back.

Julia stirred on the sofa, shifting her position in her sleep. She would have to be careful, too. She'd have to agree to stay in the house and go out only with him until they were ready to draw out Oswalt. It wouldn't do for Oswalt to learn of her location until Paine was ready. Oswalt and her uncle had an agreement for her marriage that could not be overlooked or minimised, no matter what the status of her maidenhead.

It made Paine's blood boil to think of Oswalt laying any kind of claim, even a paper one, to the beauty sleeping on his sofa. Oswalt was more than a debauched old man. He also experimented deeply in darker sexual practices that went far beyond the sacred joys Paine had initiated Julia into.

Twelve years ago, Oswalt had been an anxious man looking for a cure, any cure, for what ailed him. Paine could only make conjectures about how ravaged the man was now and how much more desperate he'd become for that cure. What the man had been willing to engage in twelve years ago had thoroughly shocked

Paine at a time when he thought he was an unshakable, jaded youth. Paine could not bear to envision what the man would be willing to do as his desperation grew exponentially over the years.

Julia had to be protected at all costs.

The force of that realisation was jarring. He had not felt the need to safeguard anyone to that extent for years, maybe not ever, certainly not a woman. But for whatever unexamined reasons, Julia brought out the need in abundance.

In his years abroad, he'd become a businessman, keen at assessing risk and profit. He seldom started a venture without an eye for how it would end. With Julia, it was different. The wealth of risk was there, as it was in any venture, but the profit was veiled at present. Still, with an intuition born of experience, Paine knew he had to see this through to whatever conclusion lay ahead. It wasn't enough that the passionate, curious, Miss Prentiss had to be protected. If it was, he could fob her off on people more sociably suitable than himself. He could probably talk his Aunt Lily into taking her. No, Julia had to be protected by him. For that to happen, he had to make himself respectable again. There were two ways to respectability: money and connections. Paine had both if he chose to use them.

Paine lowered his feet and got back to work. The first was easy. He had a shipping fortune at his disposal. From the stack of letters on his desk, there were many people in need of funds who cared far less where the money originated.

Many of the letters were from highly placed men appealing for a private loan to tide over ageing estates and emptying coffers. That would help with the second requirement for respectability—connections.

Those connections might take more time than he had and Paine had a better card to play, if he dared. His brother was the Earl of Dursley. They had been close once. His scandal with Oswalt had put a rift in that relationship, but perhaps it could be redeemed. He'd been disappointed that his brother, Peyton, had not written to him since his return. He'd loved his two brothers dearly. It looked like he would have to make the first move in that regard. Paine picked up his pen and began to write. The first letter was a long-overdue missive to his brother. The second was a terse note to one of his most trusted employees, Brian Flaherty, who was charged with the mission of seeking out news of Mortimer Oswalt and whether or not the man was hunting down his errant betrothed.

'Damn it, that's the fourth one.' Paine gave his cravat a hard tug and gave up. He'd tried for twenty minutes to fashion a *trône d'amour* knot. He was supposed to be at the hell by eight. At this rate, he wouldn't make it until midnight and all he had to show for his delay was an ignominious heap of crumpled lengths of once-pristine linen on the bed.

'Here, let me try.' Julia rose from the low bed where she sat watching him go through his *toilette*. She was dressed in his robe, fresh from a lazy bath, her hair still up in pins. She drew another length of fabric from the drawer and draped it around his neck. Standing in such proximity, he could inhale the delicate scent of her. Tonight, she smelled divinely of English lavender. If serenity and softness had a scent, this would be it. Somehow, the smell suited her to perfection.

She reached up to straighten the linen length and the overlarge robe gaped, affording him an unadulterated glimpse of her breasts. Blood heated in his groin instantly. After all their love play this morning and the night prior, he thought he'd be at least momentarily sated, that his body wouldn't be capable of rousing again so thoroughly or so soon. Evidence to the contrary made an auspicious tent in his dark trousers. Apparently he was wrong.

Intent on carrying out the intricacies of the knot, Julia was oblivious to his new state. Beyond a terse 'Keep your chin up', the linen held all her concentration. 'Make a single knot, place one end of the fabric over the knot to hide it, spread the remainder out and turn down into the waistcoat.' She bit her lower lip adorably while she muttered the 'recipe' for his knot, competent hands deftly shaping the fabric and smoothing it beneath the claret silk of his waistcoat.

'There.' Julia said with satisfaction, stepping back to survey her work. 'Much better.'

Paine peered into the looking glass above the cabinet holding his personal accessories. 'This is not the *trône d'amour.*'

'No. That was half your problem.' Julia flounced smugly on to the bed, a smile twitching at her lips, unaware how the robe strategically gaped. 'Your cravats aren't nearly starched enough for that knot and rightly so. Minimal starch in the cravats is all the rage these days.'

'How do you know so much about men's fashion?' Paine cocked his head to study the innocently provocative woman on the bed. She could rouse him without effort as the simple act of tying his cravat had proved.

'Three male cousins, two of whom fancy themselves to be pinks of the *ton*.' Julia gave him a wide smile. 'You need a valet.'

'I have a valet.' It was embarrassing to admit how heavily he'd come to rely on his valet, Jacobs, in the year he'd been home. During his sojourn abroad he'd managed to dress quite well on his own. But it had been out of the question to send for Jacobs with Julia present. He'd sent a note earlier in the day to Jacobs at his Jermyn Street rooms, telling the valet to stay away.

The fewer people who knew about her being here, the better. Until he could ascertain the current level of gossip surrounding her disappearance, it would be best to keep her hidden. That was why he felt it was so imperative he spent the evening at the club. The way Julia was looking at him right now though, he wondered if she'd ever let him leave.

She rose up on her knees on the bed, her eyes dancing with light mischief. 'I said the cravat starch was *half* of your problem. Do you want to know the other half?'

'Absolutely,' Paine sensed a game afoot and stepped towards her in anticipation of her gambit. In China, girls learned the art of seduction from pillow books, but

Julia had unerring instincts that couldn't be taught when it came to arousing a man. 'There's an ancient Chinese proverb that says "learning is a treasure that follows its owner everywhere". He encouraged in husky tones, 'I think you'll find me an excellent student.'

'Then I feel compelled to tell you that the other half of your problem was your trousers. They were *and* are too tight.'

She said it with such straightforwardness that Paine did not immediately understand until her hand reached for him, cupping him through his trousers. He gasped, the friction of the cloth against his member creating an exquisite set of sensations that made him simultaneously want to end and prolong the moment.

There was nothing for it. He'd be of no use at the club walking around in this frustrated state all night. The club's legitimate owner would have to make do without him tonight, at least for a while.

'Take my trousers off, Julia.' He managed a hoarse whisper and, in terms of words, that was all he managed for a good long while.

## Chapter Six

By midnight, Paine realised he wasn't going to the club. It wasn't too late to go. Indeed, midnight was considered early among those who frequented the hells. The real action and serious gambling would just be getting under way this time of night. If he went, he could still hear all the news about town. The truth was, he didn't *want* to go. The thought of leaving Julia and the warm bed for the dingy hell was vastly unappealing. For the first time in a year, he had somewhere else he wanted to be.

Julia stirred in his arms, her naked form pressed against him in reminder that he did not make it a regular practice to hold sleeping women at length after the act. 'Tell me about yourself,' Julia murmured, obviously unaware that that type of question after lovemaking was far too smothering. Countless times that question served to be a conversation ender, not starter, with him.

But miracles seemed to be in endless supply that evening. Not only did he not want to go to the gambling hell, he actually wanted to talk. Paine absently stroked a length of her hair. 'What do you want to know?'

'I want to know why you choose to flaunt convention, why you run a low-level gambling hell when you could move among high society, I want to know….'

'Whoa, one question at a time!' Paine protested, but only in jest. He found he didn't mind her curiosity. She was quite astute to pick up on the little contradictions of his world.

'The *ton* likes to ignore my money because it comes from a shipping business I ran for ten years in Calcutta. You and I know both know how working for money is frowned upon. But such narrow-mindedness works out because, as it happens, I like to ignore them.' Paine gave a little laugh, smiling in the dark. 'What about you, Julia? Do you like the *ton*nish world?'

'I haven't had much experience with it,' she admitted with a sigh. 'I should like to try a taste of it, though, just for fun, without the pressures of the Marriage Mart.' She spun him an innocent fantasy of waltzing in a fine ballroom with a dashing hero of a man, drinking champagne and wearing a beautiful gown. 'You must think me a foolish girl for thinking such things. I try to be practical, but every once in a while it's nice not to be.'

Paine chuckled and tightened his grip about her shoulders. 'Not at all, my dear. It's perfectly fine to have dreams.' It was a girlish fantasy, but he found he wanted to give it to her, hero, gown, waltz and all.

'Enough about me, Paine. This was supposed to be

about you. Was shipping one of your dreams? Is that why you were in India?'

The vixen was clever. She'd noticed the shift in conversation and had redirected it back to the original topic. Her comment also reminded him just what an ingénue Julia was. She hadn't been in town long enough to hear all the sordid details of his exile, only the more romantic rumours of his exile. She was young and untouched in so many ways. His thirty-two years seemed eons from her innocent nineteen.

Paine shifted his position for more comfort, rising up on an elbow so he could look at her while he spoke. 'I suppose you could say that. Shipping was a necessary dream. I am the third of three sons. You know *that* story—eldest gets the title, second son gets the military commission, third son gets the church or whatever else he can muster up. Well, it was obvious at a young age that I would never suit the calling of a church—something to do with getting caught with a village blacksmith's daughter when I was twelve.'

'No!' Julia gasped in mock surprise.

'Your lack of faith in me is touching. I must add in my own defence that there was some hope I might become a missionary. I did love to travel. I spent most of my school days poring over atlases and studying geography.' Paine drew down the bed sheet covering Julia and traced a delicate circle around the aureole of a breast. 'I think if my tutors had impressed upon me that more of the world went topless than naught, I might have gone the missionary route,' he said in seductive tones.

'You would have been a horrible missionary.' Julia laughed.

'Or a very persuasive one,' Paine whispered, tracing a ticklish line to her stomach. 'Have you ever read the Song of Solomon?'

Julia batted at his hand. 'Stop it. You're getting off track again. So you went to India and became a shipper?'

'Hmm.' He was losing interest in the story. Julia's body was far more entertaining. He could not recall the last time he was so captivated. 'In short, I ran an export business for ten years. I travelled the breadth and depths of India in search of rarities. I even went to China once. I would have gone to Burma if the war in 1824 hadn't closed down the borders. I sold the business, though, when I came back, and banked the profit.'

'What made you decide to come back?'

'I don't know. It just seemed like it was time. I realised that if I could build a business and thrive on my own, I could certainly handle any repercussions, if any, from the duel with Oswalt. Usually, the police are too busy with real crimes to worry about cases of the Quality fussing over honour.'

Julia opened her mouth to ask another question, but Paine silenced her with a finger to her lips. 'That's enough questions about me, my sweet. The less you know about me, the better.' At some point, part of him feared Julia would realise the kind of life he'd have led to acquire the knowledge he had and then she'd be completely appalled by the man she'd associated with. 'I have a better idea. We can play forfeits. We can each ask a question and the other can decide if they wish to answer the question or pay a forfeit to forgo the question,' Paine suggested. 'I'll go first since you've have your questions already. How did you come to live with your aunt and uncle?' It was admittedly a highly personal question, but Paine found he wanted to know everything about her and not because he was risking so much for someone he knew so little about. He wanted to know everything about the delectable Julia Prentiss.

'That's an easy question, so I'll answer it,' Julia said, rolling on to her back. 'My parents were killed when I was small in a freak boating accident. I've been with my father's family since I was five.' She looked over at him, her gaze intense and demanding of his attention. 'You don't know them. They're very good, very simple people. Whatever they've done, or whatever comes out of this mess with Oswalt, I want you to know that. What my uncle is attempting to do with Oswalt is appalling, but he's not a practical man. The world does not always deal fairly with philosophical men like him who love their theories and ideologies more than the realities of the day.'

'You don't have to defend them, Julia. They've certainly not defended you,' Paine shot back, unnerved that, even at this late date, Julia's goodness would try to countenance such inexplicable behaviour.

'Now it's my turn,' Julia said, setting aside the brewing quarrel regarding the culpability of her uncle. 'How many women have you been with?'

Paine groaned. 'What kind of question is that?'

Julia gave an insouciant shrug. 'My question. Are you refusing to answer?'

'Absolutely—a gentleman never brags of his conquests.' Paine put on a great show of gentlemanly affront.

Julia scooted towards him, a hand caressing his chest. 'You will pay the forfeit? Anything at all that I want?'

'That was the rule,' Paine drawled, his curiosity piqued at wondering what the inquisitive Julia would demand.

'Very well.' She put on a show of thinking, then said at last, 'Teach me the sutras.'

The request stunned him. 'Why ever would you want to learn that?'

'Why should you be the only one who knows the secrets of pleasure?' Julia challenged, smiling.

The minx thought she'd got the better of him and maybe she had, but not in the way she most likely thought. He guessed she'd meant to shock him. But the shock was the idea of Julia using such techniques with another man besides him at some point in a far-off future. 'These are intimate skills, Julia,' Paine warned. 'The sutras are about more than studies of sexual congress. They're about managing marriage and love quarrels as much as they are about the physicality of lovemaking.'

Even as he recited the admonitions his own teachers had given him, he knew Julia would heed them as much, or as little, as he had. In the beginning of his education, he'd seen them only from the English perspective of positions and sexual prowess. It had been much later before he'd begun to see them in the Hindu way, in the sacred way of being an exalted religious expression of oneness—the whole point of life.

'You agreed to a forfeit. Are you reneging?' Julia pressed.

'All right, I'll tell you about Kama.' Paine relented. Kama could be used by anyone for establishing peace of mind, it needn't be only sexual in orientation, although it was hard to remember that with Julia snuggling against him in expectation.

'Kama is the experience of enjoyment through utilising all five of the senses,' Paine said in a low voice.

'Ah, like the oranges this morning,' Julia said.

Paine chuckled softly, pulling her closer to him. 'Yes. Intercourse should be an experience of sights, sounds, scents and touches. A good lover sets the scene, from his own grooming to the place where he intends to be with his partner. A good lover is concerned about trust on all levels. Without trust, sex cannot attain its sacred plain.'

'Your sheaths,' Julia put in quietly, lying content in his arms, happy to listen to him carry out his forfeit. 'They're about trust.'

'It is a lover's duty to ensure a fulfilling sexual experience. If either partner is worried about the after-effects of their liaison, then the experience is minimised,' Paine said simply. These lessons had become so ingrained in him that he couldn't remember thinking otherwise. But hearing himself speak these lessons out loud reminded him how foreign these practices might be to someone else and a thought occurred to him.

'If you hadn't found me, Julia, where would you have gone?'

'I'd thought of a brothel,' Julia said sleepily. 'I am glad I found you, though.'

'Me, too,' Paine whispered as he felt her drift off into a contented sleep. And in truth he was. He'd had relationships with many women, most of them far more experienced than Julia. With them, no matter how short their acquaintance, he tried to obey the teachings of the sutras. He would not wish any of them subjected to the rigours of Oswalt's perverse demands.

It was a long while before he joined her in sleep, his mind racing about next steps. What would Oswalt be doing? Where would he be looking? What would the man do once it was clear Julia had disappeared from the usual avenues?

'Are you complete idiots? How can one innocent bit of muslin, who has never been up to town and has no friends here to speak of, give every last one of you the slip?' Oswalt bellowed to the panel of henchmen sitting in his offices on the London docks.

He jabbed a rough hand at one of the men. 'You, tell me again everywhere you looked.'

The big man named Sam Brown began his recitation one more time. Oswalt leaned back in his chair, hands intertwined over his belly. He did nothing to disguise the fact that he was furious. The girl was gone, completely vanished. How the hell had his crafty plan gone so drastically awry after having gone so smoothly?

He'd expected she would run. She'd shown far too much spirit to mildly abide by her uncle's wishes. He'd seen it from the start and he'd counted on it. She would run. He would drag her home in disgrace and make an agreement with her uncle to marry the disreputable piece of baggage before a scandal could erupt. All this benevolence in exchange for returning already advanced funds—funds he knew Lockhart couldn't repay. Then he would spring the trap that would net him Lockhart's ship in repayment of the loan. The cargo from the Americas was valuable, but that wasn't the reason he wanted it.

It was the first stage in the ruination of the poor, unsuspecting viscount. The second stage would follow in quick succession. Once bankrupt, the viscount would be stripped of everything but his title. The crown couldn't take the entailed estate, but anything else that wasn't nailed down was vulnerable to the creditors in payment. It wouldn't be long before the already pinched viscount would be stripped of anything of value. His estate would be worthless. That's where he came in. Oswalt would be waiting to redeem the estate of his beloved bride's family with his wealth. Oh, yes, he'd be waiting with his new bride, the viscount's luscious niece, in tow. Marriage to Julia would ensure he'd get the estate and look bloody honourable doing it. Julia's marriage to him would allow the Lockhart lands to stay 'in the family'. Such a noble act on behalf of a peer of the realm and years of economic servitude for the crown would surely help him clinch his long-coveted knighthood. The king couldn't overlook such generous favours.

Certainly, he could still move forwards with some pressure to retrieve the funds from Lockhart, but without the girl, he'd look like the opportunist he was. The girl made him look noble.

Oswalt cracked his knuckles with relish. He felt better thinking of the elaborate plot he'd concocted. The plan had been meticulously laid out. He had no feud with the viscount; the man was simply vulnerable, a veritable chicken waiting for plucking. It was hardly Oswalt's fault the man was in debt up to his eyeballs and, while sharp at the ideologies of politics, less astute when it came to personal economics.

The man would have made a good professor of philosophy, but Lockhart was out of his depth here. Oswalt knew. He'd hunted this sort of prey among the nobility before. It served those peacocks right for treating him with disdain all these years just because his money was earned instead of inherited. If Lockhart wasn't careful, he just might find himself bereft of his three sons and looking to Oswalt and Julia's children as legitimate heirs to the title.

'Where do you suggest we look next, boss?' The big man's question interrupted Oswalt's daydreaming.

'Try the ships. She might think to flee to the Continent.' Oswalt edged a piece of dirt out from under a shabby nail with another equally ragged nail. 'Try the gambling hells, too.' If she'd been foolish enough to go to ground in the darker sections of London, perhaps the gambling hells had word of it.

He hadn't sent men to those places earlier because it

seemed unlikely Miss Prentiss would find shelter there. According to his logic, she would have been more likely to seek out her one friend, Elise Farraday, or attempt to go back to the country. But since Elise had told the viscount she'd not seen her friend and the posting inns reported no one who matched Miss Prentiss in description or situation, he was forced to expand his search.

He was also forced to consider the risk that if his intended had tried to lose herself in the slums of London, she might have also lost her virginity. He grimaced at the prospect. 'Try the taverns and whorehouses; maybe she fell into trouble,' he added as an afterthought. The idea brought a leer to his dry lips. If he didn't need a virgin so badly, it would serve the beautiful Julia Prentiss right to be subjected to such embarrassment after shunning him so overtly in front of her uncle.

Once he had her back, he'd teach her how to be humble. His groin stirred at the thought, numerous images passing through his mind. He dismissed his men with bags of gold for bribes and drinks and spent the rest of the afternoon lasciviously contemplating all the different ways he'd instruct the errant Julia Prentiss in the art of humility.

# Chapter Seven

'What do you think, monsieur? *La fille est très belle, n'est-ce pas?*' the petite French dressmaker trilled for the countless time that afternoon.

Julia grimaced at the sound of the woman's ingratiating, high-pitched voice. For the past three hours, she'd been reduced to the role of a doll, standing at attention, draped in fabrics and pins in the middle of Paine's spare bedroom. The woman had immediately recognised Paine as her benefactor and had ceased asking for anyone's opinion but his. Indeed, Paine had been in charge all day, a fact that was growing increasingly annoying.

They'd slept late and, after breakfast, Paine had decided it was time to remedy the deplorable condition of her wardrobe. Actually, there was no 'condition' to remedy since she technically had no wardrobe beyond the robe of Paine's she'd worn for the better part of two days.

Two days! Those days seemed to have flown by, melding into each other, and yet two days hardly seemed enough time to countenance all that had passed between her and Paine. She felt she'd known him for far longer than the space of a few days. She twitched and the dressmaker reprimanded her.

Julia rolled her eyes and appealed to Paine. 'How much longer will this take?'

Paine ignored her. *'Non, le rose, madame.'* He gave a dismissing wave to the length of soft green muslin Madame held up to Julia's hair and gestured to a rose-coloured swatch instead.

*'Ah! Très bien, monsieur!'* the woman exclaimed. 'You have an excellent eye for women's clothing.'

Julia fought the urge to childishly stomp her foot. With all the aplomb she could collect, she said, 'I think we have enough for today.' She tossed her head and stepped down from the impromptu dais of a large square ottoman.

The woman gasped. She appealed to Paine. *'Monsieur*, we are not finished.'

Julia thought for a moment Paine would call her back, but he merely laughed, spearing her with a gaze that held myriad messages.

Julia waited for Paine in the sanctuary of his extraordinary bedroom. This gold-and-crimson room had become her refuge. It was shocking to think of how little she'd been out of this room in the past two days, how little desire she had to leave this room.

But the dressmaker's visit was a sharp reminder that she had to do more about her situation than sit in Paine Ramsden's bedroom. The dressmaker was also a reminder that she'd uncharacteristically let someone else take the reins. Since she'd landed in Paine's arms, he'd decided everything, from the course of action to be taken with Oswalt to the very colour and type of dress she'd wear. Was it really a good idea to let a virtual stranger plan her future? Aside from the pleasure he gave her, what did she know about him?

In some ways, Paine Ramsden was more than a stranger. Not even the rumours she'd heard about him had been accurate, so she didn't have gossip to fall back on. Paine Ramsden was a conundrum; for starters, it seemed unlikely that a purported gambler would bother buying property and devote the time needed to turn it into a business venture. Such effort spoke of long-term commitments, something she didn't associate with gamblers who didn't look further than the turn of a card or the throw of the dice.

Further confusion arose from his foreign but noble outlook on intimate relations—an outlook that permitted copious amounts of sex, but with a strong sense of ethics that was currently lacking among members of the English *ton*.

The concept was intensely juxtaposed to that of the hypocritical *ton*, making it impossible for the English mind, steeped in virginal traditions, to countenance. Julia doubted the rakes peopling the *ton* had the scruples to which Paine ascribed.

At the core of her conundrum was the reality she'd personally encountered in Paine. She'd deliberately gone looking for a man who wouldn't take an interest in her affairs after the initial act was done. Instead, she'd found a man who had his own reasons to stay inter-woven in the current events of her life. In a city of thou-sands, she'd managed to find the one man who wanted revenge on Oswalt.

Julia did not fool herself into thinking that Paine allowed her to stay out of any romantic attachment. He let her stay because she could assist in his retaliation. She was useful to him for that reason alone.

The rest of it—the love play, the instruction in intimate arts—meant nothing particular to him. He was a man used to a different code of conduct, a different code of honour. The English gentleman's code of honour abhorred the deflowering of virgins. Apparently, Paine's foreign codes didn't abhor the deflowering so much as it abhorred a poor bedding.

It would be too easy to misunderstand his intentions, to view his actions through English eyes. She must be careful to remember how Paine saw the world or else she'd start entertaining impossible notions about a future with Paine Ramsden—a man who would be easier to love than he would be to forget.

She *would* have to forget him. Eventually, this gambit would end in some fashion and she'd have to move on. Paine Ramsden certainly would. He'd go back to his cryptic lifestyle, his exotically conducted affairs and forget about the viscount's niece who had begged him to deflower her. The vision was a difficult one to stomach.

Downstairs, a door shut at the back of the house, sig-nalling the dressmaker's departure. Within moments,

Paine's footfalls sounded on the steps and shortly afterwards the bedroom door opened.

'Julia, love, you have the patience of a flea!' he proclaimed in high spirits. 'That is Madame Broussard, the finest dressmaker in the city by many accounts. One does not order her about like a common servant. She might leave pins in your gowns.'

Paine came to sit beside her, pulling the tails of his shirt out of his trousers' waistband. 'But you were right. That was enough for the day. I didn't think I could stand another minute of looking at your delectable body clad in nothing more than a shift. I thought my trousers would burst.' He tugged on her hands. 'Come, relieve me, Julia. I'll show you "the splitting of the bamboo". You'll like it.'

He looked boyish and carefree; it took an enormous amount of will power to resist. 'Wait, Paine.' Julia shook her head. 'We need to talk. It's been two days and I'm no closer to knowing what my future holds than I was the night I walked into your club.'

Paine shrugged and lay back on the pillows, hands behind his head. 'Go ahead, then, talk,' he offered expansively.

'What's the meaning of all this?' Julia began. 'What's the purpose of all the gowns? Why am I staying here? What's to become of me? This is not what I had planned at all.' She could hear the frustration rising in her voice and resented it. The last thing she wanted to do was sound like a hysterical girl.

Paine tried for humour. 'Well, I will want my robe back at some point in the future.'

'Not funny. Really, tell me, what am I doing here?'

Paine sat up. 'You are staying safe until I have all my pieces in place, Julia. Oswalt is dangerous. We cannot rush out and challenge him. He's too smart for that. I have asked my investigators to make inquiries about Oswalt's business. We need to know what he is up to and plan accordingly. I've asked for inquiries about your uncle, too. I know you say he's an honest fellow, but I am a bit more cynical.'

'Inquiries! I did not give you leave to pry into my family's private matters,' Julia protested, further exclamations silenced by the soft press of his finger against her lips.

'As for the dresses,' Paine went on, overriding her dismay, 'we'll need the backing of the *ton*, some of them at least, for what I have planned. I mean to reclaim my good standing.'

'Good lord, that could take years!' Julia cried without thinking.

Paine chuckled. 'Again, your trust in me is overwhelming, my dear. I think you'll see it will only take a matter of weeks.'

'And you'll be wearing the dresses while you reclaim this good standing?' Julia probed wryly, not following his logic in its entirety.

'You'll be by my side, Julia. You're the key to my reform. The influence of a good woman's love is a powerful source of conversion.'

'I haven't converted you,' Julia said carefully. A man who knew such colourful expressions and methods for lovemaking like 'splitting the bamboo' was in no way reformed. 'When did you decide on this story?' Here was yet another example of Paine Ramsden's managing ways.

'Yesterday afternoon when I was taking care of some correspondence, I started thinking about it. Today, somewhere between the blue silk and the green muslin, it all seemed to come together. The *ton* will like the story, it's a fairy tale come to life and it will make a good explanation for how I turned up with you.'

Paine's eyes glinted with the excitement of the drama. 'We'll tell everyone it was love at first sight. When I saw you, I knew my erring days were over. It's a plausible reason for being together and it will give me a valid excuse to keep you close. Once Oswalt learns that you're with me, the game will be fully engaged. He'll stop at nothing to have you back. We just have to draw him out into the open and expose him for what he is.'

Julia recognised the plan wasn't quite that simple. They needed the *ton* to accept them, or rather to accept Paine, so that there would be support for exposing the issues with Oswalt. That support would be needed to bring Oswalt down. Apathy could be a powerful non-weapon. If no one cared enough to buy into their cause, the status quo would remain the norm. That norm would see her wed to Oswalt, the contract with her uncle upheld. For Julia, that outcome was unacceptable.

'And until then?' Julia asked, moving back towards the bed.

'Until then, all we have to do is pretend we're in love.' His eyes were mesmerising in their persuasion. Who could resist those blue eyes, dark with desire? 'Are you ready to split the bamboo?' he whispered, nipping at her neck with soft kisses.

'I see this has nothing to do with trees,' Julia managed to flirt between kisses.

'No, not trees, love, but it has everything to do with your deliciously long legs.' Paine moved and knelt before her on the bed, running a hand down the length of one leg and gently lifted it over his shoulder. 'Make your legs into a raised V for me, Julia. We'll start with the "yawning position" and take our "bamboo" from there.' He leaned forwards to kiss her mouth. 'And no quips about the "yawn" being boring. I assure you it is not. In fact, it's quite exciting.'

'Why?' Julia murmured.

'You'll find out,' Paine offered in cryptic reassurance.

After that, she had no more thought for questions. Julia gave herself over to Paine's exotic instructions. In the wake of his persistence and passion, Julia found it wasn't hard to convince herself his plan made sense. Neither was it hard to do her part and pretend she was in love with him. As he knelt before her and showed her how to alternately raise her legs to his shoulders, thus 'splitting the bamboo', she suspected she was already half way there.

There was no question of Julia going to the gaming hell with him, although it was the devil convincing her of that. He might have been able to take one night away from the club, but he could not afford to be absent another night. Not only would it deprive him of valuable information, but his absence was sure to be noticed. Julia had finally consented to be left behind on the condition that he bring her back a wig.

Thinking of her saucy demand as he left brought a smile to his lips even now. Bringing Julia with him had a certain appeal. He might even teach her a few of the club games. Just the thought of Julia's bosom leaning over the dicing table stirred him and he'd only been gone from her an hour. Paine set the tantalising image aside. Tonight, he had work to do, work that mattered to him and to Julia.

John, the doorman, was waiting for him when Paine arrived at the club shortly after eight-thirty. 'We all missed you last night.' He gave a short nod to the group of dandies led by Gaylord Beaton, talking too loudly in the corner. 'They want to play faro with you. The bunch of them came in last night.'

Paine nodded, sizing up the rowdy group. He'd bet they would be in more sombre spirits by midnight. He'd hoped the earlier loss at Commerce would have taught Beaton a lesson about playing beyond one's means. Apparently not. 'Anything else?'

'The gel that came looking for you has a man looking for her.' John lowered his voice. 'That man over there has been asking about her. She matches the description he's been giving, anyway.'

Paine's eyes narrowed, taking in the burly, unkempt man by the wall, slumped over a glass of cheap brandy. 'What did you tell him?'

John shook his head. 'Nothing. I didn't like the looks or smell of him. The gel doesn't fit with him, so I thought the worst.'

'You're right about that. The girl's from a good family. Until I instruct anyone otherwise, we've never seen her. Make that clear to everyone—the dealers, the bartender, the other girls.' Paine bounced on the balls of his feet, organising the evening's business in his mind.

'John, send a bottle of our best brandy to the dandies with my compliments. I'll join them for faro at ten. I'll be in my office settling accounts until then. When Brian Flaherty comes in, I want to see him directly.'

Flaherty was a stocky Irishman with a balding pate and good humour in spite of his dark career as a private investigator. In the past year, Paine had come to trust the Irishman implicitly when it came to the business of the gambling hell.

The man was a veritable bloodhound, able to sniff out the backgrounds of Paine's sundry clientele. No credit was extended, no deal struck, without Flaherty's stamp of approval. The man's ability for research had saved Paine countless pounds. Tonight, Paine was hoping Flaherty had information regarding Oswalt and his search for Julia.

'The man is definitely looking for her,' Flaherty said, easing himself into a chair in Paine's office. 'Oswalt has his men everywhere. The three coaching inns I asked at indicated others had inquired about the same girl early yesterday. The good news is that it appears he didn't think to start searching gaming hells and other such establishments until tonight. That means he's still guessing with nothing substantial to go on,' Flaherty reported.

Paine nodded. He'd expected as much, but it was good to have those suspicions confirmed. 'And the uncle?'

Flaherty shook his head. 'I am still working on that. It's hard to say. Oswalt had visited the uncle, but to my knowledge the uncle has not been asking around for the girl except for inquiries at the Farradays.'

'Thank goodness for that at least.' Paine sighed. He'd take all the luck he could get. He'd hoped the man had enough sense to keep Julia's disappearance quiet and it seemed he had. If no one was aware of her disappearance, it would be far easier for her uncle to cover it up, explain it away with a believable story, or even with Paine's story that he and Julia had fallen in love at first sight. As things stood currently, only Julia's family and Oswalt knew she was gone.

Paine preferred it that way. 'Can I trust the uncle?' Paine mused out loud. The man had shown surprising discretion so far. Perhaps he'd judged Barnaby Lockhart too harshly, too soon. He'd thought he might go to the uncle and assure him of Julia's safety.

Paine also had other reasons for seeking out Uncle Barnaby. Paine wanted to 'help' him concoct a safe story that explained Julia's absence. It would be easy enough to use the sick relative in the country story and neatly tack on that while there she encountered him, under the watchful eye of chaperons, of course. Romance bloomed, allowing their 'courtship' in London to take place upon her return.

Paine most definitely wanted to have a hand in that alibi if he could manage it. Julia's situation demanded concentration if one was to avoid a scandalous misstep. It could not be left to an amateur.

So far, his luck was holding. The uncle hadn't raised the hue and cry. But his silence wouldn't last long. Even if the uncle didn't say anything, people would be asking for Julia. Like any busy débutante, she was no doubt committed to events ahead of time. When she didn't appear at the places she was expected, people would miss her and her uncle would have to explain. Paine wanted an alibi in place before that happened.

As much as Paine wanted to pay Uncle Barnaby a visit, Paine worried that Oswalt's hold on the man would be too strong for the keeping of any secrets. The last thing he needed was to face Oswalt's henchmen in an unequal fight. It was a daunting reality to acknowledge that he was literally the only person standing between Julia and Oswalt. If he fell, Julia would be entirely at the man's mercy.

Flaherty affirmed his misgivings. 'No, the uncle is under too much pressure. He sees Oswalt as his only way out from under the burden of his debt. Already, Oswalt is bargaining for the girl's return. He says he'll marry her anyway if she's found, but he'll pay less than the originally promised sum. If she doesn't reappear, he is seeking a return of the funds he's already advanced.'

Paine's eye brows perked at the mention of a new deal brewing between the uncle and Oswalt, his brain working quickly to assimilate the new details. 'Is there a chance the uncle can pay?' He didn't believe there would be, but he had to be certain.

'I don't think so.' Flaherty rummaged through a battered black bag at his side and pulled out a sheaf of papers. 'Here's what I managed to get from the uncle's solicitor.'

Paine took the sheaf and whistled. 'Your skills never cease to amaze, Flaherty. I don't want to know how you managed this.' He quickly scanned the documents, records of the uncle's latest finances.

The outlook was dismal, but not unexpected. Viscount Lockhart's pockets were to let except for the ship that Julia had mentioned. If Julia didn't return, the family's collapse would be immediate. The ship's cargo, should it return, would be used to pay back what the family owed Oswalt. There would be nothing left over. If Julia returned, there was no telling how far the reduced sum would go in alleviating the family's financial concerns. Paine wagered it wouldn't go far enough. Oswalt wanted something that the viscount's financial viability blocked.

'Help me think, Flaherty.' Paine drummed his fingers on the desk. 'Why would Oswalt go to all this trouble to ruin a man who is already on the brink of it? He's deliberately pushing Lockhart over the edge. He's singled Lockhart out for a reason.' Paine rubbed at his brow, gathering his thoughts. 'Flaherty, look into Oswalt's business dealings and, while you're at it, find out what cargo Lockhart's ship is carrying. There might be something telling in that. Let me know when you have news.'

Paine had a feeling that marriage to Julia was merely part of a larger plan Oswalt had set in motion. She was one of many steps—a critical step at that if the amount of manpower behind his search for her was any indicator—but Paine had no idea what that larger game might be, only a feeling that if Julia wasn't found, Oswalt's game might be hampered. Oswalt was a man who didn't like to be thwarted. It made him an exceedingly dangerous opponent. If Oswalt felt cornered, he would become more volatile. On the other hand, he might also become more desperate and that could work in Paine's favor.

He would also send an anonymous note to Uncle Barnaby, letting him know Julia was safe and that he should give out the story she was tending a sick relative in the country if he wanted to minimise scandal. He wanted to do more, but under the circumstances, the meagre effort would have to be enough.

There was nothing to do now but reassure and wait. He would reassure Julia that he'd taken some short-term steps to alleviate her uncle's worry and to pre-empt the potential scandal. Regardless of his thoughts on the worm her uncle was, Julia obviously regarded him in a more friendly light. And he would wait; wait for the responses to the letters he'd sent out; wait for Flaherty's news regarding Oswalt's pursuits. Then there would come a time of action.

Between now and then, he would skin the young bucks waiting for him at the faro table and teach Julia to gamble. The thought of the last brought a lingering smile to his face.

# *Chapter Eight*

'I'm ready,' Julia said with a touch of uncertainty at the top of the stairs. She nervously smoothed the skirts of the deep rose evening gown Madame Broussard had delivered earlier in the day. The gown was of the first stare of fashion, far beyond any of the pale, virginal gowns in her débutante's wardrobe at home. There was no disputing the quality of the gown with its exquisite tailoring and stitching.

'How do I look?' She moved slowly down the stairs, highly conscious of the plunging neckline and the way the gown clung to her silhouette. Perhaps the colour was too bold after all? She would never have dared such a bold colour either. She suspected only Paine Ramsden would have the audacity to pair the rose with a cinnamon-haired girl and carry it off. She had to admit the shade Paine had chosen complemented her hair rather than clashed. Not that it made any difference tonight. Her auburn tresses were securely tucked up under a black-haired wig.

Julia reached the bottom of the staircase and gingerly touched a gloved hand to her head to check her wig one more time. 'Say something, Paine. Do I look all right?' But she already had her answer. Apparently the gown achieved its desired effect if Paine's intent gaze was any indicator.

His eyes were hot; the wolfish smile spreading across his lips were approval enough. There was a certain thrill in earning the approval of a man like Paine Ramsden. He didn't have to say anything. She knew with her new-budding woman's intuition that he liked what he saw—that he desired her.

'You're absolutely ravishing, Julia. I can't decide if you're Snow White or Red Riding Hood. You look like a fairy tale come to life, even with that wig.'

Julia gave a faux-pout. 'Little Red Riding Hood? That makes me sound like a child.'

Paine leaned close to her ear and nipped the tender flesh of her ear lobe. 'No, not a child, Julia, a delicious ingénue,' he drawled. 'When I look at you, I see an intoxicating mixture of innocence and sensuality, a lady about to awaken to the pleasures of the world.'

Warm heat rushed to Julia's core at the images his low tones conjured. There was no doubt as to what those worldly pleasures might be and how they might be provided. The man flirted so well, it was impossible not to be taken in. 'Then perhaps you are mistaken. I am neither Snow White nor Red Riding Hood, but Sleeping Beauty.'

Paine laughed near her ear, enjoying her witty efforts. 'If you're Sleeping Beauty, what does that make me?'

Julia bit back the first reply that sprung to her lips— that he was the prince come to awaken the princess with love's first kiss. That would never do for a man like him. It implied too much. 'Why, that's easy,' she said instead. 'You're the wolf. You're always the wolf.'

Paine stepped back, his eyes dancing. 'Then let's away to my lair.' Her answer had pleased him. Julia wondered if the banter had been a test of sorts to make sure she wasn't entertaining any romantic notions.

The idea to go with Paine had been an exciting prospect in theory. Dressing up in a low-cut gown, donning a wig and becoming someone else altogether for the evening had been exhilarating—right up to the part where they arrived at the gambling hell.

Paine's coach lurched to a halt and Julia's stomach did a lurch of another kind. 'Are you sure no one will recognise me?' she asked tentatively. Paine had explained to her that Oswalt's man had come the night before asking about her and that it was possible the man might come again once Oswalt knew this hell was Paine's territory.

Paine offered her another round of reassurances and leaped down. He turned to hand her out of the carriage. 'Remember, Julia. This is not a fancy place. You'll stand out like a diamond among coal. But we're counting on that. If Oswalt's man is here, there's nothing better for throwing him off the scent than a glimpse of my dark-haired lady throwing dice. He'll report back to Oswalt that the woman with me didn't resemble you in the least.'

He shot her a dazzling smile, meant to reassure. 'It'll

be fun, Julia. Relax. Tonight, you're not Julia Prentiss, you're Eva St George, an actress with many talents.'

That made her smile. Julia summoned her courage, telling herself she was on the brink of a grand adventure. When would she have the chance again to visit a gaming hell? As Julia Prentiss, the niece of a viscount, such behaviour was beyond the pale but as the embodiment of the fictitious Eva St George, anything was possible.

An hour later, she was fully into her role as the adventurous Eva St George. She stood at the head of a crowded hazard table, giddy with the thrill of it all. It was her turn to act the part of the caster. She jostled the dice in anticipation. Near her ear, Paine offered a running litany of instruction.

'Call your main before you throw, that's any number you choose between five and nine. If that number comes up, you win the stake. If you throw a two or three, you lose—it's called "throwing crabs." If neither the main nor the crabs comes up, it's your chance and you neither win nor lose on it.'

'Seven!' Julia called out, tossing the ivory cubes on to the green felt table. A six turned up first and she bit her lip, relieved to see a one showing on the other cube. 'I win!' Julia cried.

The men gathered around the table laughed good naturedly at her excitement. She picked up the dice again, prepared for another round. Paine bent over and blew on them for luck, taking a fair amount of ribbing from the other players.

'Lady Luck is supposed to blow on the dice, Ram,' one of them shouted.

'Are you kidding?' another joked, 'With Ram's luck, I'd let him blow on my dice any night of the week.'

Julia called a six and threw her main. 'I won again!' In her enthusiasm, she flung her arms around Paine's neck and pressed close against him. 'I love this game!' In reality, she thought she'd love anything that kept Paine by her side, whispering in her ear. The combination of his dark evening wear and the scent of his spiced soap was intoxicatingly potent. Tonight, he exuded a commanding aura of urbane control and powerful masculinity. He was a man in charge. He could just as easily have come from an elite club or *ton* ballroom.

Paine responded to her embrace wholeheartedly, sweeping an arm about her waist and capturing her upturned face with a full-mouthed kiss that had the table whooping. 'Let's see how that helps your luck,' Paine said with a grin, releasing her and handing her the dice. 'Third time lucky.'

'Looks like she already got lucky,' someone at the end of the table hooted.

Julia blushed. The public display from Paine had been unexpected until she remembered who she was supposed to be. A seasoned actress would not balk at such a display or at any comment made about it. Eva St George would take such a moment in her stride. Julia Prentiss would have to, too.

As he stood beside her, Paine's hand settled at her waist, steadying her as if he guessed her reaction.

'You're doing fine, quite convincing actually,' he whispered near her ear.

She threw again and the table cheered.

The raucous laughter coming from the hazard table held Sam Brown's attention almost against his will. There was a boisterous crowd tonight. The noise made it hard to concentrate on surveying the rest of the club. He'd been here the prior night, too. He'd spent that night in vain. No sign of his boss's girl had materialised. Yet, he had a hunch that someone here knew something. The glint in the big doorman's eye suggested as much. The doorman had been too quick to dismiss his questions and deny knowledge of anyone meeting the girl's description. So, with nothing else to go on, he'd come back to wait and to watch.

From his small table against a back wall, he had a clear view of all the comings and goings in the place. Technically, no one was going to slip past him, but his attention kept drifting back to the hazard game. A whoop of excitement carried over the general commotion, followed by applause. The sea of people around the hazard table shifted. He caught a glimpse of a nattily dressed man in dark evening clothes and a stunning dark-haired woman dressed in a striking rose gown, leaning over the table with the dice.

The man, he recognised from the prior night. The man had been alone then and not dressed as formally as he was tonight. Still, it was the same person. His face, with its elegant cheekbones and aristocratic flair, was quite memorable.

A serving girl in a provocatively low blouse passed his table. He grabbed her arm. 'Another brandy,' he ordered, tossing a coin on her tray. He jerked his head towards the hazard table. 'Who's the gent?'

'That's Paine Ramsden.' The girl sighed, her voice full of an annoying touch of hero-worship.

He grunted, scoffing at the girl's obvious infatuation. The handsome coves had it too easy. 'Is he bleeding royalty, then?'

'He is to us. He runs this place. He comes in every night and handles all the business personally.' She smiled, but he knew the smile wasn't for him. She was remembering something about the god-like gambling-hell owner. Well, at least she was willing to talk about the object of her adoration. It was more than what he'd got out of anyone else—another telling sign that something simmered beneath the surface here. Everyone was too close-lipped.

He smiled back at the girl and nodded, encouraging her conversation. She leaned towards him. 'He's not royalty, but there's a rumour that his brother is an earl.' She sighed again. 'Just think, the brother of an earl rubbing shoulders with us in our part of the world. Who would have thought?'

The girl moved on, her stock of facts about Ramsden exhausted. But she'd given him plenty to chew on. Who would have thought, indeed? What was the brother of an earl doing managing a cut-rate gambling establishment? The place wasn't a place the Quality would frequent. He could see first hand that the people here were from London's underbelly, rough men, men of disrepute—the dandies in the corner being an exception. But Sam could imagine why those toffs had come. No doubt they were looking for the adventure and excitement they thought hobnobbing with the lower classes could provide.

The girl returned with his brandy and set it down. 'What about the woman with him? Do you know her?'

The girl shook her head. 'He's always got a pretty bird on his arm. Some of the other girls say she's an actress.'

He nursed his brandy and stared hard at the handsome couple. He could tell, even from a distance, that Ramsden was a charismatic man, but the real reason everyone flocked to the table was the woman. The deep hue of her gown was a siren, drawing men to her from across the bleak, colourless hall. Her laughter kept them. She was enthralled in the game, her excitement over winning as genuine as her disappointment when the dice betrayed her.

The man finished his brandy and edged closer to the crowd, hovering on its rim, studying the woman. Someone in the group called out, 'Come on, Eva, roll a good one!' She held up the dice for Ramsden to blow on for luck. She tossed and won. The group cheered. 'Hurrah for the St George luck!'

Eva St George. Now he had a name and an occupation. That would be something to go on. But what? According to the serving girl, it wasn't unusual for this Ramsden to have a woman by his side. There was nothing to suggest a connection between this couple and the lost girl. Another wasted evening and an unusual incident of his hunches failing him.

He gave the happy table a last look and was about to call it a night when he felt a discreet presence at his elbow. A well dressed young man with slightly dissipated features stood next to him.

The young man stared ahead at the game in progress as he talked, making no attempt at eye contact. 'Are you the man seeking information about a girl?'

He eyed the newcomer, sizing up his potential. 'Yes. Do you know something?'

'Do you have the means to pay?'

He nodded. 'But only for good information. I've got a nice knife in the ribs for liars. Meet me in the alley out back and we'll see what you've got.' He hadn't survived this long as one of Oswalt's henchmen for believing every tip he received.

The young man waited out in the alley for him, clearly nervous. Good. It gave him a chance to assume the upper hand. 'All right, tell me what you know. I have a fifty pounds if your information is good.'

The young man brightened at the prospect of money. Excellent. The buck could be bought.

'The girl was here a couple of nights ago. She wore an aquamarine silk dress and had reddish-brown hair.' The boy blurted his information quickly. 'Can I have my money?'

He narrowed his eyes. 'Not so fast. Why should I believe you? Perhaps you overheard me describing her.'

The boy swallowed hard, his Adam's apple bobbing. 'I saw her with my own eyes. I was sitting at a table, playing Commerce with Ramsden himself. He went to the door and met the girl. Then he took her back to his office. Ramsden didn't return that evening or the next.'

He nodded. 'Very good.' He'd noted the hardness to the boy's voice when Ramsden's name was mentioned. It explained much, like why the finely dressed young man was out in the alley talking to the likes of him. He turned friendly. 'Did Ramsden clean you out?'

'Yes.' A sigh followed. 'I didn't think I'd lose as much as I did, but Ramsden has the devil's own luck. If the pater finds out I've lost my quarterly allowance already, I'm in the suds.'

He smiled in the dark. From the sound of it, this wasn't the first time this bucko had had a run of bad luck. 'How much do you owe Ramsden?'

'A hundred pounds,' the lad said dejectedly.

'Tell you what, I'll give you a hundred pounds— fifty for your information tonight and there's another fifty in it for sticking around the club and letting me know if the girl resurfaces.' He tossed a leather purse full of sovereigns at Beaton. 'There's good money in information,' he assured the lad.

'How shall I contact you?'

He clapped the boy on the shoulder with false bonhomie. 'Don't worry, I'll find you.'

From the hazard table, Paine covertly watched Gaylord Beaton re-enter the club after a ten-minute absence. It took all of his will power to refrain from dragging the boy outside and doling out the pummelling he deserved. The boy was a poor loser and a stupid one at that. After losing at Commerce, followed with a losing streak at faro the other night, the boy hadn't learned his lesson about playing within his means. Paine knew the loss had cost him dearly. He'd hoped it would teach the boy to keep away from the tables.

The lesson hadn't taken and now the boy was bent on revenge, no doubt seeing Paine as the arbiter of his ill fortunes. Unfortunately, the boy wasn't all that good at skulking. Paine didn't have to ask John where the boy had gone. He'd tried too hard to slip out into the alley unnoticed by the back door.

Paine could guess, too, who he'd met out there. Oswalt's man had been back. He'd had his eye on him all night. He'd watched the man chat to the barmaid. In spite of his best efforts to keep Julia's appearance at the club secret, it appeared the secret was starting to surface and his connection to Julia along with it. It was bad luck that Gaylord Beaton had been at the club the night Julia had shown up and that he'd found the courage to share that information with Oswalt's henchman.

Paine grimaced at the consequences. By dawn, if not sooner, Oswalt would know he ran the club where Julia was last seen. Oswalt would correctly surmise that Julia was with him, knowing that he'd not let an innocent loose to be caught in Oswalt's clutches. The only secret that hadn't been exposed was that Julia was the dark-haired woman with him.

The disguise of Eva St George had been a resounding success on all levels. At times, Paine had struggled to remember the woman beside him was the gently reared niece of a viscount. Julia's *joie de vivre* was utterly convincing. But it would not hold. The henchman might not have put two and two together, but Oswalt was clever. He'd see through the disguise and the coincidence that two new women had shown up at the club within two nights of each other, especially after he searched the playbills of London and determined there was no actress named Eva St George currently treading the boards.

Paine shot a look at Julia, laughing as she tossed the dice. He didn't want to alarm her. She was having so much fun. The men around the table were utterly charmed. But he needed to call an end to the evening. He only had a handful of hours to get Julia to safety, somewhere where she could be protected.

He was a loner, used to relying on himself. It was rather difficult to think of anyone or any place where he could take Julia. But one place did surface, as hard as he tried to fight it. He could take her home. Not to Jermyn Street or to the anonymous town house on Brook Street, but to his family home, the seat of the Earl of Dursley, deep in the sheep country of the Cotswolds.

He hadn't been there for twelve years, and he'd left in disgrace, but it was still the one place he thought of when he thought of being safe. Between the influence of the Earl and the thick sandstone walls of his home, Julia couldn't be safer, no matter what kind of reception he himself would receive from his brothers.

He sighed and edged to Julia's side, placing a possessive hand at her waist. He murmured something into her ear about leaving. It was time. The prodigal was going home.

# Chapter Nine

Something was amiss. Paine's playful whisper in her ear about going home didn't match the iron grip he had on her waist as he guided her to his carriage parked in front of the hell. That was odd, too. When they'd arrived, they come in the back door and left the carriage in the wide alley.

'What's happened?' Julia asked the moment the carriage door was shut behind them. 'Why are we parked in front?'

'Because I wasn't sure who was waiting in the alley for us,' Paine said tersely.

Julia didn't need further explanation. She knew what that implied. She swallowed hard. 'Oswalt knows.'

Paine gave a short nod. 'He will know shortly. Gaylord Beaton, one of the dandies who comes slumming, went outside with Oswalt's man. I don't have to be a fortune teller to know what transpired. Beaton was here the night you came to the club. He's been losing heavily. I am sure he saw this as a prime opportunity to get a little of his losses back and some revenge against me as well.' Paine sighed. 'Oswalt will put the pieces together when his man gives him the news.'

'Then Oswalt will come looking for you.' Julia supplied the rest, concern evident in her tone. This was the very scenario she'd wanted to avoid. She didn't want anyone entangled in her problems. She'd sought Paine out because he wasn't likely to take an interest. But just the opposite had occurred. She didn't want him to become a casualty of her folly.

'Don't worry,' Paine said. 'He's got to find us first.'

'Where are we going?'

'We're going to my family home in the Cotswolds. I don't know what kind of reception we'll get, but I know my brother won't turn us away. We'll stop at the house briefly, just long enough to pack a few supplies, no more than an hour. I don't know how much time we have before Oswalt sounds the hunt.'

Julia didn't like the grimness in Paine's tone. At the house, she tore upstairs with single-minded efficiency, throwing necessities into the first satchel she could find. A travelling valise was right where Paine had said it would be. She dragged it out from under the low bed and stuffed a few items of clothing for them both into it. Paine was downstairs furiously dashing off notes.

He'd said no more than an hour at the house. She thought an hour was too much. Julia dashed downstairs fifteen minutes after going up them with a jumble of cloaks and a spare blanket draped over her arms, the valise in one hand, the small satchel full of toiletries in the other. She couldn't attest to how well the garments she'd haphazardly packed would hold up, but at least they'd be clean and warm when they needed them.

Paine looked up at the sound of her racing feet on the steps. 'I am just finishing a note to Madame Broussard about your clothes,' he said, too casually for Julia's taste.

'My clothes? How can you think about something like that at a time like this?' Julia scolded, breathing hard from her exertions. 'Let's go. Hurry.' She hated the desperation welling in her voice, but there was no hiding it. She was scared.

Paine came to her, placing a hand on each arm. 'Everything will be fine. I will not let Oswalt lay a hand on you, not even a finger. But for me to be successful, we can't let Oswalt drive us off course from our plan. When we return to London, you'll need those clothes for all the events we'll be attending. I rather Oswalt not get wind of this residence because a delivery boy comes poking around with trunks of lady's clothing and starts asking questions because he doesn't know where to leave them.'

Julia hardly heard the last part of his rationale. Her mind was still stuck back on the 'for me to be successful' part. 'That's just it. I don't want you to be successful. I didn't want anyone involved at all and now you're in this up to your neck and we're racing off to implicate your brother, the earl, too. Why don't we just drive over to the Buckingham Palace and involve George IV, too?'

'Well, if you thought it would help,' Paine drawled, sending the last of his quick missives.

'Arrrgh! Men!' Julia stamped her foot in irritation. No, that wasn't nearly strong enough for what she was feeling. How could he be so calm when Oswalt could be out in the streets looking for them already? Men had no sense of righteous, warranted, fear.

Paine came around from his desk. 'I am sorry, Julia. I shouldn't have joked. It was poorly done of me.' He drew her into his embrace. 'Go to the carriage. The coachman is hitching up my travelling team. You can get in and arrange the luggage.' Paine kissed the top her head. 'I'll be there in a minute.'

Julia nodded, offering Paine a tremulous smile. He was doing his best to be strong. She should do the same. But she knew Paine was worried too. She'd felt the hard steel of a pistol at his waist when he'd held her. She didn't have to be told that it would be a mad dash to the Cotswolds and a dangerous one at that. It was at least two hours until dawn. Thank goodness for the full moon. It would be the only thing keeping them on the road instead of in a ditch. But, Julia rationalised, any head start would be valuable.

Sam Brown gave his boss the news over breakfast in the 'white room' of Oswalt's London town house. In the five years he'd served in Oswalt's employ, he'd never come to the house or any of the man's residences. All their business was done in the dock offices. He wished they were there now. He much preferred the plain plank floors and the inevitable dirt to the starkness of this room. The room made him overly conscious about the city mud on his boots.

The use of so much white was an odd choice for décor in a city well known for its abundance of soot. But he'd heard talk among the other men about Oswalt's unusual penchant for purity. This was the first time he'd seen actual evidence of it.

He stood at attention, making his report and trying not to worry about what was on the bottom of his boots while Oswalt cut into the thick sirloin with relish. 'The club she was last seen at is owned by a cove named Paine Ramsden. I saw him last night. He's a right handsome ladies' man. I wouldn't be surprised if—'

'What did you say?' Oswalt's fork stopped halfway to his mouth, his eyes going hard.

'I said the girl was spotted at a club operated by a Paine Ramsden,' Sam repeated hesitantly, shocked by the vehemence of Oswalt's response. He had not thought his boss would take the news so poorly. All the others had reported nothing. He had a lead to offer. To his way of thinking, the boss should have been jubilant to have some news at last, a place to begin the search and a name to go with it.

Oswalt's fork clattered on to the white china plate, the sirloin forgotten. 'She's with Ramsden?' he growled.

'I don't know that, sir. My informant said only that he saw her the night in question.'

'Who's the informant? Anyone we know?'

'None of the usual.' Sam Brown knew the boss was

referring to the regular snitches they bought information from when the need arose. 'This was a blue-blooded buck who'd lost his father's allowance. He was scared and ready to talk. I found out his name is Gaylord Beaton. He saw her go into the back room with Ramsden and she didn't come out. But that doesn't mean she's still with him.'

Oswalt brought his fist down on the white tablecloth. 'Of course she's with him, you dolt. Where else could she be? She went into his office and didn't return. No one else has reported a sighting. He's probably spirited her away somewhere.'

'It's just that he was with a different woman last night at the club and no one has seen the girl since,' Sam Brown said nervously, twisting his cap in his hand. He seldom had to argue with his boss to make a point. But he'd yet to see his boss so upset over an individual that logic risked being overlooked.

'Who? Who was he with last night?' Oswalt shouted, his eyes glinting.

'An actress, Eva St George.' Sam Brown was doubly grateful he'd been astute enough to pick up that information last night.

'She had black hair and didn't match the description of your girl. She was definitely not a débutante. Her gown was cut low, she wore cosmetics and she and Ramsden were quite affectionate in public.' He shifted his feet, awkwardly remembering the very passionate, very public kiss Ramsden had given the woman and how the woman had responded whole-heartedly, clearly enjoying it. From what he'd heard of débutantes and high-society ladies, they never enjoyed it.

'Really? What else? Tell me about it—their "affection", as it were.' The boss seemed over-eager for a detailed accounting of the couple's intimacies.

Sam did his best, thinking the request one of the queerest requests ever made of him. 'I don't know how to describe it, sir. She leaned into him and he pulled her so close it was hard to tell where one began and the other ended. They looked like they were in love, sir. That's why I didn't think there was a need to look into the woman's background further.'

'More's the fool you,' Oswalt sneered. He raised his bushy eyebrows. 'An actress? Are you sure about that? Have you checked the playbills? What role does she have? What theatre does she work at?'

Sam Brown didn't like to be treated as an idiot. He was good at his job. Oswalt would never have hired him otherwise.

The boss was apoplectic by this point, his face red. 'Perhaps the woman wore a wig. Did you think of that? I bet that's what the conniving bastard, Ramsden, did— passed her off as someone else beneath our noses!'

'I'll go back to the club and when they turn up again tonight…' Sam began.

'Why wait until tonight? Find out where he lives and check his quarters,' Oswalt demanded. 'If he saw you make contact with anyone, or if the informant—this Gaylord Beaton—was seen, your hand's been tipped. With luck, you'll take him by surprise, maybe even *in flagrante delicto.* You'd better hope so, because if luck fails, it'll be a race to the Cotswolds.'

Sam was relieved to see some of the anger ebb from Oswalt's features. His boss calmed down considerably once the man started to plan. 'Why the Cotswolds, sir?' Sam ventured to ask. He couldn't imagine why a man about town with one foot in the underworld and one arm around a gorgeous, willing actress would happily head to the bucolic Cotswolds.

'Because that's where his brother, the earl, lives. The family seat is in Dursley.' Oswalt's piggish eyes narrowed. 'If we don't catch them on the road, there'll be no getting to them once they're under Dursley's jurisdiction.'

'Seems like you know the family pretty well,' Sam hedged, wondering how his boss had come to know so much about a family of peers.

Oswalt leaned back in his chair, hands folded across his corpulent belly. 'You could say I've had dealings with them before.' His interest in the sirloin returned, the crisis had passed. He jabbed his fork into a fresh piece of meat. He waved it at Sam before taking a bite. 'Mind you, I won the first encounter and I'll win this one, too.' The gleam in his eye suggested he was looking forwards to the challenge laid down before him.

There were more questions Sam would like to ask, but didn't dare. There was a deeper game in play than Oswalt was letting on. The name, Ramsden, had upset his boss greatly, more so than his men's inability to unearth any useful information on his escaped betrothed. One thing was clear. His boss knew and disliked

Paine Ramsden. There was a bad past between them. That much was obvious, although the reasons for it were not. Now there was bound to be a bad future, too, since the boss's coveted virgin bride had given him the slip and fallen right into Ramsden's hands. There was no denying Ramsden's attractiveness to the opposite sex. Sam Brown thought it highly likely that the boss's bride wasn't a virgin any more. Perhaps that was what had the boss worried.

Sam Brown turned gingerly on his heel, careful not to leave behind any more markings on the carpet than necessary, and careful not to think too much about why his boss wanted a virgin bride so badly. The men had talked about it, speculating that Oswalt had the pox, that his physician recommended a virgin to cure it.

Like many of the rumours surrounding Oswalt, that one, too, was nothing more than drunken conjecture over ale in the dockside pubs. As such, Sam Brown didn't have to regard it with any amount of seriousness. There were many things in his dealings with Oswalt he was careful to treat in the same manner, for fear of looking too deeply into the issues that paid him a handsome salary.

After all, he was not paid to think, not in that vein, anyways. He was paid to act and, right now, he needed to round up a few of his trusted men to search out Ramsden's residence and if needed, track the man and his actress to the Cotswolds.

# Chapter Ten

Julia dozed fitfully, her head bumping against the carriage wall. The coach was well equipped enough with its squabs and padding to minimise the constant jounce of the road, but she wasn't. Paine had encouraged her to sleep, but sleep was impossible. Her mind whirred with the unreality of it all.

Tomorrow was the fifth day. If she'd stayed in London with her aunt and uncle, she'd be facing Oswalt and his physician. The thought made her shudder. But was this any better? She'd run away in the hopes of simply losing her virginity to the one man of her meagre acquaintance immoral enough to take her maidenhead and not think twice. Her plan had succeeded in terms of achieving her goal, but her plan had been naïve, not nearly enough to stop Oswalt if Paine was to be believed.

Apparently, she *did* believe him. That was what contributed most to her restless napping. In four days, she'd come to rely on Paine Ramsden, a dark rake, as a man of honour. She trusted him with her future and that of her uncle's. That trust was based on precariously little beyond instinct. Instinct had convinced her that her best hope in eluding Oswalt was to take Paine's advice and not return to her home. That same instinct now had her making a mad dash across country before dawn in the hopes that his family would take them in and cloak them in protection.

Instinct had led her down a slippery slope with Paine Ramsden and not all of it was about her problems with Oswalt. For better or worse, she'd allowed herself to see Paine as more than a means to an end. She had yet to decide how foolish that choice had been.

She had known girls back home who had become infatuated with young men from the village and in their infatuation had constructed entirely unrealistic pictures of the objects of their affection, only to be disillusioned later when their fantasies failed to come true. Had she done that with Paine Ramsden? In her panic, had she been so desperate for a hero that she'd fashioned one out of whole cloth and put the guise on Paine, determined to make it fit?

The mistake would be an easy one to commit even without the duress of her situation. He was sinfully handsome and had all the makings of a Gothic hero: a man with a scandalous past, a man decent women were warned away from, the perfect creature waiting to be redeemed by love's healing power.

The bit about 'waiting to be redeemed' was the problem. Julia couldn't imagine Paine waiting for redemption, no matter what story he'd concocted to tell the *ton* about them. She shot a look at Paine from beneath her eyelashes. He wasn't asleep either, although his eyes were shut. There was a tenseness to his body that belied his otherwise restful repose. He was waiting for something right now, but redemption wasn't it.

No, Paine Ramsden seemed quite content with his life, sutras and all. When she'd walked into the gambling hell and seen him striding towards her, all causal confidence in his rolled-up shirtsleeves, he'd seemed a man who was supremely at ease in the world around him. He'd found his place. Julia thought it highly unlikely that anything or anyone could entice Paine to give that up. 'Normal' living would hardly be appealing to a man who enjoyed 'splitting the bamboo'.

Perhaps normalcy was the reason behind his aversion to the *ton*. Such a lifestyle like the one available to him as a traditional younger son was bound to be too confining for a man of his ilk, its rules too foreign to him The choice to remain aloof from society had also forced him to stay aloof from his highly respectable family. A difficult choice, and not all that different from the choice she'd recently made.

Of course, she might be reading too much into that in her desire to see the similarities between her and Paine. Again, the niggling worry arose that she was fashioning a hero out of a man who did not wish to be cast in that light. He simply might not like his family. The choice to remain aloof might have been an easy one. She knew very little about his family besides the few facts floating about the *ton* that new-come débutantes were allowed to hear and the information she had read from a dry page of *Debrett's*. His brother was the Earl of Dursley, of course, and Paine was the third of three sons. On top of that, there was the scandal that seemed to follow Paine everywhere like a calling card. Julia had known precious little of the details when she'd decided to seek Paine out, only that he had been involved in a quarrel twelve years prior over the virtue of a woman. Julia did not know for sure. The quarrel had escalated into a duel and become a public spectacle. The rest was murky after that. She knew only that Paine had been exiled when the duel had been exposed to the authorities. Since then, she'd learned from Paine that the quarrel had been with Oswalt.

She wondered what it was costing him now to go home and face his family. Certainly, he'd made something of himself during his time abroad. But the past was a potent demon and it could not be easy. Yet, he'd done it without any hesitation for her sake. She had not suggested it; indeed, she hadn't even been fully aware of the imminent danger she faced in London.

Julia gave up any pretence of resting. She sat up straight against the leather cushions. 'Why did you do it?' she asked.

Paine's eyes opened quickly, alert and blue, giving every indication that she'd been right. He hadn't been sleeping either. 'Do what?'

'Decide to go home.'

'There was nowhere else to go. The decision was

painfully easy,' Paine said bluntly. 'I could think of nowhere safer than my brother's house.'

'Will he be glad to see us?' Julia queried, wanting to know what kind of reception they'd get.

Paine gave a wry smile. 'In his own way, I expect he will be. Don't worry, Julia. He'll love you.'

'What will you tell them about me?'

'I shall tell them the truth, although I doubt my brother will be glad to hear of my latest run-in with Oswalt.' Paine's face was grim. 'But he'll help us.'

'Oh,' Julia said quietly. She'd thought for a moment he might tell his family the story they'd made up about love at first sight. It was surprisingly disappointing to hear the real truth spoken out loud. But she nodded as if that was the tack she'd expected all along.

Paine didn't seem inclined to pursue the conversation, so Julia forged ahead on her own. 'What's your brother like?'

'Which one? I have two you know. Peyton, the earl, and Crispin, who is also older. I imagine it's quite possible that they'll both be at home. Crispin despises the Season and Peyton won't come up until the end of June. He puts it off as long as he can. At least he used to.'

Julia experienced a moment of fear. What if they'd come all this way and the earl wasn't home? 'Is there a chance your brother has already left for London?'

Paine shook his head. 'No, a note I'd sent earlier to the town house was returned and my footman said the knocker wasn't on the town-house door. I'd sent out two notes, just to be sure—one in town and one to the country.'

Her momentary fears were eased. But other concerns presented themselves. 'So, I am going to a bachelor estate and setting up house with three brothers.' Julia tried to make light of it. She felt ridiculous for suddenly worrying about propriety at this late date. Technically, she'd broken every rule a débutante could break. It was entirely illogical to be concerned over such a little thing now. Still, old habits died hard.

Paine laughed. 'Peyton has convinced our Cousin Beth to take up residence. My Aunt Lily tells me that Beth runs the house these days and Peyton finds the arrangement much more amicable than finding a bride to do it.'

Julia thought of the tall, poised older woman Paine had been escorting the night she'd seen Paine from a distance at the ball. That must be Aunt Lily. She and Paine had the same raven-dark hair and had looked congenially at ease with one another. 'Why doesn't he marry? Cousin Beth can run the house, but she can't provide him heirs.' Most men she'd encountered put a supreme importance on producing a successor for the family.

But Paine dismissed the concern. 'Perhaps Peyton hasn't met the right woman yet. No matter, Crispin is an admirable heir in that case. The family will go on.'

Paine leaned forwards and pulled back one of the curtains, assessing the growing light. 'We'll be able to stop soon and refresh ourselves,' he said, clearly changing the subject. Julia had to content herself with what she'd learned, although the answers he'd given had spawned more questions.

Other than Aunt Lily, he'd apparently not made any

contact with his brothers in the months he'd been in England. She wondered why. It was obvious he held them in affection and he was interested in what his family was doing. Was this lack of contact reciprocal? Had the earl tried to contact Paine? Surely he knew Paine was back. It seemed unlikely to Julia that Aunt Lily would let such a thing go unnoticed even if the earl didn't make a habit of coming up to town.

The sun had been up for two hours when they stopped at an inn to break their fast and change the horses. Paine reserved a private room for them so they could eat in quiet and with as little attention as possible. Julia's gown was wrinkled, but the colour and cut would still stand out. At Paine's suggestion, she kept her dark wig on. At least now the innkeeper and his wife could deny in all truth that a cinnamon-haired woman had passed that way with a man of Paine's description.

Julia felt better after washing her face and hands and eating. She saw to the packing of a hamper in the kitchens while Paine dashed off another note and sent it with a rider.

'Who's the note to?' she asked coming up at Paine's side in the stable yard.

'My brother. I thought we'd better tell him we were coming. He doesn't like surprises.' Paine smiled and tried to tease her, but Julia missed nothing. There were lots of reasons beyond the obvious why Paine would want his brother on the lookout. If Oswalt's men caught up to them and they failed to arrive on time, Dursley would come looking for them. That could hardly be what Oswalt's men preferred.

Julia hoped it wouldn't come to that. She knew her etiquette well enough to know that Paine was a mere mister, the title of 'Honourable' only applying as a written heading. Tangling with him was one thing. Engaging in a violent act against the Earl of Dursley was another.

Paine handed Julia into the coach and took his place on the top of the box to give the coachman a break. They couldn't afford the luxury of stopping for sleep and the coachman couldn't drive for ever. A man could be pushed no more than a team of horses without risking the safety of the journey. Such action would be complete folly. It would do no good to outrun Oswalt's minions only to be caught by the side of the road with a broken carriage wheel.

Paine clucked to the team and slapped the reins. It would be a tiring two days on the open road. Part of him longed to be inside the coach with Julia to distract him. He would have given a monkey to know what she'd been thinking about so hard this morning. Her eyes had been shut, but he could practically have seen the wheels of her fast-moving mind whirling at top speed.

While he was flattered to think those thoughts might have been about him, he hoped they were not. He was dangerous for Julia. Usually he limited his relationships to women who understood the game, women who were satisfied with the temporary pleasures he could give them, women who knew that, like all games, theirs would come to an end. Julia Prentiss was a different

kettle of fish, which was the exact reason he felt so compelled to protect her, even to the point of going home to
face Peyton and all the things he had to apologise for.

Whether she would admit to them or not, or was
even aware of them or not, Julia had expectations. She
needed a hero right now and he was more than glad to
oblige for the short term. But he wasn't capable of being
her hero for longer than that. There was too much rest-
lessness in him. Paine already knew he'd leave England
again. Maybe not tomorrow, or next month, but eventually within a few years he would leave again. There
was a huge world to explore and Britain was well placed
to conduct those explorations. Julia had grown up in the
country. She would want a husband who was stable,
reliable, able to stay in one place and put down roots.

Whoa. Paine jerked on the reins, avoiding a near run-
in with the ditch on the side of the road. Husband?
When had he gone from short-term hero to husband?
Commitments didn't get any more long term than that.
He couldn't be anyone's husband, especially not Julia
Prentiss's. She would give him all her trust, all her
passion, all her heart and he would hurt her. She
deserved more than a restless man. Before he could
consider being a husband, he had to find peace for
himself. Maybe that peace was in Bombay, or Burma,
or in some mystical place he had yet to explore.

*Maybe it's with her. Maybe she brings you peace,* a
tempting voice quipped in his head. *That's why you
showed her 'splitting the bamboo' and the 'yawn.' You
know that position lets each lover view the other's re-*

*actions without any obstacle. The position renders you emotionally exposed. That's why you climax so intensely with her and her alone. Go on, slay her dragons and win the fair maid's hand.*

Paine yanked hard on the reins, pulling the coach away from a deep rut in the side of the road. Lucifer's bells, he was going crazy! He'd nearly wrecked the coach with thoughts of playing husband to the delectable Julia. Now, his mind had wandered from eastern sexual sutras to the chivalry of England. What was he thinking?

Oh, he knew *what* he was thinking, and he knew what he *ought* to be thinking. He ought to keep his thoughts on the tasks at hand; goodness knew there were several of them more worthy of his time than impossible fantasies about peace and Julia Prentiss.

London was already seven hours behind him. Tomorrow's sunset would see them on his brother's doorstep. He was cognisant, too, that the game with Oswalt was irrevocably in motion now. Tomorrow would see him and Julia at Dursley, a day closer to both a reunion and a reckoning that had been twelve years in coming.

Paine drove all afternoon. The idea of a reunion with his brothers, coupled with the soft rolling green hills, proved to be too potent of a temptation to resist, making it easy to indulge the memories he loved so well.

Around him, waving fields of golden summer wheat not yet knee high spread like a haphazard quilt, so similar to the landscape near his home. In his mind's eye, he saw three boys rollicking in the fields, trousers rolled up and fishing rods slung over their shoulders. A stranger would not see much difference in them. Not much separated them in physical appearance except for their stair-step height. All had jet-black hair and blue eyes that sparked with constant mischief.

Those had been halcyon days when they'd lived as brothers and friends under the spell of an English summer. Each year upon year, it had always been that way for as long as Paine could remember. The tutors dismissed for the warm months and the boys free to roam at will. Paine was six years younger than his oldest brother. He'd thought such summers would last for ever.

But they ended when he was eight and Peyton left for school that autumn, leaving a huge chasm behind. Peyton had been the mortar that bound all three of the boys together. Without Peyton, he and Crispin were lost. Peyton had been the one to create their fantastical adventures, to lead the way on their expeditions. He'd been the one, because of his age, to act as both brother and father in the absence of a real father who lived almost exclusively in London.

Paine recognised now that, if his father had been home more often, Peyton wouldn't have been allowed to attain the ripe age of fourteen before going off to school. Most heirs were long gone from the family estate years before then. Still, everything had started to change the day the coach pulled out of the drive, taking Peyton away.

He didn't want to think about those dark days today, not with the sun shining on a perfect mid-morning summer. He wanted to be a boy again, innocent and fresh-come to the world. Not too young, though—not so young he couldn't celebrate this glorious day with a maid.

Paine laughed out loud, startling the horses. If it was his fantasy, he would do it right. He'd be sixteen and only modestly experienced in the ways of the world and flesh. Yes, he'd be sixteen and in love—a pure, unadulterated love with a girl as pure and curious as he was. She'd be a country girl, of course, so they could pack a picnic and hike through the woods to a field of wildflowers. They'd lay out their picnic of brown bread, a cheese wheel and a jug of cold ale on an old faded blanket. There'd be no need for chaperons or fancy delicacies or mating games with intricate negotiations.

Paine thought of Julia, snug in the carriage. Of all the women he'd known, she'd perhaps like such a picnic best. Certainly, she was by far the most innocent he'd ever known. It seemed something of an irony that she'd come looking for him to ruin one of the qualities he admired about her most. He knew as she did not that innocence was more than the physical manifestation of her maidenhead. He'd met virgins who weren't innocent in the least. She'd meant for him to take her innocence and now, he'd wound up protecting it. He would fight Oswalt with every weapon at his disposal before he'd let Julia see what that man could do. He would examine the reasons for such motivations later.

# *Chapter Eleven*

When they stopped for a short lunch in the afternoon the next day, Julia begged to ride up on top with Paine. She'd had enough of being cooped inside with a snoring coachman. The man had driven through the night for them and deserved his rest. Julia wasn't convinced, however, that it entitled him to expose her to such a noise.

She was also convinced that they'd eluded Oswalt. There were only two hours to go until they arrived at Dursley. The fear that had formed a continual knot in her stomach since London was starting to unravel.

Julia was contemplating the pleasure of a hot bath and cooked food when the shot rang out. Julia screamed. Shards of lacquered wood grazed her cheek from the impact of a bullet piercing the side of the coach. The horses whinnied in fright, galloping recklessly down the rutted road, dragging the coach behind them. The strength of Paine's arms were the only barriers between the horses and certain doom if the carriage veered into the ditch. At this speed, even a shallow ditch would cause the vehicle to flip, flinging its occupants to imminent injury or death.

'Julia, how many are there?' Paine shouted over the jangle of the coach, all his attention focused on keeping the coach on the road, on keeping them alive.

Julia clutched the seat rail and hazarded a quick backwards glance. 'Four.'

'Get down!' Paine shouted as another shot rang out.

'Julia, listen to me. We'll have to stop the team. I can't hold them for ever; if they keep running, it's only a matter of time before a corner is too sharp or we hit a rut. At this speed, we die most assuredly. When I stop the coach, you get down and run for the trees. Just keep running. Stay under cover and keep your sense of direction. You'll run into Dursley Hall.'

'Where will you be?'

'Here, fighting them off. Then I'll catch up.'

'Four men?'

'Don't fight with me over this, Julia. It's you they want. The last thing I need is to have my concentration divided between you and them. I can't fight you both. It only takes one man to swing you up on his horse and ride off while the other three keep me busy.'

Paine sawed hard on the reins, bringing the frightened team to a stop. 'Go, Julia!'

Julia tumbled over the side and ran for the woods, hoping Paine was right and that no one had seen her yet. With luck, Oswalt's men would assume she was inside the carriage. The shots that had been fired hadn't necessarily been aimed at the driver.

Julia gained the thick copse that grew near the road side, worry for Paine filling her. *The shots had been aimed at Paine.* Julia's hand flew to her cheek where the wood shards had scratched it. At a distance and with the blur of motion, the men had no way of knowing Paine was the driver. They'd assume Paine was in the coach with her and, as the gentleman, he'd be riding with his back to the box, facing backwards.

Paine's words came back to her. *You're the one they want.* That had made logical sense. Oswalt wouldn't want her dead. He needed her definitely alive. But Paine was expendable and, given their history, perhaps it was even preferable that Paine was dead.

She turned to look back. One man lay still on the ground, probably from Paine's single pistol shot before he'd got too close. Another grappled with Paine on the narrow box seat. Paine drew back his arm and delivered a debilitating punch to the man's jaw, sending him staggering off the edge. But two men remained and they'd had time to get into position. One of them had drawn a knife.

Julia watched in horror as they dragged Paine off the high seat, one of them swiping at Paine with the blade. The trio hit the ground, Paine rolling free of the punches they threw. He reached swiftly into his boot to withdraw his knife. He crouched, arms held wide, ready to fight, but he was already bleeding. In the close confines of the box seat, the blade had found purchase.

Julia could see a slow stain forming on his arm—the

right arm that held his knife. The steel blade Paine possessed suddenly seemed inadequate to her. How could such a thin piece of steel keep those burly men at bay? How long would Paine's wounded arm hold out? Where was the coachman? Surely he hadn't slept through all the commotion and the bone-jarring ride? He should be out there, helping Paine.

One man moved and Paine stabbed with his knife. The man danced away. The other one feinted, drawing Paine's attention. Julia bit her knuckles. This could go on for ever and, if it did, Paine would come out the loser.

Julia glanced around and picked up some rocks, an idea taking shape. Decisively, she ripped the silk gown, tearing it above her knees. Now she could run and, now, thanks to summers spent roaming the estate with Cousin Gray, she had a weapon.

Julia crept quietly to the edge of the trees, careful to stay hidden so that a flash of colour from her vibrant gown didn't give her away. She was close enough to recognise one of the men as the man from the club and close enough to hear the ragged banter exchanged between the men and Paine.

'What do you want with me that would be worth dying for? I'll get one of you before you get me,' Paine argued, invoking his wit as a weapon.

'We want the chit with the cinnamon hair. You have her. The boss wants her. The boss *owns* her. We've come to reclaim stolen property.' The big man's tone was menacing.

'I don't have her. You can check the coach, but

there's nothing inside except my dead coachman,' Paine replied.

Julia blanched at the news, thinking of the bullet that had pierced the side of the coach. The men confronting Paine were not bothered by the results of their errant bullet. 'That bullet was for you, Ramsden. If you'd been where you were supposed to be, this would all be over now.' The smaller of the two men lunged for Paine, opposite side to the hand that held the knife.

Julia fought back a gasp. It would be difficult for Paine to reach across his body and make an effective effort with his weapon. Instead, Paine kicked out with his leg in a fluid movement Julia had never seen before. The sweep of his leg caught the man at the knees and brought him to the ground. Quickly, before the last man could react, Paine delivered a sharp jab to the downed man's abdomen, rendering him temporarily useless.

But Paine wobbled as he spun to face the last man and the man saw it for what it was—weakness that would only grow with time. He had only to wait and he would be victorious. He'd used his comrades and their failures to take Paine's measure. He'd seen Paine's arsenal of wit and strange, foreign moves. Now Paine was exposed.

He charged Paine like a bull, head down and fast for a man so large. His head caught Paine in mid-torso, the impact taking Paine to the hard ground and causing the knife hand to release its grip. The knife spun out of reach on the road.

Julia went into action, loading one of her stones into

the hastily fashioned sling from her torn dress. She could hear the grunts and yells of the men's fight, Paine taking the brunt of it in his weakened state.

She had more rocks at her disposal but her first shot would be her best shot, full of surprise. She edged closer to give herself better range. The man reared up over Paine, giving her a clear target without the risk of hitting Paine instead. Julia cocked the sling and called out, using her voice as an additional distraction. It worked. The man kept his head up, glancing about to find the source of the sound. With dead-set determination, Julia fired the sling. The stone found purchase in the centre of his forehead. He slumped forwards.

Paine oomphed at taking the burden of the heavy weight and shoved at him, quickly gaining his feet, then looked around warily for the unexpected assistance. Julia rose up out of the brush and strode towards him. 'Paine!' She ran the last of the short distance.

'You? It was you?' Paine asked, his expression inscrutable, taking in the pink sling dangling in Julia's hand.

'Don't be mad. I looked back and saw those four men coming after you. I couldn't let you face them alone.' The words came out in a rush.

'Shh, Julia.' Paine's face cracked into a smile in spite of the bruises it had sustained. 'I'm not mad. I'm amazed. I am sure Madame Broussard would be. I'm not certain she ever envisioned her precious satin being used in such a manner.' Paine took the sling from her hand and held it up, saying with an amount of jocularity, 'Yes, I think this just might be the most expensive sling shot in the world.'

'Well, it won't last for ever. Let's get going.' Julia insisted, tugging at Paine's hand. The scene of such violence was starting to unnerve her.

'Wait, Julia, there's time for this.' Paine pulled her back to him and kissed her hard on the mouth. 'I was never so glad to see someone as I was to see you come out of the woods, striding like an avenging tree nymph,' he whispered. 'I do believe you saved me today.'

'And I will continue to do so,' Julia said with a bravado she didn't feel. She trembled, fighting back the shock that threatened to settle over her now that the ordeal was done. But Paine still needed her. 'Sit down and let me tend that wound. It's a nasty gash, Paine. I don't like how it's bleeding.'

Paine sat on the carriage step without complaint. It worried Julia that he'd given into her request so easily. Part of her had hoped he'd protest, declaring the wound only a 'scratch'. But anyone could see it was more than a scratch.

Julia bit her lip and gingerly probed the cut through the slashed fabric, wishing she had some medical skill, but beyond a few instances of cleaning up minor hunting accidents, she was vague on what should be done. Well, she would make do with what she knew and rely on common sense for the rest, she told herself steadfastly.

Fortunately, there was water in the coach from the last coaching inn where they'd taken on some provisions. Julia tore the tails of Paine's shirt to make a rag and some spare wadding. She poured water in the rag and sponged the affected area.

'Wounds always look better after they're cleaned.' Paine said, far too cheerily.

'Hmm,' Julia answered noncommittally. She wished she could agree. The wound did look cleaner, but it also looked more vivid. The bleeding seemed to slow. As long as the bleeding stopped, she could bind the arm. Otherwise, the blood would make the bandage sticky and hard to remove, not to mention painful. She took the second length of cloth and began to bind his arm.

'Ouch!' Paine winced as she pulled the cloth tight.

'If it's not tight, the binding won't do any good.' Julia said firmly, tying a knot high on his upper arm. 'That should hold. At least the fabric will keep the wound clean between now and reaching Dursley.'

Julia stood up, breathing deeply to steady herself. The sight of gaping skin was not one to which she was accustomed. Lord willing, it would never be a sight she would count in her repertoire of regular experiences.

She turned her attention to the coach and the horses and the carnage around them. The remaining men were still out cold, but it had been a while. 'Paine, will they wake up soon?'

Paine grimaced. 'Get a shirt from the valise. We'll rip it into shreds and bind them. It won't prevent them from following, but it might slow them down.'

Julia followed the instructions, nervously watching while Paine toed one of the unconscious men in the stomach. There was no reaction. With Paine's injured arm useless, it was up to Julia to bind the men's arms and legs.

She stared at them and then at Paine. He'd risen and

was trying to mount the driver's bench. It took him three awkward tries to pull himself up with one arm. She made a quick decision, one he wouldn't like. But there was no choice.

Julia scrambled up beside him and picked up the reins he was struggling to grasp in his good hand. 'I'll take those. You're in no shape to drive the coach.'

'We're not walking to Dursley,' Paine retorted.

'No, we're not walking, you stubborn man. I'm driving,' Julia informed him of the decision she'd made.

Paine snorted. 'You don't know how to drive a coach and four.'

Julia looked straight ahead down the empty road, her tone determined. 'No, I don't. But I think this is the perfect time to learn. I do have some experience with a pair. Now, this rein here—I take it this is for the lead horse?'

'Julia…' Paine protested.

'Paine, you can't drive and we must continue. You can't be so dense as to ignore the realities of our situation. If we stay here, we're literally sitting ducks. Any mile we make it towards Dursley is a mile closer to safety and whatever help your brother can offer,' Julia argued. But Paine didn't like being weak or being bossed about.

She softened her tone and tried a different tack. 'I thought you were magnificent today.' She leaned closer and managed a kiss without falling off the narrow seat. 'You did your part today to keep us safe. Let me do mine.'

'Well,' Paine said reluctantly, 'if you insist. I'll let you drive.'

* * *

Julia doggedly gripped the reins that separated the narrow box seat from the ground several feet below. Her shoulders and arms ached from the strain. She needed all her strength to keep the team of four on the road as the coach bounced towards Dursley Hall. They had conquered Oswalt's men, managing to subdue them. Once they recovered they would have to spend precious time regrouping, redrafting their plans. It was unlikely Oswalt's men would catch up to them before they reached Dursley Hall. But that victory had been accomplished at a great price.

The coachman lay dead in the carriage and Paine was wounded. The cut must be a burning torture on this rutted road. Beside her, grim-lipped and pale, Paine had his eyes fixed on the road before them, watching for any sign of trouble as a way of staying alert.

A man dead and another wounded. All because of her. Julia could not overlook the facts. Her mad scheme to elude Oswalt had led directly to the coachman's death. She had meant to be smart in outwitting Oswalt's perverse desire for a virgin bride. At the outset, she'd honestly believed she was only risking herself. The falsity of that belief had been made painfully clear to her today.

'Are we still clear?' Julia asked, trying to make conversation, fearing Paine might lapse into unconsciousness if she didn't keep him engaged.

Next to her, Paine dared a glance backwards, checking to see if Oswalt's men had caught up and were even now darting out of the woods that lined the road.

'Nothing. We're safe,' he breathed.

'How much farther?' she asked. It seemed she'd been driving for ever. Time had become meaningless. Darkness would settle shortly and she feared that the most. If they were far enough from Dursley Hall, perhaps Oswalt's men were waiting for the light to fail. In the dark, she and Paine would be hard pressed to out-manoeuvre them again.

'Just two miles.' Paine grimaced, turning paler than he had been. 'Julia, listen to me, there'll be a turn in the road, it marks the entrance to the Dursley parkland. Turn and then head straight, the road will lead you to the hall.'

Just two miles. Julia said the words over in her head like a Catholic litany. They had to be the longest two miles she'd ever travelled. Then, just when she thought they were safe, five riders loomed in front of them as they neared the turn in the road.

Five magnificent dark horses spanned the road like a barricade. Julia felt her panic rise. She would never make the turn or be able to crash through them and remain unscathed. Her skill was only hours old. Julia fought back her terror, but she couldn't refrain from the scream that bubbled up in her throat.

Paine laughed beside her in spite of his injury and weariness. 'Don't be frightened, Julia love, it's merely my brother. We're safe now.'

Julia's fear turned to relief. At last, she could lay down her burden. She pulled the carriage to a halt with the last of her arms' strength.

A black-haired man rode up and smiled up at Paine.

'Welcome home, little brother. Somehow I am not surprised you've returned with a beautiful woman at your side and the hounds of hell at your heels.'

'Crispin—' Paine's voice was full of emotion, although he couldn't speak more than the one word.

'He's hurt,' Julia broke in, eager to get Paine off the road and to see the journey completed. 'I can drive the team well enough if you can manage the leader on the turn.'

'Where's Peyton?' Paine managed.

'Waiting for you at the house with Cousin Beth.' The brother called Crispin tossed the words over his shoulder as he edged his horse up to the where the leader stood, blowing hard after the run. 'No more questions until we get you settled. The lady's given her orders,' he joked, but Julia thought she sensed worry in his voice.

Paine did look quite awful with his myriad cuts and bruises, the ragged bandage on his wounded arm showed signs of new bleeding—bright red blood still damp to the touch. Remnants of their encounter on the road and two days of unending travelling had worked great changes in Paine's appearance. No one would guess the man beside her had been turned out with sartorial elegance two nights prior.

Julia knew without the benefit of a looking glass that she appeared no better than Paine. The expensive silk was ripped and stained beyond repair. Her hair hung tangled and matted from wind. But just as she knew how awful the pair of them appeared, she knew his brothers wouldn't care. There'd been abject devotion in Crispin's eyes and underneath his teasing words of welcome.

Beside her, Paine tried to slip off to sleep or into un-consciousness—she couldn't tell which. She elbowed him gently. 'Don't you leave me now. Your brother will never forgive me if you arrive asleep after a twelve-year absence.'

'How do you know?' Paine mumbled, his speech slurred with exhaustion.

'Because he's coming down the lane right now,' Julia said, unable to hide the smile from her voice. Crispin had led them around a bend in the road and the house came into view as they gained the drive. Two figures stood on the wide steps, dark in the fading light. At the sight of them, one of them started moving.

Nearing the figure, Julia could see he was running, a swift, athletic sprint. When he was close enough he called out, 'Crispin, is it them? Paine? Paine? Is it you?'

The voice roused Paine. 'Julia, stop the carriage. Help me down.'

Julia protested, 'We're nearly there. Can't you wait until we reach the steps? You're in no shape, Paine.'

'Please, Julia. I want to get down and meet him on my own feet,' Paine persisted, his tone sharp and sur-prisingly alert.

Julia pulled on the reins, calling to Crispin to halt. She helped Paine steady himself. His injured arm made his descent ungainly, but he had his wish. Then Peyton had him wrapped in a brotherly embrace that nearly moved Julia to tears.

'Paine, you're home, at last. Thank God. I thought I had lost you for ever.'

Paine murmured something Julia couldn't hear and sagged in his brother's arms, spent at last. She watched Peyton and a footman haul Paine indoors and presumably upstairs to a chamber to rest. She felt bereft. The one person she knew in this strange place could be of no assistance to her now.

'He'll need a doctor. There was no time to stop on the road and nowhere to stop, in any case,' Julia said to no one particular, feeling at loose ends.

'He'll be fine.' A woman of middle years with dark hair and kind eyes spoke in soft tones, coming up to the carriage. 'Crispin!' she called out. 'Come help Paine's lady down.' The woman turned a gentle smile in Julia's direction. 'I'm Cousin Beth; you're in good hands now. Don't worry about a thing. We'll get you settled in no time. There's nothing wrong with Paine that rest and good cooking can't cure and you, too, for that matter. You look as if a meal and a long sleep would be welcome. I'll send for the physician from the village.'

She meant her words kindly, but she could not dispel the loneliness that swamped Julia. Julia let Crispin swing her down from the high seat. She let the eminently capable Cousin Beth lead her through the house to a beautifully appointed lady's chamber. She was appreciative of the friendly welcome, but she desperately wanted to be with Paine, even if it was to watch him sleep.

Only now when Paine was out of her reach, did she

fully realise how much she'd come to rely on him—not simply for protection, but for companionship. In a short time he'd become her buffer between herself and the world.

# Chapter Twelve

Cousin Beth's prediction proved unerringly true. After seventeen hours of sleep and poultices, Paine looked and felt immensely more like himself, with the exception of a stiff arm. Peyton and Crispin had rummaged their wardrobes for spare clothes to replace the tatters he'd arrived in. They were all of a similar build and the fit was good. The few personal effects Julia had grabbed at the Brook Street house were laid out on the dresser. He recognised his comb and his razor.

Out of curiosity over what had become of the rest of the clothes Julia had packed in the travelling valise, Paine opened the wardrobe and peered inside. Paine laughed to himself. It was empty except for his trousers, hopelessly wrinkled and entirely unsuitable for wearing. He remembered then that his shirt had gone for a good cause. He hoped Julia had been as fortunate with a makeshift wardrobe as he. Whatever she'd packed for herself was probably in the same wrinkled state his own clothes were in. But he did not doubt Cousin Beth's efficiency in managing every detail. He was certain suitable clothes had been found for Julia as well.

The sight of his crumpled clothes brought an image to mind of Julia upstairs in the Brook Street house, madly opening drawers, rummaging for clothes. At first, the image seemed humorous and touching. Even in her haste, Julia had thought of what he might need—the comb and razor were evidence of that. Then, the image lost its warm edge. His Julia should never have to flee in the middle of the night. His Julia should never have to know the fear she'd known during their flight from London. A fierce protectiveness awoke within him. *His Julia.*

Paine took a final quick look in the long mirror. He would do. A shave would be nice, but he didn't want to take the time. He wanted to see Julia. Paine felt he had been somehow remiss in his duty to her. She was his to look after. He'd left her alone in a house of strangers to find her own way. Not that there was much need for worry. Peyton wouldn't let her go wanting. Neither would he let her out of his sight. Paine had been very clear in the note as to the dire situation of her circumstances.

Thoughts of Julia, of wanting to assure himself that she was well, propelled him downstairs in his borrowed clothes. The sun was up and it was mid-morning of what promised to be a glorious May day. Voices floated out of the breakfast room, Julia's among them, chatting and laughing with his brothers, and Beth was joining in the light banter around the table. It was an easy sound, a comfortable sound, one that made Paine smile.

Julia had the seat across from the door. She spied him immediately, a brilliant smile lighting her face upon seeing him. 'Paine, you're awake.'

He could have basked in the sun of that smile all day. Paine couldn't recall the last time a woman had smiled at him with such genuine warmth that had nothing to do with wanting something from him.

'How are you feeling?' Peyton was all concern from the head of the table.

'Quite well,' Paine assured him, suddenly feeling awkward in his brother's presence. He had much to reckon with in regards to the family and Peyton. He fought the urge to shift from foot to foot like an errant schoolboy called on the carpet instead of a thirty-two-year-old man with a self-made fortune. Paine turned from Peyton and busied himself at the sideboard, filling a plate with the traditional breakfast offerings that had adorned the Earl of Dursley's sideboard since he could remember. There was a quiet joy in lading his plate with sausages and eggs and a stack of buttered toast—the comfort foods of his boyhood.

He took the seat across from Julia, feeling conspicuous. The happy chatter he'd heard coming down the stairs had faded away, replaced with silence while they waited for him to be seated.

Paine unfolded the square of linen next to his plate. Perhaps the reckoning would come now at breakfast. He rather hoped not. He'd prefer to explain things in private with Peyton. He didn't relish the idea of being called to the carpet in front of Julia. He'd come to like the idea of being her knight in shining armour, a hero instead of the dark rake.

Having to explain the last twelve years to Peyton in front of her would tarnish his image. A year ago, he wouldn't have cared what someone thought of him. But in the time they'd been together, it had suddenly come to matter very much what Julia thought.

'It will be a fine day,' Peyton began, drawing everyone's attention easily, falling back on the faithful topic of any English conversation. 'The weather is perfect for taking Julia out and showing her the estate.'

'I'll have Cook pack a hamper if you like, Paine. You can pick strawberries. They're in full fruit right now,' Beth suggested eagerly.

Julia beamed at the idea. 'I'd love to see everything,' she exclaimed excitedly and then sobered. 'But it can wait. I don't want to take you away from your brothers. There must be a lot to talk about.' She meant it kindly. Paine knew she had no idea just how much there was to talk about.

Peyton was quick to assure her. 'There will be time to talk later.'

Paine felt a flicker of anger lick at his conscience. He could make his own decisions. He wasn't the baby brother any longer. He didn't need Peyton's permission to show Julia around.

He tamped down his temper, disappointed that the old kernel of his discontent was still there, so readily accessed at the smallest provocation. He'd come home to keep Julia safe. He knew the choice would mean making amends and explanations. He could not let himself be angered so easily or Peyton wouldn't see him as a changed man, a man who knew the world.

'Then, we'll go,' Paine offered with a tight smile, but he felt Julia's eyes linger on him as if she could see the turmoil beneath his seemingly easy acquiescence.

Dursley Park was easily several times larger than her uncle's modest estate. Julia marvelled at the sheer vastness of the parkland, the immense stretches of green, manicured lawn reaching up to the woods that bordered the southern flank of the house. Paine told her the woods were full of bridle trails leading out to various follies. There would time to explore those later. Today, they were headed to the west side and the grain fields that beckoned with an undulating golden wave in the light breeze.

Paine drove them about in a plain pony cart pulled by a cob, the sleeves of his linen shirt rolled up past his elbows, the steady, slow pace manageable with one hand on the reins. He was jacketless and the shirt was open at the throat. He exuded a natural male beauty in his simple attire. Julia thought she could stare at him for ever. She might have continued casting covert glimpses at him from under the brim of a borrowed straw riding bonnet if he hadn't caught her.

'What is it, Julia? You're staring.'

'I was thinking how you look today reminds me of the first night I saw you. You had your sleeves rolled up then, too,' she stammered, embarrassed at being caught in her perusal.

'A whole week ago,' Paine said wryly.

'A lot has happened since then,' Julia replied, struggling to keep her gaze fixed forwards. She was reluctant to talk of the business between them on such a lovely day, but it seemed dishonest not to acknowledge it. 'I never meant for it to come to this,' she said quietly. It had to be said. The guilt of it all was too much to bear silently.

She felt Paine's eyes on her. 'How much have you told Peyton?'

Julia shook her head. 'Hardly anything. I wasn't sure what you wanted me to say. I thought you should be the one. I wasn't sure...' she faltered, repeating herself. She was entirely out of her depth here. She did not know the extent or quality of Paine's relationship with his family. She had not meant to involve an earl in her plan or to even develop an association with Paine Ramsden that went beyond one night.

Paine pulled the cart over to the side of the path they'd followed and jumped down. 'No more talk of such things. Today is for us.' He came to her side of the cart and swung her down.

The easy grip of his hands at her waist felt welcome. She'd missed his touch while he'd slept. She'd missed his presence. Of course, she couldn't tell him that. This thing between them was strictly business. That he gave her pleasure, that he stirred longings in her, was not part of their agreement, merely a by-product. A shared by-product.

Mutual attraction might not be part of the contract, but it had developed. Julia took comfort in that.

Whatever his emotional attachment to her was, she knew Paine desired her physically. When this was over, such knowledge would have to be consolation enough.

Paine's hands stayed at her waist long after her feet found the ground. He pulled her to him, causing her head to arch back to look up at him. She revelled in the feel of his body, hard and muscular against hers. Without hesitation, he took a swift kiss, bending with expert precision to avoid the brim of her hat.

When he pulled back, he was all carefree boyish charm. 'Where did you get such a contraption?' He made a gesture towards her hat. 'Tell me you didn't pack it all the way down from London?'

'No, it's an old hat of your Cousin Beth's. Do you like it?' Julia did a pirouette.

'Absolutely not. It's awful, just awful!' There was laughter in his voice. 'Peyton needs to give Cousin Beth more pin money if she's been reduced to such a travesty.'

Paine held out his hand. 'Here, take my hand. I don't trust you can see the path plainly with that thing on.' He kept her hand gripped in his own. With his other hand he swept up the hamper and led the way to a shady spot. Julia was thankful for the strength of his hand. She would have tripped without him to steady her on several occasions. The terrain was uneven and awkward to traverse in Beth's slightly too-long skirts and slightly too-big shoes. Still, Julia was grateful for Paine's cousin's generosity. Otherwise, she would have been tramping the countryside in a torn silk evening gown.

'We're here,' Paine exclaimed at last, dropping the hamper and blanket.

Julia looked about her, trying to grasp what 'here' was.

'Take a deep breath and just listen,' Paine coaxed softly.

Julia did as instructed, the allure of the place becoming immediately apparent. The scent of summer wafted gently from the fields behind them, the sound of a nearby creek mixed with the errant chirps of meadow birds filled the air. She didn't have to open her eyes to know it was summer.

'We can pick strawberries later.' Paine grinned and pointed to a patch. He spread the blanket. He sat down and began to tug off his boots.

'What are you doing?' Julia asked.

Paine chuckled. 'Getting comfortable. Sit down, Julia. Take off your shoes. We can be ourselves.'

His good humour was infectious. Julia plopped down and took off her shoes. 'I think your sutras would like this place. The site appeals to all the senses.'

'You're a quick learner.' Paine said, stretching out beside her. 'Although I think the sutras would prefer fine furnishings and music to our ragged blanket and chirping birds.'

'I like our setting. It's simple,' Julia said, casting a coy glance sideways at Paine. She would have to store up all the images of him she could. She would have to share him with his brothers, and then with society, if their plan were to succeed. And that success would be the end of their association. She'd once thought it would be a facile trick to walk away from him. But she'd never dreamed a man like him existed.

Julia tossed her shoes aside and reached for her stockings. Paine's hand stopped her before she could roll them down.

'As I recall, you like to have me do this for you,' Paine whispered huskily, his eyes glinting with mischief. His hands reached up beneath her skirts, skimming her hidden curls as he grasped the top of each stocking.

Julia bit her lip against the sensual play. She knew she was damp when he reached for the second stocking. It was embarrassing to note how wanton she was with him. 'Paine...' she began uncertainly. 'We're outdoors.'

'On the contrary, nature is the perfect place for this. The sutras suggest that male and female take inspiration from nature for inventing their own love-play,' Paine whispered in his low, seductive tone. He pushed back an errant strand of hair from her face. 'There are several positions named for animals: the mare, the elephant, the blow of the boar, sporting of the sparrow. The list is quite extensive.'

Julia blushed furiously. 'You have the most scandalous conversation of anyone I've ever met.'

'Hush, Julia.' Paine rose up over her, turning his attention to her face. His hands crept to the bow that secured her hat. 'We'll have to get rid of this monstrosity.' He untied the hat and tossed it aside. 'It's far too hard to kiss you with this thing on.' He kissed her hard on the mouth, easing her gently back on to the blanket, his body covering her. 'That's known as the "kiss that kindles".' He nuzzled the side of her neck. 'What shall we try today?'

Julia struggled a bit, pushing him away long enough to speak. 'You don't have to do this, Paine. You've held up your end of the bargain. I am thoroughly ruined. You don't have to continue your instruction.' Indeed, she didn't want him to, not if that was all it was—lessons conducted much in the fashion that one might receive a piano lesson.

'I thought you liked my "instruction".' Paine reared back slightly.

'I do,' Julia stammered. How could she explain she didn't want to be the student, but a partner, an equal, without driving him away? Such an implication would send Paine fleeing, validating everything he believed about virginal débutantes and their obsessive goal to capture a husband.

'I'm sorry. I was cow-handed in my approach a moment ago,' Paine said, his gaze studying her, no doubt seeing more than she wanted him to see. 'I want to do this and you want this, too.'

Julia felt her face burn, knowing he had not over-looked the effect of his hands on her legs, knowing he had proof that his actions had aroused her. She returned his gaze, seeing in his eyes the rise of his desire. It was enough to convince her he understood her dilemma. There was something else in his gaze, too, she couldn't name—perhaps a desperation that had clawed its way to the surface. But she couldn't imagine what a man like Paine Ramsden had to be desperate about. He bent over her, taking her mouth in a long, searching kiss, until her body gave him compliance.

* * *

He shouldn't have done it, Paine thought ruefully. He lay on his back, one hand thrown over his eyes against the sun, on the blanket next to a dozing Julia. He told himself she'd been a willing participant in what had transpired on the blanket. But the argument was a weak one, only a technical justification at best. She was an innocent, untouched by any but him. He was experienced in the art of pleasure and arousal. He'd known he could easily coax her submission. He'd used her own body against her. In truth, she'd hardly had a choice.

It wasn't that the coupling hadn't been enjoyable for her. It was just that he had done it for the wrong reasons. He'd wanted her from the moment he'd seen her in the breakfast room and so he'd taken her with no regard for the uncertainties surrounding them.

Her requirements of him had been met. She was thoroughly ruined in both reality and circumstance. No well-bred young lady put herself in the hands of Paine Ramsden for a night, let alone an entire week spent in his company, a week that had her visiting gaming hells and making a mad dash across country unescorted. They had not spoken of continuing their sexual relationship beyond the confines of the agreement. There were many things they'd not talked about and should have. Their association was quickly spiralling far beyond the parameters of their original intent.

Certainly, acting as her self-appointed protector hadn't been part of the deal or even discussed. Yet, the role had been implicitly affirmed. That was at the core of what bothered him. He had brought her here to Dursley Park for her own safety because it was the right thing to do.

He didn't want Julia thinking that she had to pay for his favours, that his protection was bought only with the currency of sex or that she would suddenly find herself set adrift if she failed to comply with his wishes. His pride couldn't bear such a notion. More importantly, his honour would not tolerate it. For a man believed by many to have very little honour, the thought was humbling.

Yet, he had perpetrated the act with utter carelessness, all in the name of selfish need. He'd even gone so far as to couch it in terms of 'education'. Julia had seen right through that ruse, just as he'd immediately seen her reasons for refusing to accept it under the guise of such educational experience. She was not mentally or emotionally equipped to transmute their congress into simple terms of physical gratification and leave it at that. He was partly at fault. He'd not given her the tools to adjust her way of thinking. Instead, he'd prattled on about the Hindus seeing sex as a sacred expression of religion. Now, he was facing the consequences. Julia wanted him as more than a tutor in the sexual arts. Worse, he could not, should not, allow her to believe more was possible and yet he craved her.

He wanted her with a desire so intense he'd been willing to put all other considerations aside, pride and honour be damned, just to caress her body, to be inside her again, to feel the hot pulsing rush of his seed and know that the shuddering release of his climax would bring the exquisite peace he'd mysteriously found with her.

No matter how short lived that peace was.

He would need her again.

Already his coveted peace was slipping away. He'd expected it would. The eastern scholars he knew in India had taught that only true peace came from within. No one could give peace to another, at least not permanently. One had to find permanent peace from within oneself. They'd also taught him the key to such peace started with forgiveness of oneself. Paine often doubted he'd ever be able to do that. Julia's purity was a stark reminder of how far he'd fallen.

He thought of the story he'd fabricated to explain Julia's association with him—that her love had reformed him. It made a nice fantasy to ponder, starting with the bit about her falling in love with him. A gently bred girl like Julia would come to rue the day she fell in love with a man like him. She'd been very clear the night she'd come to him about why she was there. He was the most immoral man she could think of, who would do what she asked, all because he lived by a different code she could not completely understand.

Still, she'd put her trust in him. She'd followed him to the country and she'd fought beside him on the road. She never doubted his ability to protect her and when she turned those green eyes on him, they were not full of calculation, proving she no longer thought of him as only a man to stand to stud. The thought gave him some hope and, in his experience, hope was a dangerous thing, especially for a desperate man.

Beside him, Julia stirred, her hair loose and warm from the sun. She was beautiful and he felt his body surge, wanting to take her again and lose himself in her. But he was a man of honour now, and he could not justify such selfishness again.

'How long did I sleep?' Julia asked, raising up on one arm.

'Not that long. A half-hour,' Paine said carelessly. He reached for the hamper. 'Hungry?'

He waited until they'd finished off the picnic before bringing up the subject plaguing him. He smiled as Julia wiped her hands on a cloth napkin. Even outdoors with bare feet she had good manners. He'd known from the first she was a lady, a real lady.

'Julia, we have to talk about our future,' he began.

Julia looked up from folding her napkin, a small frown knitting her brow. 'I thought we'd agreed not to talk about Oswalt today.'

Paine shook his head. 'This is not about Oswalt. This is about us. You and me.' He rushed on before she could break in or misunderstand him. 'I must apologise for what happened on the blanket. We should have talked about this before anything like that happened. Our agreement has been fulfilled and I don't want you to feel obligated to have sex with me as any further part of our relationship.'

He felt awkward saying the words with Julia. In the past, he'd talked about sex quite conversantly with numerous women. In his past liaisons, such negotiations had been commonplace.

Julia coloured at his frankness. Then she surprised him, putting her hand over his where it rested in his lap. 'You have done me an enormous service by bringing me here. Without knowing me, you have offered yourself as my protector. It never crossed my mind that you were a man to provide those services and expect an exchange of favours.'

'Perhaps it should have,' Paine said wryly. 'You know what I am, how I live. I'm a dark rake. I sleep with hundreds of women and play in the underworld. I am thoroughly debauched by the *ton*'s standard.'

Julia gave a soft laugh. 'So they all say. I am hard pressed to believe it. They don't understand you.' She looked down at her lap, biting her lip in contemplation. 'Paine, I owe you an apology. I came to you for sordid reasons, but even so, you've treated me with far more respect than what I reserved for you. I looked at you through society's eyes and I misjudged you.'

'And now, Julia? What do you see?' He was heady with desire, swamped by it, in fact. He exhaled heavily, fighting her effect on him. She had no idea how much he wanted to wrap his body around her.

She reached up to stroke his cheek. 'I see a good man who hides his true self from others.'

There it was.

Was it possible that in one sentence, she'd seen what everyone had missed? Julia made him think the impossible—that he could be saved, drawn back from the abyss, that perhaps he could offer her more than he thought.

He wrapped a strand of her heavy hair around a finger. 'Why do you think that is?' he mused.

Julia shrugged. 'I don't know. I am sure this good man has his reasons.'

'No, that's not what I meant,' Paine whispered. 'Why is it that you see a good man when everyone else sees a rake?'

Julia tilted her head and gave him a contemplative smile. 'I'm not the only one who sees it. Your family sees it, too.' She tugged at him. 'Now, make love to me because you want to. No more talk of agreements, Paine.'

## Chapter Thirteen

Peyton was waiting for them, for him, when they got back. Paine hid a smile. Peyton wasn't overtly waiting for them in the foyer, that wasn't his style. But he'd been on the lookout for them. The sudden hustle of servants upon their return indicated as much. Paine would have bet good money he'd barely turned into the stable yard before news of his return reached Peyton in the study.

The door to the study was open. It would be difficult to get by there without being seen. This was, of course, what Peyton had planned. Paine turned to Julia in the wide main hall and nodded towards Peyton's open door. 'I need to see my brother. Will you excuse me?' There were many things he and Peyton had to talk about. He wasn't ready to have Julia hear the family laundry aired and he wasn't sure how diplomatic Peyton would be about it. But he was ready to face it, armed with Julia's confidence and a new sense of hope.

Paine saw Julia up the stairs and then strode towards

the office, prepared to reconcile with Peyton for the first time in twelve years.

Peyton looked up from the papers on his desk at the sound of footsteps. 'Paine, you're back. Did you have a good time?' he asked as if he hadn't known they'd arrived twenty minutes before.

'Yes. Julia is upstairs, resting. I thought we could talk. There are things that should be said,' Paine said, taking charge of the conversation.

Peyton nodded. 'Would you like a drink?' He motioned to the polished cabinet that displayed a series of cut-crystal decanters.

'No, thank you,' Paine declined, taking a chair across from the expansive desk, marvelling at Peyton's nervousness—Peyton, who had always been decisive and in control.

'You've changed so much, Paine. I can hardly take it in when I look at you,' Peyton began. 'You're a man now. It's hard to countenance that my baby brother is two and thirty.' He shook his head. 'I still think of you as much younger. But you're a man full grown...'

He foundered there and Paine knew Peyton was thinking of the long years in exile when there'd been no letters from India assuring him of his brother's safety and well-being; of the long months Paine had been home in London, but sent no word.

They stared at each other, lost in awkward silence. Paine shook his head and shrugged. 'I should have written, but I didn't know how. I'd been so foolish, so stupid. I didn't know even where to start. I was a complete disgrace.' Or even if his brother would want to hear anything. Peyton had been so angry, Paine was sure his older brother would be glad to simply have him out of the way, no longer a blight on the family name.

'My sentiments, exactly, only about me. I have regretted my behaviour, my choices, every day since you left. I was so stupid, so foolish, a complete disgrace.' Peyton used Paine's words and gave a sad smile, one that showed the deep brackets at the corners of his mouth. For the first time, Paine was struck by the amount of time that had passed and how close he'd come when they'd been attacked on the road to not having this moment with his brother at all. Perhaps he was still foolish.

'I want to hear what you've been doing, how you've spent your years,' Peyton said.

'I'm sure you can guess most of it,' Paine said, reluctant to roll out his accomplishments like a litany and even more reluctant to share his sins. The East was a different world, half a globe away. He wasn't sure Peyton would understand what it meant to move in that world.

'Please tell me,' Peyton asked softly. 'Ridiculous pride has kept us from communicating too long.'

It was all he needed to let the stories come. Once he started talking, Paine was surprised how easily the telling came. The wanderings into strange countries when he had no sense of direction, setting up the shipping business when he found he needed a purpose, selling the shipping firm when he'd made his fortune and decided it was time to come home. There were other stories, too, that tumbled out. Stories of the people he'd met, the cultures and lifestyles he had encountered, the beliefs that had challenged him in his own thinking. Long shadows were falling outside on the lawn when he finished.

Peyton looked impressed. 'It seems you've come full circle then, Paine. Home again with a fortune at your disposal and years of hard-won wisdom. What are your plans now?'

'I own a gambling hell, which I am sure Aunt Lily told you.' He saw Peyton trying not to wince at the mention. He moved on. 'I recently bought a house in Brook Street that I want to turn into a hotel.' Paine held Peyton's gaze. 'There are things to do, however. Oswalt is still a menace. That comes first. Then we'll see.'

Peyton raised his dark brows and steepled his hands. 'And Julia Prentiss? How does she fit into all this? Is she a pawn or something more?'

Paine heard the challenge in his brother's voice and he clenched his jaw to hold back his rising temper. Peyton was trying to see him as a new man. But he couldn't expect Peyton to change over night. To him, he would probably always remain the little brother in some capacity. 'She came to me, if that's what you're asking. I didn't go looking for a chance to get at Oswalt.'

'But you certainly didn't turn her away once you heard she was connected to Oswalt.' Peyton's challenge was no longer veiled.

'How could I? I of all people know what Oswalt is

capable of. I could not turn my back on her, especially when I have the means to stop him.'

'Do you? Have the means to stop him? You thought you could handle him the last time, too. You were lucky you weren't killed.' In his temper, Peyton had risen behind the desk to his full height.

'I'm not a naïve stripling about town these days,' Paine warned, gaining his feet to match his brother. 'I know how to handle men of his ilk.'

'No. You have come here for my help. If you want it, you'll let me handle everything,' Peyton insisted, eyes flaring over being gainsaid.

'I didn't come home to let others fight my battles,' Paine growled in a near shout.

'For once, can't you do what you're told?' Peyton barely refrained from yelling.

'Why? I won't hide behind you or anyone else.'

'Because I can't stand to lose you again. Because I need to make it up to you.' The admission tumbled out of its own accord, bringing the brothers' argument to a halt. The tension dissipated.

'I should never have let you go the first time,' Peyton said quietly, years of remorse clear in his eyes. 'I thought taking on Oswalt would teach you sense. I never dreamed it would lead to a duel, that it would come to a head over a woman. But you and your misplaced chivalry wouldn't hear otherwise. By the time I realised what was really happening, it was too late to protect you. It won't happen again. I didn't mean to fight with you, Paine. I only meant to say I was sorry.'

Paine sank into his chair, trying to absorb it all. 'All these years, I thought you were ashamed of me. I couldn't face you afterwards, knowing that I'd disappointed you.' All this time, he'd not once thought that Peyton had anything to apologise for.

Peyton shook his head. 'I won't fail you again, Paine. This time, we face Oswalt together. Tell me what you have planned.'

And just like that, he was absolved.

Paine was at peace and he savoured it, even though he knew it couldn't last long. He let himself bask in the knowledge of his brother's love and Julia's honest affection. It would only be a matter of days before the fruits of his hastily dashed notes in London would arrive at Dursley Park.

Within a week, Flaherty's news would catch up with him, giving him insight into why Oswalt was after Julia's uncle and what the bastard planned next. Mail would also arrive regarding the business loans he'd proposed to influential members of the *ton*. Soon, the plan would be in motion. They would return to London and the issue with Oswalt could be resolved, leaving Julia free of the man's shadow.

Free to do what? He hadn't been able to adequately answer his brother's questions regarding Julia. In terms of his feelings for Julia, he feared he'd picked the very worst time to fall in love. But what else could it be when the thought of her being free to pursue another caused his stomach to churn?

* * *

Paine's short idyll lasted approximately a week and a day; the end heralded by a note from Flaherty that arrived neatly tucked inside a trunk full of Julia's clothes from Madame Broussard. Julia discovered the letter while shaking out the last of the gowns from their meticulous tissue wrappings. It fluttered to the floor, the plain brown-paper envelope a stark contrast in a room filled with a riot of flounces and lace.

Julia bent and scooped up the envelope, concluding immediately that the note was not an additional note from Madame Broussard, whose correspondence had been on top of the tissue wrappings and strongly scented with lilacs. She turned the envelope over, noting the masculine scrawl.

She doubted the letter was for her. First, this letter had been secreted in the trunk in such a way that implied the writer was worried about discovery. Second, the letter was clearly not for her. No one would know where to send a letter for her. No one knew she was with Paine Ramsden, and certainly no one knew she'd visited Madame Broussard's. No one would know she was expecting an order of clothes.

Only Paine knew. Julia smiled to herself over Paine's consideration for her. In the rush of their departure from London, he'd thought of everything, dashing off that note to the dressmaker so that Julia would have her gowns, at least enough of them. The rest—her evening gowns and fancier town dresses—would be waiting upon her return.

She didn't have to be a mind-reader to deduce that the note she held probably had something to do with when that return would occur. That return worried her immensely. Going back to London would force her to deal decisively with Oswalt as well as bring her association with Paine to a head. Once her situation with Oswalt was resolved, she reasoned that her situation with Paine would be dissolved as well.

More than that, her future, whatever it would be, would begin when they returned to London. There was her family to consider in all this. What were they thinking right now? Did they miss her? Worry for her? Understand why she had taken such drastic action? Would they receive her when she returned and give her a chance to explain? She'd known when she embarked on this mad scheme that after she was ruined, she might very well be turned out of the family. She'd known it was a very real risk she was running. Still, she wanted a chance to explain.

Who knew one simple envelope could cause such turmoil?

Julia made a face at the envelope. There was nothing for it. She had to go and find Paine.

She found him in what had become his customary place—sitting at the long table that dominated the length of the book-lined library. She could easily understand the appeal of the room. The far end was graced with floor-to-ceiling windows that provided both the ability to flood the room with light and the ability to soothe an agitated guest with a view of elegant expanse of verdant grass.

Paine was dressed casually in a lawn shirt and paisley waistcoat, a simple cravat tied at his neck. The ledgers in front of him held all his attention as he tallied columns and wrote sums. Peyton was with him, sprawled on a leather couch near the windows, immersed in a book.

A peaceful scene. Julia hated to interrupt it. She'd much rather stay buried in the country with Paine at her side. However hard it had been for Paine to come home, the choice had served him well. She still didn't understand all the dynamics behind his separation from his brothers, but it was easy to see he was loved here and forgiven.

She bit her lip and felt her cheeks heat at the thought. Since the picnic, they'd been together every night. Peyton had given them separate rooms, but that hadn't stopped Paine from visiting after the house quietened. She looked forwards to those hours spent in the dark, when Paine was by turn both lover and teacher. Even now in the bright light of the afternoon, she was nearly giddy with anticipation of the evening ahead at the very sight of him.

Julia pushed the door fully open and stepped into the room.

'Hello, Julia.' Paine looked up from his ledger before she'd had time to speak. Was he that aware of her presence that he could sense when she was in the room? It was a novel fantasy. 'How are your dresses? Don't tell me you're done trying them on already?'

'They're lovely. But, no, I haven't tried any of them

on yet.' Julia approached the table, aware that Peyton surreptitiously watched them from the couch. 'This came for you. It was tucked inside the trunk.'

Paine took the envelope and studied it. 'Thank you. It's from Flaherty, one of my investigators. I've been hoping to hear from him.'

'Is it about the club?' She asked as he scanned the note.

'No,' Paine said without looking up.

Julia waited, hoping to hear more and feeling left out when nothing more was forthcoming. 'Is it about my uncle?' she pressed. Paine had mentioned such an inquiry before.

Paine looked up from his perusal of the letter. 'No, not directly anyway.' He smiled, but Julia was not fooled.

'I will not be treated like a child, Paine. If that note concerns me, I want to know what's in it.' Julia could feel her temper rising. The blackguard was trying to dismiss her.

'Julia, there is no need for you to worry,' Paine said pointedly, looking up from the document in irritation. 'Everything will be taken care of.'

Peyton rose from his couch and came to stand behind Paine, reading the letter over his brother's shoulder. Paine made no attempt to shield the letter from his brother's perusal. That was the final spark that ignited her temper.

'I see. Only men are allowed to worry.' She placed her hands squarely on the table and leaned across it. 'Well, that's not good enough, Paine. There is every need for me to worry. A coachman is dead and my uncle faces financial ruin, all because of me. You cannot fob me off with a smile and false assurances. I am in this up to my neck.'

Peyton eyed her speculatively, seeming to weigh the situation. 'I suspect your uncle faces more than financial ruin, Miss Prentiss.' He nodded towards the note. 'Let her read it, Paine. It's best she knows the worst straight away. Sugar coating never makes things better in the long term. I'll ring for tea and have a footman search out Crispin.'

Paine gave a tight laugh. 'Tea and Crispin? Speaking of "sugar-coating", dear brother, is that your way of calling for a family meeting?'

'Why, yes, it is.' Peyton said without prevarication.

'I don't really understand any of this,' Julia said, waving the now well-worn and -read note in her hand. Tea and Crispin had arrived and the letter had been passed about. It was thankfully short, but informative. 'I'm not sure what marriage to me has to do with the cargo on Cousin Gray's ship.'

Paine spread his hands on his thighs and drew a deep breath. 'Those two occurrences are not linked to each other, but they are both linked to a larger plot.'

'Which is?'

'That's the part that is still unclear.' Paine looked at her with his sharp eyes. 'What is clear though, Julia, is that you're in danger and your family is in danger when it comes to Oswalt. He's convinced your uncle that they're on the same side, that you're the enemy. In reality, your aunt and uncle are in as much danger as you are, although it's a danger of a different sort.'

'Oswalt can't marry them.' There was a touch of acid to her tone. Paine had let her read the letter from Flaherty, but he was still trying to protect her by speaking in vagaries. He knew more of the puzzle than he let on.

Paine stood up and began pacing, making his familiar gesture of riffling through his hair as he spoke his thoughts out loud. She would have found it endearing if she hadn't been so annoyed with him. This was her plan, her choices. How dare he exclude her?

'Here's the story we know so far,' Paine began. 'Oswalt makes a habit of ruining noblemen. Usually— in fact, always—it's ruination of a financial sort. He likes the challenge of the chase. That's what makes the situation with your uncle so difficult. There's no money to speak of, except for this potential cargo, and there's no challenge—the two things Oswalt traditionally thrives on. Bottom line, Oswalt is not after your uncle's money.'

'But the cargo is valuable,' Julia cut in. 'Uncle Barnaby says it will cover our debts.'

'Certainly that's true.' Paine gestured to the letter Julia held. 'Flaherty confirms that the indigo and cotton carried on the ship will be valuable to your uncle. However, Oswalt is a merchant. He has a fleet of his own ships at his disposal. He doesn't need to go after your uncle's cargo. He could have one just like it with less risk and more efficiency.'

'Then why?' Julia furrowed her brow. Admittedly, her sheltered experiences with the world provided little for her to draw on in terms of options. 'If he doesn't need money, what does he need that my uncle has?'

'That's the question we are trying to answer,' Peyton put in, reaching for another sandwich from the tea tray. 'Can you think of anything your uncle might be dabbling in? Investments? Agriculture?'

Julia shook her head. Nothing came to mind. 'I can't think of anything he's mentioned over dinner. Most of our dinner conversation is about his Parliament work.'

'Could that be it?' Paine asked slowly.

'I see what you're thinking,' Crispin spoke up in excitement. 'Perhaps Oswalt wants a voting politician in his pocket. If he financially bails out Julia's uncle, the viscount will feel beholden to him.'

'That wouldn't last long,' Peyton mused cynically. 'That's a fairly terminal exchange of goods and services.'

'Not if Oswalt married the viscount's niece. Then he'd be in the family and the expectation could go on indefinitely,' Paine pointed out.

'And cure his pox at the same time,' Crispin added flippantly from his corner, forgetting his present company.

Julia sucked in a quick breath. 'Pox?'

'Crispin!' Paine shot his brother a quelling look.

Crispin shrugged, unapologetic. 'Everyone knows.'

'I didn't know!' Julia cried in a choked voice. 'Did my uncle know?' she whispered, unable to keep the horror from her face. The more she knew about the backdrop against which her wedding contract had been negotiated, the darker it became.

Paine shook his head and reached briefly for her hand in a comforting gesture. 'I don't know.'

'Sorry,' Crispin muttered into his teacup.

'Let's focus on one issue at a time.' Paine resumed his pacing. 'Perhaps Oswalt is playing for the right to pull the puppet strings in Parliament. Are there other ideas? What else does the viscount have that Oswalt would want?'

'Land? An estate?' Peyton suggested.

It was Julia's turn to respond. 'My uncle's estate isn't nearly half as big as Dursley Hall. It's hard to believe anyone would go to so much trouble for a small manor when there are larger prizes out there. Besides, Oswalt couldn't get the estate anyway. It's not for sale. It's entailed. Surely a master planner like Oswalt would know that.'

'That's it,' Paine pronounced, hardly needing a moment to think. 'He's after the title.'

'Paine, that's an enormous leap of logic,' Peyton cautioned.

'I don't see how he could get it.' Julia agreed. 'Titles are bestowed by the Crown and my uncle has an heir. Why, Oswalt isn't even related.' A hand flew to her mouth. 'Yet. Marriage to me would change that. Children of ours might inherit if Gray or the others don't marry. But it seems unlikely that all three of them wouldn't produce a single son between them.'

Paine shrugged. 'There are other more direct ways to get a title than staking it all on a roll of the genealogical dice. Oswalt could be made a knight,' he put in.

'Perhaps the king would knight him as a favour for saving a peer financially, especially if he was already married to that peer's niece. The king might even see that Oswalt is named the trustee for the estate since it's his money propping it up and he would have a connection by marriage.

'I'll have Flaherty dig around and see if Oswalt's put a petition in motion to that end. Additionally, perhaps Oswalt can argue years of economic servitude to the Crown. There's no contesting that he's made money for the empire.' Paine's eyes assessed her face and she felt herself smile in spite of herself.

She felt better until Crispin said, 'There's always murder, too. He could simply marry Julia and then arrange to have the three brothers encounter untimely demises.'

Paine and Peyton shot him quelling looks, but the damage was already done. Julia blanched at the blunt assessment. It was what she'd been thinking. Was Oswalt capable of seeing three young men dead? What kind of tortured soul could wilfully engineer such atrocity? Julia shivered at the thought.

'None the less, all this speculation assumes the ship comes back,' Paine continued, trying to gloss over Crispin's blunt assessment. 'Need I point out that Oswalt's job is much easier if the ship doesn't return? Without the cargo, the viscount owes creditors *and* Oswalt.'

'Gray's ship will come back. He's never failed,' Julia said with grim conviction.'

'Ship or not, the most important issue now is what

we will do about Oswalt, assuming that our assumptions are correct.'

'That's simple,' Paine ground out. 'We go back to London and expose him before he can act on all the machinery he's put into motion. Once the *ton* gets wind of his conspiracy to undo one of their own, society will do the rest.'

'Exposure will require proof. There will be an element of risk,' Peyton reminded the group sternly.

'Anything worthwhile contains risk. I am well aware of the risks involved when dealing with Oswalt, probably better aware than most. That makes me eminently capable of seeing this situation resolved to my satisfaction.' Paine spoke confidently, refusing to be cautioned.

Julia gave him a searching glance. There was so much she didn't know about his past with Oswalt. His motivations for so fully engaging Oswalt were more than a fleeting concern. Although it was flattering to believe that he did all this on her behalf as her champion, reality suggested there were other, stronger forces at work that prompted his choice.

Paine needed her protection as much as she needed his. Oswalt was dangerous to them all. Around her the men talked of risks and benefits, but she'd had enough. She had to end this before another man, one she cared for immensely, ended up injured or dead. She had to get away from Paine Ramsden for his sake.

Julia stood up and smoothed her skirts. Her voice was firm as she made her pronouncement. 'Gentlemen, I thank you for your input and your services. It has helped me see the situation I face and, in part, the situation I created when I left my uncle's home. It is also clear to me that I cannot in good conscience continue to implicate others in a web of my own making. Tomorrow, I would kindly request the use of a travelling coach so that I can return to London.' She turned to face Paine directly.

'I am afraid we can't let you do that.'

Julia looked around in confusion for the voice. She'd certainly expected to hear those words of refusal, but she'd expected Paine to be the one to say them. The feminine tone came as a complete surprise.

Julia stared in amazement as Beth set aside her needlework and rose from the chair she occupied near the work table. Julia had been so wrapped up in the discussion over Oswalt's motives, she hadn't heard or seen the woman come in. Beth gave her a kind smile and moved to stand beside her, tossing Paine and his brothers a scolding stare. 'Shame on you all, you can't simply ride back to London and declare war on Oswalt. Think about what it will mean to Julia. She'll be beyond the pale if she shows up in your company.'

'We'll be discreet, Cousin,' Peyton began in a placating tone. 'We'll take her to Dursley House where she'll be well guarded, and we'll be with her whenever we're out.'

Beth gave an unladylike snort that made Julia like the woman immensely. 'Just like a man, even a well-meaning man. Men don't have to think of these things, so they don't,' she said dismissively. 'How will you explain Julia's return? Especially, how will you explain why Julia is at Dursley House and not back with her family? And who will be at Dursley House? She can't stay there with the three of you! She needs a chaperon, a very formidable one at that. What would the *ton* say if they knew she was living with three men? Have you thought of that?'

Julia smothered a giggle. In spite of the seriousness of their circumstances, there was a modicum of hilarity behind watching the Ramsden brothers shuffling from foot to foot, staring at each other, waiting for one of them to pick up Cousin Beth's social gauntlet. In truth, there was no arguing with Beth. She was entirely correct. They had analysed Oswalt quite thoroughly, but had not addressed the immediate concern of what to do with Julia.

'Point well taken, Cousin,' Peyton said after a bit more shuffling and staring passed between the brothers and they somehow decided Peyton got to eat humble pie because he was the eldest and the earl. 'You're precisely right, as always, about these matters. To start with, I'll write to Aunt Lily. She's in town and can take up residence at Dursley House immediately. That will provide Julia with an appropriate chaperon. A chaperon doesn't get much more proper than the Dowager Marchioness of Bridgerton, fondly known as our father's sister or Aunt Lily.'

Beth would not be satisfied with half-measures. 'That's a fine beginning, but what about the rest? I think it will look exceedingly odd for her to stay with friends with her family so close at hand, mere streets away.'

This was more difficult and for a while Julia thought

there was no viable explanation. Surely she wouldn't have to return to her uncle's home? She wouldn't be safe there for a moment and all this would have been for naught.

'If Julia and I were engaged,' Paine offered slowly, giving the impression that they were hearing his thoughts the instant he thought them, 'we could say I wanted her to meet my family and get to know them without the bother of commuting between homes, that I wanted her to spend as much time at Dursley House as possible with my Aunt Lily, since Aunt Lily will be handling the bulk of the wedding plans.'

It wasn't a perfect explanation, but it was all they had and it did make sense. After all, Julia's aunt and uncle didn't move in the same lofty circles as the Earl of Dursley. Commuting between the grand town house of the earl and the shabby, only marginally acceptable neighbourhood occupied by Julia's family could be viewed as commuting between levels in the social hierarchy and that was awkward for everyone in the *ton*.

'Julia's presence at Dursley House suggests that my marriage has my brother's full support and, by consequence, that Julia has my brother's full support,' Paine said, his conviction growing as his thoughts came together.

'Well,' Beth said hesitantly, 'it might work, but people will still look askance at the speed of such a declaration.'

'If they do, I doubt they'd dare to speak such a thing out loud. Peyton here will burn their reputation to a cinder,' Paine said jokingly, but knowing very well that Peyton held power amongst the *ton* and few dared to cross him.

'I believe Paine is right in this case, Beth. If people believe I support the match, they might question in private, but won't dare to breathe a scandalous word in public,' Peyton averred. 'Now that's settled, I think we should proceed to dinner and celebrate an engagement.'

'It's just pretend,' Julia blurted out.

'Don't let anyone hear you say that. Our success depends on our believability,' Paine scolded and Julia sensed the scold was not a tease. He was in dead earnest, as they all were.

That decided it. She had to put a stop to these mad schemes. They risked too much for her and she was cognisant of it to the extreme.

'I cannot let you all do this. It is too much to ask and it is not your concern, not really. I never meant for this to go so far.' Julia turned to Paine. 'Paine, you are chivalrous to a fault and for that, I relieve you of all obligation with my thanks.'

She saw his jaw tighten as she swept past him to the door, but to his credit he did not explode. To her surprise, he actually let her leave the library and make it up to her room. It was disappointing, but for the best. She'd expected him to rant or at the very least follow her upstairs and make an effort to protest her request. But he did none of those things. Yet. Or, perhaps like her, he would soon realise just how out of control things had got and that severing ties with her was in his better interest.

# Chapter Fourteen

Upstairs, Julia folded a few gowns back into the tissue paper and placed them in the trunk she'd so recently unpacked. When she'd gone downstairs to give Paine the note, she'd known the missive's contents would dictate their return to London. But she had not planned to so abruptly sever her ties with Paine. Then again, she had not known the full danger of her situation. She bent over the trunk and heard the door open behind her.

'Obligation has nothing to do with it,' Paine drawled. 'You cannot relieve me from that which was never a duty.'

Julia turned from the trunk, summoning her resolve. She couldn't extricate herself from this web, but she could set Paine free. Her growing feelings for him dictated she do as much. 'Don't do this, Paine.'

'Don't do what?' Paine lounged in the doorway, leaning against the white frame and looking somewhat intimidating in his maleness in her feminine abode.

'Don't confuse reality with fantasies and suppositions,' Julia said meaningfully.

'Perhaps you're the one doing that,' Paine returned, coming to take the clothes she held from her hands. 'The reality is that you are in very real peril from Oswalt in every way possible, both physically and socially. The fantasy is that you think you can go back to London alone and manage to untangle his deceits.'

Julia shook her head, finding his closeness intoxicating as always. 'Please don't try to seduce me out of this.' She sounded like she was begging and she was. She had no idea what she would do in London, if her uncle would even listen to her and believe her claims, if he would protect her from Oswalt.

Paine's eyes were intent on hers; her resolve all but collapsed at what she saw in them. 'Paine…'

His mouth took hers softly. The kiss was slow, kindling a heat in her that would not be rushed. This would not be a frantic, desperate coupling. Nor was it a farewell. Nothing in his demeanour suggested he felt it would be the last time for them. This was a lover's seduction of a beloved partner and she revelled in it.

Paine unhooked the buttons at the back of her dress, pushing the gown off her shoulders to the floor, his mouth intent on hers. He guided her back to the bed, sweeping away the piles of new gowns with his arm. He eased her back, leaving her only long enough to strip out of his clothes. Then he joined her on the bed, lowering himself over her, fitting himself between her thighs. His slow thrusts were as powerful as any of the more heated couplings they'd shared. Julia found herself powerless to resist the call to pleasure he offered. She fought his temptation valiantly. She knew why he did this.

'Paine, I can't allow this,' she tried to argue between languorous kisses.

'This is not about rules and contracts, Julia.' Paine stared down at her. 'This is an aide-mémoire. When you came to me, you became mine to care for.' His phallus, rigid and warm and deep inside her, could not have been a more potent reminder.

Paine was gone from her side in the morning as usual. Julia took it as a good sign from the fates. It would be far easier to leave without having to face him. Facing him would mean a quarrel and she'd learned last night that Paine didn't fight fairly. Still, she was exceedingly grateful to have one last night with him. What Paine did not understand was that her feelings for him were nearly as hazardous to her as the situation with Oswalt.

Julia rang for a maid and laid out clothes for travel. She would send the maid for a footman to carry her trunk and to see to the coach.

Although it was early, a maid appeared promptly and hurried off to carry out her orders. That made Julia suspicious. The earl's cousin ran an efficient household, but Julia had expected some resistance since it had been plain that her solution was not welcomed by the stubborn Ramsden brothers. Perhaps the maid had gone to inform Paine instead.

Julia dressed hurriedly, pushing aside her qualms. She didn't have time to create conspiracies out of whole cloth—not when she had a very real conspiracy to unravel back in London. When the maid returned with a footman, Julia half-expected to see Paine follow her into the room. She experienced a twinge of disappointment when he didn't.

Without questions, the footman shouldered the trunk and politely inquired if that was all. He and the maid left the room and Julia swallowed hard. All she needed to do was walk downstairs to the coach. No one was going to stop her. She should be exuberant. She held her head high, although there was no one to see her this time of day except the servants, and swept down the stairs.

Outside, the sun was just up, heralding a good day for travel. The horses stamped in the crisp air. The coachman, dressed in Dursley livery, touched the brim of his hat when he saw her. Julia nodded. She took one last look at the house and stepped inside the coach. Paine would thank her later for this.

'Beautiful day for a drive.' The object of her ruminations was sprawled on the seat of the roomy coach, impeccably turned out in riding gear, Hessians and a well-tied cravat, the clean smell of his morning *toilette* subtly filling the carriage.

Smiling would definitely hurt her position. It would be hard to convince Paine she was angry with him, but she found herself smiling nevertheless.

'Happy to see me?'

Julia settled on the front-facing seat. 'I asked for a loan of a travelling coach and driver so that I could leave this morning.'

'And my brother has graciously supplied all that you asked.'

'That's an understatement. I didn't ask for company.'

'Aha, but you didn't not ask,' Paine countered smoothly.

Julia frowned. 'How is that? I don't think that's even a grammatically correct sentence.'

Paine's eyes were dancing in jest. He warmed to his game. 'You didn't not ask,' he repeated. 'You merely said you would be returning to London. You never stated we couldn't come along, or specifically that I couldn't come along.'

Julia grimaced. 'I said you were relieved of obligation.'

'But that doesn't mean I can't come. It only assumes that I am not obliged to come or that I was obliged to do anything in the first place, which I've already pointed out that I was not.'

'You're being obtuse. It was implied that I wished to return alone,' Julia snapped.

'And I *implied* that I disagreed with that choice.' Paine smugly rapped on the coach. 'Let's be off!'

'You're insufferable,' Julia huffed, although inwardly she wasn't nearly as upset as she appeared because, at that moment, the carriage door opened and a smiling Cousin Beth poked her head in. 'Good morning. Be a dear, Julia, and move over.'

'What is this, Beth?' Paine protested, his surprise at her appearance evident.

'A young woman of virtue can't ride around the countryside in a carriage alone with a man,' Beth scolded. 'You might have played fast and loose with the rules to this point, young man, but, from here on, it's by the book.' Beth took a seat next to Julia and took out her knitting. 'I'll have a nice scarf by the time we get to London,' she said with far too much cheer.

Paine groaned. 'Now who's being insufferable?'

'That makes two of you,' Julia replied stiffly.

The house disappeared behind them and Paine leaned forwards. 'You cannot tackle Oswalt alone, Julia. It is the height of foolishness to think so.'

'So you've said. You seem quite certain of that. Would you care to tell me why? It's a long ride to London—days, in fact—and I think it's time I knew what it is exactly that lies between you and Oswalt.'

Beth looked up from her knitting. 'Yes, Cousin. Tell her. She has a right to know.'

The sharp eyes that pierced him from across the carriage were acutely reminiscent of the way Julia had looked at him that first night in his office when she'd put her request to him. She'd given him that same un-wavering gaze, so forthright, so honest and so bold that he'd known there would be no refusing then. And he knew it now. It was an ironic quality of hers that she possessed such an abundance of feminine beauty and none of the covert wiles that usually went with such attractiveness. Nothing escaped her notice and nothing was safe from her comment.

Julia tapped a foot impatiently, her eyebrow giving a supercilious quirk. 'You may begin.'

'Why should I tell you at all?' Paine protested. He seldom shared his past with anyone; now, he would have shared it twice in quite recent times—once with Peyton and now with Julia.

Julia narrowed her eyes. 'You should tell me so I can determine if I will let you meddle in my business.'

Paine would have teased her if she hadn't looked so serious. 'Meddling, is it?'

'Yes. Meddling. This was my problem from the first and it's still my problem, even if the parameters I thought I was dealing with have been a bit altered in their scope,' Julia insisted. 'I say who has access to my life.'

'You'd better decide I do. You will need me before this is over.' Paine matched her blunt tone.

'Convince me.' Julia sat back against the seat and crossed her arms, challenging him to deny her request.

She softened slightly for a moment, becoming the image of the Julia he liked best—the Julia that moaned beneath him on the picnic blanket, who thought he could slay dragons, who brought him his secret peace. 'Come, Paine, how awful could it be?'

He gave a small smile at that. 'It could be pretty awful, Julia.'

'Let me be the judge.' She leaned forwards, all rapt attention.

Paine drew a deep breath. 'I was a rowdy youth. I ran with a fast crowd of young bucks when I came up to town. Most of the people in my set were younger sons and rather cynical about their lot in life. It became the trade-mark of our group that we flaunted the fact that we were the spares and in some cases, like mine, the spare to the spare. We were "non-essential" to our families so we lived hard, pushing convention as far as it could be pushed with outrageous feats: races, affairs, bets and dares.'

Julia made a quizzical frown. 'I can't believe Peyton made you feel that way.'

'Of course not, not directly, but Father had done the job for him. By the time Peyton was earl and I was ready to storm around town, I felt pretty "non-essential". Peyton was head of the family, Crispin was doing a stint in the military as an officer—and a fine officer he was, too, I might add. Then there was me. Peyton sent me to Oxford. I think he hoped I'd find direction there. However, I finished with no particular purpose in mind, although I received a first-class degree in the classics and loved history. Peyton wanted to set me up as an estate manager on one of the smaller family properties, but I wasn't interested in land management. Without any direction and with too much time on my hands, I was a prime candidate for falling in with that crowd.' Paine chuckled. 'It's amazing how clear the pattern seems from a distance of years.'

'That's understandable. You're not the only young man to run into that sort of trouble,' Julia offered sagely.

'Trouble with your cousins?' Paine probed.

'The two younger ones are something akin to hellions. I wouldn't be surprised if their antics have heavily contributed to the family situation these days.'

Julia dismissed the subject, wagging a finger at him. 'You won't get off that easily, Paine. Now, you said you pushed convention as far as it could be pushed. Go on.'

He didn't mind her direct probe this time. Now that he'd started talking, it was easier to continue. 'Yes, I pushed convention and one day it pushed back. There was a…um…"party" for gentlemen only at an estate out in Richmond, far enough out of town to avoid real trouble or censure.'

'Party, Paine? Don't mince words. What kind of party?' Julia pressed, sensing his hesitation.

Paine cast an uncomfortable look at Cousin Beth, who looked back blandly.

'Don't mind me. I've seen more than you think, Paine. I am not so shocked by the world as you might think.'

'It was an orgy. Do you know what an orgy is?' Paine asked, shifting in his seat with acute embarrassment. If they were being blunt, he might as well ask.

Julia blushed. 'I have some idea.'

Paine nodded. 'Well, this was worse than the usual masked *demi-monde* affair, if that's what you're thinking of.'

Julia bit her lip and shifted uncomfortably. He felt ashamed for having brought it up. He easily forgot she'd only seen parts of his world for a few days. It was a sharp reminder of the type of life he'd been leading, so far away from the standards of the *ton*.

He went on, wanting to get the next part over with, to spare her. 'The gathering was to be held at a place Oswalt owned. Peyton encouraged me not to go when he heard about it. Apparently, Oswalt had acquired the property from a baron in a card game. Peyton felt it was wrong to attend an event at a place acquired in such a manner by such a person. But I didn't listen.

'In all honesty, I didn't fully understand the depth of depravity that would be on display there.' Paine waved a hand negligently. 'I thought it would be high-class prostitutes and a few wild moments in the dark. At that time, it seemed like a lark.'

He shook his head, trying to shake off the memories of the altar-like marble block set up in the ballroom, surrounded by candles and silken ropes, and of the young woman Oswalt had forcibly bound to the altar and then begun accepting bids for public congress with her.

Paine could not look at Julia or Beth, who helpfully kept her eyes on the knitting needles, as he spun his morbid tale. He'd thought it was a game at first, that the woman was a high-paid prostitute hired to play the role of sacrificial virgin. Although telling himself that did not make the spectacle any more palatable. Then it had become clear to him that the woman was not there of her own accord.

'I thought someone would speak up, someone close to Oswalt, who would carry some sway with Oswalt. Surely all these men gathered wouldn't condone such an act. But no one did and the girl was clearly terrified.' Paine swallowed hard here. 'I pushed my way through the crowd and demanded this activity be halted. I had stupidly thrown off my mask in my outrage and Oswalt merely laughed at me. He said, "Or what? You'll tell your brother, the earl?" Well, I was on the outs with Peyton, knowing he was displeased with my choice to attend in the first place and my pride was stung that Peyton had been right after all. I could not settle for such a remark that night. I threw down my glove and challenged him to a duel in front of everyone.'

'That's very noble of you,' Julia offered softly.

'No one else thought so. I wasn't the only nobleman or nobleman's son in the crowd that night. No one wanted breath of their attendance reaching the proper circles of high society. When it became known that the girl was the daughter of an unremarkable merchant, it was implicitly decided that the event simply didn't exist, it hadn't happened. No one ever spoke of it. No one acknowledged what I had seen. The event suddenly became nothing more than a squabble between me and Oswalt over a girl of questionable background, hence questionable virtue. The girl was ruined from the gossip and I was expendable as a third son whose brother had already inherited the title.'

'And the duel?' Julia asked, expectantly. At least she hadn't completely shunned him yet. That was a good sign.

'It happened. Almost. I was determined to see it through, even though I knew what had happened to the social understanding of the events. But either London society or Oswalt himself decided that the duel would not take place. Suffice it to say, someone tipped off the authorities.' Paine shrugged. 'You know the penalty for duelling.'

'Exile,' Julia supplied. 'But what happened to Oswalt?'

'Nothing. I think he bargained with the authorities to

overlook his participation in the duel. When the authorities showed up, Oswalt pressed for exile as my punish-
ment. The outcome was decided so swiftly, Peyton
could do nothing in time to intervene. He had left a few
days prior to attend business at an estate not too far
from London. But it was far enough away that he didn't
get the news in a timely fashion.' Paine shrugged. 'Not
that I would have wanted his assistance. I was too
stubborn then.'

'Just then?' Julia teased.

'Vixen.' Paine smiled. 'That's the story. I think
Oswalt feared what would happen if I stayed in London
and had a chance to rally support and re-introduce the
issue, so I had to be sent away.'

'That's awful.' Julia sighed, worry shading her eyes.

'It's the truth. I want you to know that this incident
with your uncle and Oswalt is not an isolated occur-
rence. The man has been ruining peers, quietly and
subtly, for years. He's been preying on innocent girls for
much longer than that.'

'I can't believe no one has done anything about it.'
Julia shook her head in disbelief.

'That's society's way. If we talk about it, it gives the
problem validity. If it's ignored, then it must not exist.'
Paine spread his hands on his thighs. 'But it's not my
way, Julia. That's why I want to help you.'

Julia smiled at him gamely. 'And that's why I'll let
you help.'

'*Let me*, is it?'

'Yes, *let you*.'

Paine pulled out his pocket watch and flipped it open. 'And my brothers, too, I hope?'

'Why is that?' Julia eyed him curiously.

'Because, by my calculations, they're an hour behind us on the road.'

Julia shot him a considering look. 'I was never going back alone, was I?'

'No, you never stood a chance,' Paine confirmed, although the reason that was true was the reason he was hesitant to acknowledge, even to himself. The idea that he should at last find himself falling in love was too new, too foreign to his way of thinking. He would need some time to get his metaphorical hands around the distinct possibility that Julia Prentiss had permanently garnered his affections.

# Chapter Fifteen

**D**ursley House glittered a regal welcome in the summer twilight after a dusty, jouncing two-day journey back to London. Inviting as the town house looked, Julia also found it imposing, with its four storeys of long elegant windows. Dursley House on Curzon Street was an enormous step up from the home her uncle had rented on the fringes of Belgravia, which was still a respectable location, but just barely.

Julia tossed Paine a longing glance as he helped her down from the carriage. She knew it was important for her to be at Dursley House, but it didn't stop her from wanting to be alone with Paine. She'd much rather be at his Brook Street property, just the two of them, where they could shut out the world. She wondered if he felt the same.

Paine seemed to read her thoughts. 'We have to think about your reputation,' Paine said seriously in a tone that caused her stop and stare. When had he become the arbiter of the moral code? It certainly hadn't been last night at the inn. He'd hardly waited a decent interval before showing up in her room, although he'd been very quiet so as not to wake Cousin Beth in the antechamber or Peyton next door.

'My reputation?' Julia had to remember to shut her jaw. 'I thought the whole point was to *ruin* my reputation.'

'It was, but we can't openly flaunt society while we're living under my brother's roof. Remember, for the public we're a case of love at first sight. My Aunt Lily will be in residence at Dursley House with Cousin Beth, so everything will look legitimate, less like a bachelor household.'

They climbed the steps and were greeted by the butler at the door. Peyton and Crispin entered behind them, Peyton making a low-voiced inquiry of the butler as he passed. Aunt Lily met them in the large foyer, looking for the world like an efficient hostess instead of a woman who'd been uprooted from her London residence that morning to see Dursley House opened and ready for five impromptu guests that evening. She was indeed the woman Julia had seen with Paine earlier and Julia liked her immediately. She seemed the complete antithesis of her own aunt, who worried and fussed herself into a state over unplanned happenings.

'Aunt Lily, thank you for coming. May I present to you Miss Julia Prentiss?' Paine made the necessary introductions.

Aunt Lily fixed Julia with a gimlet eye and a slow inspection. Julia imagined the woman was weighing whether or not she was worth the trouble of moving residences. It seemed that even the brothers held their collective breath. At last, Lily spoke. 'So you're the gel that has Paine running in circles. That boy's a lot of trouble. Are you sure he's worth it?'

'Julia, Aunt Lily will show you to your room. You can freshen up. A maid will see to the unpacking,' Paine said before Aunt Lily could impugn him further.

Aunt Lily shot Julia a conspiratorial glance. 'Just like a man. Paine has no desire to stand in the foyer and be taken to task by his aunt any more than he wants to hear your answer to the question. But you can tell me upstairs if the boy is worth all this fuss. Come with me, dear. I'll show you to your room and you can enlighten me as to what is *really* going on. Dursley's note made a lot of demands, but little sense. You come, too, Beth. At least I'll get sense out of you.' She shot Peyton a quelling look and Julia fought back the urge to laugh at the Ramsden brothers being taken to task like errant schoolboys.

'I hope you will find everything to your liking,' Peyton put in. 'Tell Aunt Lily if there's anything you need. I've instructed Cook to lay out a light supper in the dining room in an hour, if you'd like to join us.'

To their credit, Aunt Lily and Beth sensed Julia's need to gather her thoughts and they didn't stay long in Julia's chamber in spite of Lily's comments to the brothers. Julia was certain the two women were down the hall right now, exchanging news, and was glad for the privacy to settle into her new rooms.

Julia's room overlooked the gardens and the open

windows caught the scent of the climbing roses that grew below. As town gardens went, Dursley House boasted quite a large one by urban standards.

She was glad for it. The trees and the greenery blocked out the city din and provided a soothing calm. Her nerves were on edge at the thought of being back in town. She would have preferred going to Paine's house and being alone with him in his exotic bedroom. Perhaps he would have, too. She was starting to understand what had goaded his passionate display at the inn. It was doubtful he'd be able to come to her room as long as they stayed here under the watchful eyes of Peyton and Aunt Lily, who occupied the room next door to her. It was all part of her 'protection'. Paine had made it clear that he didn't want her left alone at any time and Peyton had staunchly supported his brother's wishes.

In his residence, there would be just the two of them and a handful of day servants. Here, she was surrounded by him, his brothers and the family servants, whose loyalty was unquestionable. If need be, Dursley House could be her fortress.

She appreciated their efforts to see her well guarded. But it was both stifling and unnerving. Peyton was probably downstairs now, meeting with the staff, coaching them about their latest guest.

Julia leaned out the window to inhale the roses. She closed her eyes and breathed in their peace. She would need the peace of the garden in the weeks to come. Paine's arguments of propriety and protection aside, there were other reasons they *had* to be at Dursley

House. Dursley House was about status. She and Paine needed the credibility of the Dursley name behind them for their plan to succeed.

Paine waved up at her from the terrace, looking casual and fresh in a clean shirt and breeches. 'Julia, come down!'

Had it been an hour already? Julia changed into a simple yellow-sprigged muslin from Madame Broussard's in record time and flew down the stairs. The brothers were waiting for her in the drawing room. 'I'm sorry to be late,' she apologised.

'You look lovely. The yellow becomes you,' Paine said, coming to stand next to her and lifting her hand to his lips in a soft kiss. The gallant-suitor act startled her for a moment until she remembered the plan. Ah, the play had begun. She must remember to play her role as well. That would mean no sparring with Paine or arguing in public or private.

Beyond them in the dining room, dinner had been set out on white cloth-covered tables lit with candles, footmen waiting to remove the covers. Peyton and Aunt Lily led the way. Paine offered her his arm for the short distance and she smiled up at him as they walked. 'This is a nice fantasy,' Julia said, hoping to convey to him that she understood his behavior and that she would act her part. Paine merely smiled. He pulled out her chair and seated her, letting his hands linger on her shoulders before taking the chair next to her.

After a short round of small talk, while the covers

were removed and the footmen departed to let them eat in privacy, Peyton turned the conversation immediately to their mission at hand. Julia suspected this was the very reason they'd chosen to dine informally inside instead of outside on the terrace, enjoying the summer evening. Here, they could serve themselves and not be interfered with; indoors, they wouldn't risk the sound of their conversation being carried to unwanted ears.

'We've arrived without mishap.' Peyton raised a glass of the excellent white wine served with the fowl. But there was no rest for the weary. They'd barely taken two bites before Peyton raised their business.

'I have already met with the staff here at Dursley House and given them my strictest instructions regarding Julia. They are not to discuss her presence in this home. To do so will result in being dismissed immediately. Additionally, I have instructed them that Julia is not to leave the house without one of us with her plus an appropriate escort of footmen. Is that clear, everyone?' Peyton fixed them all in turn with his regal stare before continuing. 'Preferably, I'd like Julia to stay put. As soon as Oswalt knows the knocker is on the door, there's no doubt he'll set men to watching the house as a precaution. None the less, we will not hide like scared rabbits. Tomorrow, we tackle the *ton*. We need to talk about that.' He turned to Lily. 'You've looked over the invitations—which gathering do you recommend?'

'Invitations already?' Julia broke in. 'We've only been in town a few hours.'

'I had the knocker go up on the door before I even arrived,' Aunt Lily said as if another eight hours' notice made all the difference. The message was clear. The Earl of Dursley was a sought-after commodity.

And why not? Julia couldn't help but cast a glance at the man who sat at the head of the table. He was an older, more mature image of Paine, who was nigh on irresistible with his good looks. It had not occurred to her before just how much of an eligible *parti* Peyton Ramsden would be for the matchmaking mamas. Stable, wealthy, titled and handsome—all eminently desirable and rare characteristics to find in a marriageable man. But not for her.

Julia dropped her fork in a clatter at the realisation. Paine had ruined her for other men, even handsome look-alike peers with titles and money.

'Do you have something against the Worthington soirée, my dear?' Lily inquired innocuously from across the table.

Worthington soirée? Was that what they'd been talking about? Julia feigned attention. 'No, of course not. It should be a lovely evening.'

'Do you have something to wear?' Peyton, always the detailed planner, asked.

Julia didn't get to answer. 'Another trunk arrived from Madame Broussard's today. I put it in her room,' Aunt Lily supplied.

Julia smiled to herself. She'd seen the trunk, but hadn't had time to open it. Apparently she didn't need to. The efficient Aunt Lily probably knew the contents of the trunk down to the last button. She was getting used to the Ramsden way of managing everything and everyone. It was even starting to be entertaining, watching them try to manage each other. She would have to pick her battles and they would have to learn that Julia Prentiss could manage things, too. The Ramsdens weren't the only capable people in the world. She would miss them when all this was over and that was a sobering thought indeed.

Plans were laid quickly after that and Julia was careful to pay attention lest she become swept away in the ardent wave of Ramsden plotting. In the morning, Paine would go over to Brook Street and check on his house. She and Aunt Lily would pay calls on some of Aunt Lily's more influential friends at their at-homes and attend a ladies' lunch. That evening, they would make their 'grand' entrance into society at the Worthington soirée.

'What about my family?' Julia asked as the planning session drew to a close. 'There's a chance we'll run into them or a chance that they'll hear of me being in town.'

'There's every chance of that. We're counting on it,' Peyton offered, pouring the last of the wine.

'The servants won't talk, but we can't really hope to keep your presence here a secret and, truly, there's no point in making this covert. After all, we'll be out in public. We *want* to be seen together,' Paine said. 'As soon as your uncle knows you're with us, I'll pay him a visit.'

Julia didn't like the sound of that. It sounded exclusive and very Ramsden-like. 'I want to be with you when you visit. I want them to know I chose this and that I am fine. They've probably been worried to death.'

'We'll see, Julia. I won't have you put in unnecessary danger,' Paine said tersely. He pushed back and rose. 'Time for bed, I think. Tomorrow will be busy and today was long.'

Julia rose to go with him. 'You did that on purpose,' she scolded in a low voice as they exited the dining room.

'Did what? Excuse myself from the table?' Paine said obtusely. 'I tend to do that on a nightly basis.'

'Absolutely. You did it so I couldn't respond to your dictates about visiting my uncle.'

Paine glanced over his shoulder, then, apparently satisfied with what he'd seen or not seen behind them, pulled her into a dark corner of the terrace. 'You're a horrible minx to try to out-think,' he teased, attempting to steal a kiss in the shadows.

Julia put him off, twisting her head out of reach. 'No. You are not going to distract me with kisses either.' Although she wasn't at all sure of her ability to live up to that claim of resistance. 'I am not going to be left out of the visit any more than you were going to be left out of my return to London. Promise me, Paine, that I'll get to go with you.'

'All right, I promise as long as there's no danger to you.' Paine sighed in exasperation. 'Bargaining with you is the devil, Julia. May I have a kiss now?'

Julia leaned into him, arms around his neck. 'I thought you would never ask.'

'Yes, you did.' Paine gave a low laugh in the summer

darkness before he claimed her lips with a kiss that Julia thought might be quite the best goodnight kiss in the history of goodnight kisses between two people who were only pretending to be in love.

Julia stood in the long line of guests waiting to be introduced at the Worthington soirée, grateful for a few moments to gather her thoughts and happy to let the others handle whatever greetings or conversations came their way as they waited in line. At this moment, the managing tendencies of the Ramsden brothers was a very welcome trait.

The day had been a whirl of activity. She had not expected otherwise. But Julia had not been prepared for how draining the routine would be. Just changing her gowns had been a tiring chore. She'd dressed in a muslin morning dress for the calls they'd paid before the lunch. Lily had rushed her home between calls and the luncheon to change into something 'fresh' although she'd only worn the gown for three hours. Then there had been another change so she could be seen driving with Aunt Lily through Hyde Park at the crowded hour before returning home for dinner and to dress for the soirée.

Four dresses! And Lily had overseen each choice with military precision from slippers to bonnet. No detail had been overlooked. Her own aunt hadn't paid close attention to her wardrobe at all as long as the gown was considered fashionable. But then, her aunt was not Lily Branbourne, Dowager Marchioness of Bridgerton and a Ramsden by birth.

Lily had expertly shepherded her through the day, introducing her to influential women, including a patroness of Almack's. Lily had not forgotten, as the cadre of Ramsden males had, that Julia was new come to town and there were protocols to follow. Julia had barely been presented at court and had her own come-out before the trouble with Oswalt began. Lily understood all that implied. She'd gone so far as to warn Paine that Julia could not yet dance the waltz, since Almack's hadn't given her permission.

Paine had protested the notion, but had earned himself nothing but a sharp rap on the knuckles from his aunt's ivory fan.

Paine's own news for the day wasn't good. His venture to the Brook Street home had been dismaying. The home had been burgled. The few pieces of furniture the house possessed had been broken, the elegant yin-and-yang cabinet vandalised, its contents shattered on the floor. Paine could not discern if anything was missing and he reported that he doubted anything was taken.

The Ramsden brothers concluded that the break-in had been designed to scare or perhaps to catch. Somehow, Oswalt had figured out where the discreet residence was and was sending the message that he meant to flush Paine out. There was nowhere to hide.

Fortunately, hiding wasn't part of the plan. They meant to go about in plain sight. Julia spread her own fan and waved it delicately to generate a little air. The evening was warm and standing in line was warmer still. She was glad Lily had suggested the light gown of 'changeable' pale pink silk adorned with ribbon instead of the one Julia had favoured with heavier beading.

'You look lovely,' Paine whispered in her ear. 'I don't know how you manage to look both sinful and innocent at the same time. I want to devour you.'

'There'll be none of that, Paine, my boy,' Aunt Lily scolded, stepping in. 'It's our turn. Behave.'

Her tone was censorious and a sharp reminder that tonight wasn't only about Julia. It was about Paine returning to the fold with the backing of his brother's good graces. In order for them to put a stop to Oswalt's manoeuvrings, Paine had to be accepted back into society.

They were announced to the hostess and Julia fought back the impression that the announcement had been louder than anyone else's and that everyone stopped their chatter to stare at them.

'Everyone is staring,' Julia whispered.

'Of course they are. They're wondering who the beautiful woman is on my arm,' Paine encouraged softly. 'We want it this way. We want to be noticed.' Further conversation was impossible as they approached their hostess. Paine turned on his considerable charm, bowing gallantly over Lady Worthington's hand and they were through.

'See,' Paine said once they entered the ballroom, 'Ramsdens don't skulk. We don't have to slither in and be ashamed of anything.'

'Then we've succeeded,' Julia shot back. It was clear the clusters of people standing near the entrance to the ballroom were indeed staring at them. She kept her head high and dared a smile at one or two who were brazen enough to meet her eyes.

'Keep moving,' Paine counselled through a smile as he acknowledged an acquaintance here and there in the crowd. His hand never left the small of her back and Julia welcomed its light pressure, its warm reassurance while they navigated the crowd.

'Here. We'll stop here. This will be a good place to make our own,' Peyton said at last when they gained a spot near a pillar along the side of the ballroom. Within moments, people seemed to sense that the Earl of Dursley was ready to 'receive'.

People who had watched his progress from the reception line through the ballroom began to make their way towards them. Julia's fear that they'd be shunned was quickly dispelled. Within minutes, they were surrounded by mothers wanting to introduce daughters to Peyton, men wanting to meet Paine and women hoping to do more than meet him, Julia thought uncharitably. Everyone wanted to hear Paine's story.

The evening served as a pattern card for the evenings that followed. The Ramsden brothers were seen at every affair of merit hosted in Mayfair's ballrooms over the next few weeks, squiring about the sparkling Julia Prentiss with the redoubtable Aunt Lily close by. The story of Julia and Paine's supposed country romance was on the lips of every worthy gossip. Aunt Lily's chaperonage lent the tale credibility. The twosome had met during Paine's reunion with his brothers recently and had become quite taken with each other. Aunt Lily claimed having introduced them at a family dinner.

As June lengthened towards midsummer, everywhere they went, crowds surged around them. But Julia wasn't naïve enough to assume the sycophantic crowd around them meant Paine had been welcomed back. It was too soon. That judgement would occur later and the verdict would start trickling through Mayfair. As would the verdict regarding herself. Had she 'taken'? How much people liked her would hugely affect how willing they'd be to accept her story without probing too closely. But there were good indicators success was assured. She'd even survived Almack's and now had permission to waltz.

Standing next to her at the Hatley rout, Paine shook hands with a gentleman. 'I'll be staying at Dursley House. Please feel free to call and we can discuss business more thoroughly.'

'That sounds promising.' Julia nodded after the retreating figure of the gentleman.

'Yes. I've found business loans can be one way of restoring my reputation,' Paine said. 'They're starting up the music. Would you dance with me? I seem to recall dancing with a gentleman at a fine affair was on a certain Julia Prentiss's wish list,' he flirted lightly, offering his arm.

'You remember that?' Julia placed her hand on his sleeve, fighting a blush. She remembered that, too, but more vivid than what she'd said was what they'd done.

'Yes. And…' Paine's eyes twinkled as they took their places in the forming sets '…I remember other things we did that night, too.'

Crispin claimed her for the second dance, but the third dance was an energetic country dance and Julia was glad for the rest. The ballroom was warm and she was desperate for a cool breeze.

Paine read her need immediately when Crispin returned her to their court. 'Perhaps you'd prefer a stroll on the terrace,' Paine suggested.

'Just the terrace, Paine,' Peyton cautioned quietly from his side. Julia stifled a laugh. There they went, managing each other again, or at least trying to. She appreciated Peyton's reasons for it, though. They were close to success, close to laying Paine's dubious past and rowdy youth to rest. An amorous blunder now could easily put paid to their hopes.

'Just the terrace, Peyton.' Paine grinned and whisked her away.

The terrace was disappointingly crowded, but the cool air was a relief. 'I think it would be all right to walk in the gardens,' Paine suggested. 'I'll be glad when all this nonsense is over and I can kiss you when I like,' he whispered in her ear.

Julia silently agreed with that sentiment. As expected, he'd been unable to come to her room and, with all eyes on them, their opportunities to be together were severely curtailed.

The gardens were better. They were less populated and Paine adroitly found them a bench by a quiet fountain surrounded by tall hedges.

'You've been here before,' Julia said, suspicious of the ease with which the place had been located. It was well hidden enough that the casual wanderer would be unlikely to come across it.

'Yes.' Paine put an arm about her waist and drew her close. 'I can safely kiss you here.'

'Paine, you know the rules,' Julia protested. 'The evening's been going so well, I don't want to jinx it.'

'We won't get caught. Besides, anyone who catches us would have plenty of explaining to do as to why they were out here, too,' Paine reassured her, sweeping her into his arms for an impromptu waltz before she could marshal another argument. 'I've wanted you so much. It's killing me not to be able to touch you.'

Julia stumbled a bit as she tried to find Paine's rhythm. 'This is not at all like dancing with my cousins.'

Paine laughed. 'I should hope not!' He pulled her tight against him and swung a tight turn around the fountain.

'Paine, there's supposed to be distance between us,' Julia gasped, but her gasp had little to do with outrage and everything to do with the excitement of being in this man's arms. With him, even a simple dance was an adventure.

'I wonder why this dance is so scandalous. I mean, the way they dance it inside. It's just a pattern of circles and turns,' Julia mused out loud, finally falling into Paine's rhythm with confidence.

'My dear, don't you know? The waltz is a metaphor for sex.'

'I don't believe you. I think you're just making that up to shock me.' Julia laughed.

'No, watch and learn,' Paine drawled, his eyes turning dark with seductive intention. He slowed his pace, making their steps deliberate. 'The woman is in pursuit, that's why the woman is always dancing forwards, as it were. It's a chase. If we dance too close together, you can feel me through my trousers, even my most intimate parts. That's why those prim matrons in there insist on distance. But out here, we don't have to worry about such nonsense.'

'Do you know everything about sex?' Julia flirted, knowing he was dangerously aroused, but not caring. She was desperate for him after weeks of denial.

He danced her against a hedge and kissed her hard on the mouth. 'I've wanted to do that all night.'

'Devour me, you mean?' Julia managed between kisses. The truth was, she wanted to devour him, too. She'd missed his presence in her bed.

'I want you, Julia.' Paine placed a line of hot kisses down the column of her neck. Julia arched against him, a moan escaping her lips. She made a valiant bid for sanity. 'I don't think this happened to Cinderella when she danced with the prince.'

'Oh, you don't, do you?' Paine whispered huskily. 'You might be surprised. Perhaps the prince knew how to do the "twining creeper".' He lifted her skirts, baring her thighs to the summer night. 'Let me do this for you, a little of our own magic before midnight.' His hand found the nub nestled in her nether curls.

He stroked.

She closed her eyes and gasped at the intimate invasion, but she was unable to fight it. His touch was exquisite, inviting her to take the pleasure he offered.

In a few moments, he would let her soar. She was nearly there. Then suddenly he stopped.

Her eyes flew open in indignation. 'Paine, why did you—?'

'What was that you said about us waltzing?' Paine grumbled softly to her, shielding her long enough for his deft hands to adjust her skirts.

'I said it would jinx things,' Julia said, still confused as to the abrupt interruption in their interlude.

'Looks like you were right.' Paine shifted from his protective position enough to reveal their unwanted guest.

They were no longer alone. Crispin Ramsden stood in the little entranceway to their hiding spot, having the decency to look uncomfortable.

# *Chapter Sixteen*

'You were supposed to stay on the terrace,' Crispin ground out once he recovered his senses.

'I am not a toddler in leading strings,' Paine retorted, pushing Julia behind him in a belated attempt to protect her modesty. 'What are you doing out here? Did Peyton send you to keep track of me?'

'I wish it were that simple.' Julia did not miss the import of the gaze Crispin sent Paine.

Paine didn't miss it either. 'What's happened?'

Crispin held out a note. 'It's from your man, Flaherty. Apparently, he found this so important that he came here and left it with a footman.'

Paine took the note and unfolded it, reading slowly. 'It's worse than we thought. Oswalt has indeed managed to have his name put forwards for a knighthood. It seems that he means to bankrupt your uncle's estate and then prop it up financially. Flaherty speculates that he might even ask to be given custody of the estate when he's awarded his knighthood. It's not an uncommon practice for bankrupt estates to be given over to a trustee for financial management. It's a long shot, but we should be prepared for it. The estate's only protection is its entailment. Still, in terms of custody, it might not be enough.'

Paine swore low under his breath. 'It's too audacious. It's not chivalrous. I can't believe the crown would reward such blatant chicanery. He won't get away with it.'

'Yes, he will,' Julia said softly. The ramifications of the note were enormous. 'If he marries me, the request for guardianship will look benevolent. He can argue that he wants to manage the estate for me, with an eye to the future heirs. His guardianship keeps it in the family. No one will ever connect him to being the cause of my uncle's debts. On the surface, he'll look like an angel, having offered my uncle a fair settlement for me, and for tiding the family over during difficulties. It won't look like it's his fault the family continues to sink into bankruptcy.'

Julia fought the urge to sway. She grabbed on to Paine's arm. 'We have to tell my uncle. He must be warned about Oswalt's intentions.'

'I'll go tomorrow,' Paine promised.

'Correction, *we'll* go tomorrow,' Julia contradicted. The garden had lost its magic, the glitter of the evening had paled against the reality facing them. Crispin sensed it, too.

'We've accomplished enough for an evening. I'll tell Peyton to send for the carriage. We can respectfully leave,' he said quietly. 'I'll see you both inside in a few minutes.'

'It's bad, isn't it?' Julia said once they were alone.

Paine nodded slowly. 'I had hoped against hope that you were merely an accessory to Oswalt's master plan, whatever it turned out to be. I had hoped your ruination might save you from him.'

Julia took his hand. 'We did our best in that regard.' She tried for levity, but this was too serious. She didn't have to be told that she'd been upgraded in Oswalt's plan from a virginal accessory for a debauched man's cure to a key lynch pin. If Oswalt meant to seize the estate ostensibly on her behalf, he'd want her, virgo intacta or not.

Paine paced the length of Peyton's room. It was well past the time to be in bed, but he was restless, his body full of energy with no outlet and his mind a riot of options he repeatedly sorted through and discarded. 'What would you do, Peyton?' he said at last, halting briefly in front of the fireplace.

Peyton waved the question aside. 'That's irrelevant, Paine. You're not me. I can't advise you in this.'

'That's no help,' Paine snarled.

'Not my fault.' Peyton straightened up from his slouch in the big wing chair by the window. 'What do you want to do, Paine? She came to you for one thing and you've done what she asked. You don't have to do any more.'

Paine furrowed his brow. 'Are you suggesting I should just walk away?'

Peyton gave a casual shrug. 'There's really only two choices here, you know. You can walk away or you can stay with her.'

'I know that and I can't walk away. She'll be ruined or sacrificed to Oswalt's cause or both,' Paine protested. The option to leave Julia to her fate was reprehensible. 'I've squired her around the *ton*, declared to have feelings for her.'

Peyton nodded. 'It was part of the plan. Julia agreed to it, knowing full well those declarations were not necessarily real. She seems to be a smart girl, Paine. She knew what she was doing.' Peyton splayed his fingers on his thighs in thought. 'But if letting Julia find her own level is so unpalatable to you, then your choice is clear. You see this out. But have you thought what that means or where that ends? I should ask what your feelings are for the girl. Do you like her?'

'Yes. I like her a great deal.' Paine let out a breath. He supposed that was the real issue he'd been contemplating since Flaherty's news had arrived. He couldn't lose Julia. He wanted Julia for his own. This was the conclusion he'd been dancing around all night. He didn't want to go back to a life without her in it.

'You'll have to do more than make her your mistress,' Peyton cautioned.

'Of course,' Paine shot back, irritated that Peyton thought so little of him that he had to be reminded of a gentleman's duty. 'I'll ride to Lambeth Palace for a special licence as soon as the hour is decent.'

'Then congratulations are in order. You're about to become a married man,' Peyton offered.

*If she'll have me.*

He parted from Peyton, his mind lighter. The thought

of a special licence did bring a sense of peace. He had a path to follow now, a path that led to Julia if he was successful. But he was not naïve enough to think a piece of paper would solve all their problems. Unless the contract between her uncle and Oswalt was broken, no one would legally recognise his marriage. And then there was Julia's own reaction to the situation. Would she want to marry him? Would she understand he wanted to marry her for reasons that had nothing to do with the conundrum they found themselves in?

'The chit was seen at the Worthington soirée!' Oswalt threw down the note he'd received from Julia's uncle in disgust. He strode back and forth in front of the line of his assembled henchman, including Sam Brown. The office at his dockside warehouse was warm and fetid, crowded with the men who worked for him. They were shuffling their feet nervously and twisting their caps. As well they should be.

They'd failed miserably. Of the men who'd ridden with Brown to catch them in the Cotswolds, one still limped, one still had an arm in a sling and the other would bear a life-long scar from his run-in with Ramsden's knife. The others had failed to confirm Julia's return to London except for noting that Dursley House had started sporting a knocker on the front door.

'Damn you all! What do I pay you for if some incompetent nincompoop finds her first? How is it those milksop cousins of hers noticed her before you did?' Oswalt ranted.

After a long silence, Sam Brown stepped forwards. 'With all respect, sir, the likes of us aren't invited to those functions. It's one thing to get inside a gambling hell, but it's mighty awkward to skulk about a ball without drawing undue attention.'

Oswalt grunted at that. 'Still, it shouldn't have come to this. We should have been able to snatch her out of Dursley House.'

Emboldened by Sam's report, another man stepped forwards. 'We have men watching Dursley House all day and all night. She hardly leaves; when she does, she's with the Ramsden brothers and those burly footmen of the earl. We're not afraid of a fight, but it has to be one we can win. No point in losing.'

Oswalt had to concede the man made sense. 'We need an equaliser, then. Keep your posts, men. Watch Dursley House. I want to know the minute they leave. We'll follow them everywhere and look for our chance. There's a bonus in it for the man who captures Julia Prentiss. Everyone is dismissed. Brown, fetch my personal physician immediately.'

In the empty office, Oswalt sat behind the desk, marshalling his thoughts. The game was just about over and just in time, too. He needed Julia Prentiss brought to him before the solstice. Julia and the Ramsdens would get restless, secure in their own safety one of these days, and he'd be waiting to pounce on the opportunity. More than that, he'd be ready.

The door to the office opened a half-hour later. 'You wanted to see me?'

Mortimer Oswalt looked up from his papers. His physician was here. 'Yes, I need a poison ring, preferably by tomorrow and something discreet for a knife blade as well.'

Julia felt she'd been gone from her uncle's house for much longer than weeks. She stared up at the town home on the outskirts of Belgravia, waiting for Paine to instruct his tiger. Fine living with the Ramsdens had ruined her much more quickly than she'd have thought possible. The house looked shabby in little ways. Weeds pushed up between the cracks in the steps leading to the door and the windows looked drab in comparison to the tall windows and elegant curtains of Dursley House.

'Are you ready?' Paine took her arm. 'You can wait with the carriage. My tiger can drive you to Bond Street and you can shop.'

Julia gave him a sharp look. 'I am not about to go shopping while my future is on the line.' She fidgeted with the fringed edge of her summer shawl. She didn't know exactly what that future held. Either way—winning her freedom or being forced to marry Oswalt—she and Paine would part ways. Even her coveted freedom seemed to pale against the thought of saying farewell to Paine. She'd have to go away and make a new, quiet life some place where her behaviour in London would be overlooked or, better yet, never heard of. She'd known, or imagined she knew, what the consequences would be for her choice to seek ruination. But her feelings for Paine Ramsden had not been factored into the equation then.

Well, she had made her choices and there had been no going back for quite some time now. She'd best get on with it. Julia squared her shoulders and gave Paine a confident smile. 'I am ready.'

The viscount was stunned to see them. Aunt Sara couldn't decide what to do first, swoon or order tea. Their mere arrival threw the household into an uproar. Julia gave Paine an apologetic look.

'Where have you been? Your cousins say they saw you at the Worthington soirée in the company of the earl, while we've been here at home not knowing you were even in the city!' Uncle Barnaby said gruffly once the excitement subsided and the four of them were seated with teacups in the small drawing room.

That news surprised her. She hadn't seen her cousins that evening and it struck her as odd that they would have spied her, but not approached her. If they'd really been worried, wouldn't they have rushed over and greeted her? Worse of all was the realisation that, if her cousins knew, Oswalt knew. Julia tamped down her growing anxiety.

'I've been with Lady Bridgerton,' Julia said smoothly, laying out the story she and Paine had practised. It wasn't a complete lie. She had been with Lady Bridgerton, just not for as long as her aunt and uncle might be concluding. 'I have decided that I will not be marrying Mortimer Oswalt.' She couldn't repress a smile as she made her announcement. It felt good to confront the issue at last. She felt powerful. Although she knew this time it was the presence of Paine Ramsden that gave her the power. But she had an ally and that made all the difference. They couldn't force her to marry Oswalt now. They couldn't lock her in her room.

Aunt Sara wrung her hands at the news. 'Oh dear, don't you understand? You can't decide that on your own. What's got into you, Julia? You used to be a nice biddable girl. Now, you've refused a marriage your uncle has arranged for you and you've run off without a note for weeks at a time. We've been worried to death.'

In truth, her aunt did look as if she'd been concerned. The woman looked tired and was more nervous than usual. Guilt for that gnawed at her. 'I didn't mean to hurt anyone, I simply needed time to sort through my feelings.' Julia said.

'Who is this young man?' Aunt Sara turned to Paine.

'I am Paine Ramsden. I'm Lady Bridgerton's nephew,' he added politely.

Uncle Barnaby set down his teacup, eyeing Paine in much the same way one views a venomous snake. 'Julia, what you've done is of the gravest nature.' He, too, looked as if worry had taken a great toll on him. 'We have a contract with Mortimer Oswalt. He's paid for every gown upstairs in your wardrobe. He expects a gently bred bride. I have given him my word, and you've destroyed his faith in me.'

'Then break the contract, Uncle,' Julia answered unswervingly, bringing the topic around to the point they needed to discuss. This part of the conversation would not be pleasant and it would be entirely too blunt, but there was no other way.

As expected, Uncle Barnaby's watery blue eyes bulged at the mention of breaking the contract. He began to sputter. 'A betrothal contract can't just be broken! Do you know what that entails? I'll have to reimburse Oswalt for all his expenditures on your behalf, Julia, and for funds he's already advanced the family on the understanding that you would soon be wed.'

'You could just return the money,' Julia probed, hoping to determine her uncle's exact level of indebtedness to Oswalt.

'Silly chit! Oswalt was right. These kinds of transactions are too complicated for the female brain. The money has been spent. We had to have something to live on until Gray returns and Oswalt's money seemed good for spending. After all, it was an advancement on what he owed us. We didn't have to pay it back. It was ours.' Uncle Barnaby's weak chin trembled. 'At least it was ours until you ran away and Oswalt started asking for the funds back. Now, we owe him Gray's cargo unless you marry him.'

Julia swallowed hard. She'd heard Paine explain this aspect of Oswalt's plan to her on more than one occasion, but hearing the despair in her uncle's voice was difficult to bear, especially since he saw her as the cause of their woes.

Her aunt piped up cheerfully from her corner, 'All is well now, Barnaby. Our Julia is home and she can woo Oswalt back.'

Julia folded her hands in her lap and stiffened her spine. 'I am afraid that's not possible any longer. He stipulated in the contract that he wanted a virgin bride. Those terms no longer apply to me.'

Aunt Sara gasped. Uncle Barnaby's eyes flew to Paine. 'You're a black-hearted scoundrel, taking advantage of a girl about to be married. You're worse than the rumours.' He shook an ineffectual fist in Paine's direction.

Paine ignored the older man's rant and jumped into the conversation for the first time. 'What Julia hasn't mentioned yet is that we came here to warn you about Oswalt. He's planned this all along. He meant to ruin your finances, which were precarious at best. He meant to push you into irrevocable debt.'

'Balderdash. He's got no reason to do that. You can take your lies elsewhere,' Uncle Barnaby stammered.

'He's got every reason.' Paine carefully laid out Oswalt's plot to the best of his most recent knowledge. 'You cannot doom Julia to that life. You have to stand up to Oswalt and put a stop to him once and for all. You're not the first nobleman to fall victim to his plots.'

'Don't listen to him, Lockhart. He's a lying cockerel only seeking revenge for an old perceived insult,' a voice said from the doorway. All heads swivelled to see the newcomer who'd not waited to be announced.

Mortimer Oswalt stood there in a garish mockery of fashion, dressed in a tangerine afternoon suit of China silk, more appropriate for an engagement at court in the last century than a call at the shabby Lockhart residence. Julia sucked in her breath and compulsively grabbed Paine's hand.

'I'd call this a fortuitous happenstance if I didn't

know better.' Oswalt waved a beringed hand. 'But I do know better, thanks to the men I have watching Dursley House. Imagine my elation when they informed me you were headed in this direction. I had to see Viscount Lockhart today and this makes the visit so much better.' He advanced with mincing steps. 'Ah, Julia, you've returned. I knew you would once the guilt over deserting your guardians prevailed. I am looking forwards to our nuptials, my little virago.' He reached into a pocket and withdrew a tin of snuff. The gaudy ring on his middle finger flashed.

'Ramsden, I'd heard you'd got yourself entangled in this little mess.' He sniffed, sneezed, and gave a satisfied sigh. 'I think it's Ramsden's perfidy we should be discussing, not mine, Lockhart, and we would have that discussion if I didn't have distressing news to share, which is the reason I've come by. There was word today down on the docks that the ship, *Bluehawk*, has foundered at sea off the coast between France and Spain. The *Bluehawk* is your son's ship, is it not? I thought you should hear the news from a friend first.'

Aunt Sara swooned.

Julia jumped to her feet. 'You lie!' She turned to her uncle. 'Don't believe him. He could tell you anything. There's no way to verify it.'

Mortimer laughed, a hoarse, evil sound that sent shivers through Julia. 'Whatever Ramsden has been teaching you, it hasn't been manners.' He stepped towards her and Julia flinched involuntarily. Paine rose beside her, lending her the strength of his presence.

'So you like them wild, Ramsden? All those savages you bedded from your time abroad, no doubt. Well, I'll make a lady of you yet, Julia. Have no worries on that account.'

Julia's skin crawled. 'We'll be going.' She had to get out of this room. Oswalt radiated malevolence.

'Not so fast, my pet.' Oswalt said, motioning for his henchmen to approach. 'I think, under the circumstances, I'll ask permission to keep my bride-to-be under lock and key until the ceremony, which will be very soon and very quiet out of deference for the family during their mourning.'

'I don't know…' Uncle Barnaby sputtered.

'Yes, you do,' Oswalt sneered, all veneer of friendship gone from his face. 'You know Julia's marriage to me is the only thing that will keep your family financially viable.'

'I won't go with you,' Julia protested.

'Wants are of no consequence. That's what my men are for. Men, help Miss Prentiss to my carriage. You three, handle the arrogant Mr Ramsden for me. You know what to do. I believe you have a score to settle from the Cotswold road with the gent.'

Julia screamed and grabbed up the nearest vase, hurling it at the closest attacker. Various parts of the tea set followed in quick succession. All to no avail. In the end, there were more men than tea sets and thin china shards were no deterrent to men used to knives in London's dark alleys. The men seized her roughly by the arms and hauled her towards the door.

She dragged her heels and screamed for Paine, but Paine was fully engaged with three burly men, warding off snaggle-bladed knives with a delicate chair. He was doing well, having survived thus far with only a streak of blood showing on his arm. Then, suddenly, for no explicable reason he collapsed on the floor in a dead heap.

A man stood over Paine, knife ready to deal a final blow. Julia screamed again, fear for Paine giving her more strength. Oswalt called him off. 'Let's go. He can't follow us if he's dead. We want him to live a while longer.'

'Uncle! Help me, stop him,' Julia cried a desperate plea, swivelling her head around to the corner where Uncle Barnaby had retreated during the fight. Surely, now at the last, when all the masks had been pulled from the vileness of Mortimer's scheme, her uncle would do something! But the shock of losing Gray had numbed him completely. He huddled in the corner, helpless and ineffectual.

'Uncle!' she cried once more, thrashing in the grasp of her captors. But she knew, even as she called for him, she was entirely on her own.

Oswalt was not amenable to her pleas. 'I'll silence the bitch myself.' He advanced on her. Julia anticipated a blow to the head. Instead, she saw it coming too late. He grabbed her hand and scratched it with the ring he wore. The sensation rendered her senseless, no matter how she tried to fight the descending darkness in her mind.

Sam Brown didn't like the way events were developing one bit. He dutifully deposited the unconscious girl in the small chamber on the top floor that Oswalt had set aside, but he didn't like it. Swindling a weak viscount was one thing. They'd done that often enough in the past. But involving an innocent girl was beyond the pale in his book.

He sought out Oswalt, finding him in the large office on the second floor.

'Is it done?' Oswalt barked when Sam Brown came to the door.

'About that, boss…' Sam Brown began. He did not make a habit of questioning Oswalt. 'What are we doing with her?'

'*We're* not doing anything with her. I'm marrying her tonight.' Oswalt stopped long enough to cough, a harsh racking sound. He spit into a brass spittoon. 'Once I marry her, all my problems will be over.' He coughed again.

Sam noticed the papery quality to Oswalt's sallow skin. He had not realised how frail the man had become. 'You've got Lockhart ruined. You don't need her.'

Oswalt eyed him curiously. 'Is a pretty face all it takes to turn your head these days, Sam? Time was when you were immune to that.'

Sam shifted from foot to foot. 'Time was, I only dealt with the coves you were culling and it was good sport,' he dared bravely.

'Today's not the day to get squeamish. I need her to secure the knighthood and, more importantly, I need her for my cure so I can live long enough to receive that title.'

'Your cure? You can't believe all that Druid nonsense about restoring your potency,' Sam blurted out.

'Druid nonsense?' Oswalt snarled. 'It's hardly nonsense. It's the reason I've lived so long as it is in spite of my affliction.'

Affliction, hah. Oswalt's ailment was more than a minor affliction. It was pox at best, syphilis at worst, Sam Brown mused, and it would kill the young girl upstairs in a slow torturous death that was unworthy of her.

Oswalt waved him away. 'Back to work, Brown. There's plenty to be done before tonight. Send my physician in on the way out.'

Sam Brown grunted. He'd been lucky Oswalt hadn't taken his head off. What had he expected to accomplish? He hadn't really expected to dissuade Oswalt. He knew the man was intractable once he had made his plans.

He found the forest crone Oswalt loosely titled as 'physician' and went outside to the lawn where workers were erecting a large slab. He didn't like to think what it was going to be used for. Oswalt had taken great relish in outlining what would be done to purify his bride on that slab. The description had turned Brown's stomach.

No, he didn't like the direction Oswalt's plot had taken. He was a straightforward man who liked direct action. He didn't mind ruining the viscount, who was most likely ruined already by the hand of his own stupidity. Brown didn't mind picking a fight with coves like Ramsden, who knew the rules and the consequences for living in the stews and hells. He hadn't liked 'cheating' with the poisoned blades and he certainly didn't approve of what was being done to the girl.

Sam Brown glanced at the sky, tracking the sun's descent. He had a few hours left in which to do some thinking.

# Chapter Seventeen

Paine woke slowly, struggling against the intense fog that swamped his brain. He could hear Peyton and Crispin. Peyton was angry. He could hear his brother's cold 'earl' voice berating some unfortunate soul. Why would that be the case? Where was he? Wherever he was, it was hard and felt like a floor.

'Paine?' That was Crispin. 'Are you coming around now?'

Paine found the strength to push his eyes open and then wished he hadn't. The room swam. Crispin's face appeared in his line of sight like a mirage on the desert. Was he ill? He didn't recall being sick earlier. 'Help me sit up.' His tongue felt thick.

Crispin supported him on one side to hoist him up. Paine gave an involuntary groan at the motion and tried to push with his arm on the other side. His hand made contact with a sharp shard of something. It felt like china.

'Julia!' Full cognisance flooded back. Paine forced

his eyes to stay open in spite of the dizziness. He grabbed at Crispin's coat. 'Julia's gone. Oswalt's taken her. There were men, too many of them.' He was babbling, letting the last moments of consciousness tumble out in no particular order.

'Hush, Paine. It's all right.' Crispin soothed him like he had when Paine had fallen out of a tree in their youth.

Paine pushed at his brother. 'No, it's not all right.' The dizziness was slowing, less crippling now. They were still in the viscount's drawing room. He could make out Peyton with Lockhart in another corner. So that was who Peyton was giving a tongue-lashing to. He didn't pity the man at all. Whatever Peyton did or said to the man wouldn't be any less than he deserved. The coward had let Oswalt forcibly remove Julia from the house.

Peyton spied him and abruptly left the trembling viscount to come to his side. 'Peyton, tell me everything. How did you know to come?' Paine pressed, sparing his body no discomfort as he fought to recover.

'Your tiger came for us when he saw the men go into the house. He counted up numbers and realised he'd be of more use coming to us.'

'They've taken Julia. Oswalt has her. He means to marry her,' Paine said. 'I have to find her.'

'I know.' Peyton paused.

'Tell him everything.' Crispin urged when it seemed Peyton wouldn't say anything more.

'What?' Paine swivelled his head between his brothers as they shared a silent communication. He paid for the effort with a sharp bout of dizziness.

Peyton went on. 'Julia fought them. She didn't go easily. The viscount says they had to drug her, too, before they reached the carriage.'

'The bastards!' Paine wanted to explode with anger; anger at the men who did Oswalt's bidding, anger at the viscount for putting them all in this situation, anger at himself for having failed Julia.

'Calm down, Paine. You can't help Julia if you aren't thinking clearly or if you make yourself sick. The drug will wear off shortly. It's already been an hour.'

Paine touched his arm where one of the men had nicked him. The ugly blade had slipped through Paine's chair-shield only briefly. At the time, Paine had thought he'd been clever to avoid a larger slice from the wicked blade. But a larger slice had not been necessary.

'The blade was poisoned?' Paine asked.

'It seems to be the case,' Peyton concurred. 'The viscount said you collapsed suddenly and without reason. Oswalt probably had the blades rubbed with a topical poison.'

Paine nodded. That made sense. He'd encountered several types of poisons in the East that could be used in that manner and bring about the desired result. As a merchant with far-reaching trade interests, Oswalt would have knowledge of and access to such a commodity.

'Have some tea. It will help settle your head and your stomach.' Crispin handed him a mug, probably wrested from the kitchen staff. It was thick and large, not at all like the dainty teacups Julia had thrown at Oswalt's men.

The thought of her brought the guilt back in full force. 'We have to get to her fast.' The words were inadequate to express the fears rioting through him. It brought him physical pain to think of Julia suffering the effects of the drug while being alone in the hands of her enemy. *Julia, I am coming.*

'Do you know where they might have taken her?' Crispin asked after he'd had a chance to drink some of the strong tea.

'I have an idea,' Paine confirmed, calling over to Lockhart. 'Lockhart, does Oswalt still have his property in Richmond?'

'Y-y-yes. I believe so.' Lockhart was rooted to his chair across the room, looking utterly immobile except for the movement of his mouth.

'That's where they went,' Paine said confidently.

'B-b-but he's got a house in London. It's closer. Are you sure?' Lockhart took that unfortunate moment to speak up.

Paine lashed out. 'Yes, I am goddamned sure of that. I was unaware I had asked for your opinion or that you were even capable of formulating one of your own.' He pushed to his feet, spoiling for a fight now that the tea had quelled the last of his ill effects.

'Paine,' Crispin warned *sotto voce* at his elbow, a gentle hand on his arm. Paine was unsure if the gesture was meant to restrain him or offer balance if he wobbled. 'The man's lost his son and his livelihood all in one day. He's in shock.'

Paine shook off Crispin's touch and sat back down.

'Get him a drink and get him out of here, then. His valet can see to him,' he growled.

Peyton barked an order and the valet came to fetch the viscount.

'I love her, you know,' Paine said as the viscount neared the door. 'I mean to marry her when all is settled, if she'll have me.' He had the special licence in his pocket to prove it. He'd interrupted the archbishop's breakfast for it just this morning.

But he didn't think the archbishop minded too much by the time their business transaction was done. Paine had his paper and Lambeth Palace had a new illuminated map of India from Paine's own collection of atlases. It was one of his favourites, acquired from a Hindu map-maker in Calcutta. The Archbishop was thrilled at the prospect of sending missionaries to all the secret, heathen kingdoms on the map. Paine could care less what the Archbishop did with the map. The only soul he wanted to save was Julia's and he would have given anything in his possession to do it.

'It's been two hours since they took her,' Paine said restlessly.

'You're sure it's Richmond?' Peyton queried.

'Yes. Oswalt could have had me finished off during the fight—a lethal blade or a stronger poison would have done it. He meant for me to live and he means for me to find Julia. He knows I'll guess he went to Richmond.'

'All right, we ride and then we wait,' Peyton said. 'We wait for the cover of darkness and make our move then, unless there is good reason to move sooner. We'll stop at Dursley House and collect my footmen. They'll be useful in a fight, but we'll still need every advantage the darkness can provide.'

Paine nodded. Peyton was right, but it was six hours until dark and it seemed an eternity to wait. Foolish bravery would earn Julia nothing.

They collected Peyton's footmen and set out the short distance to Richmond. Paine rode with grim determination, the sound of his horse's hooves pounding out the litany that rang through his mind: *Julia, I am coming*.

Paine would come. *He would.* Julia paced the confines of the tiny attic room she'd been stuffed in. It was windowless and eight feet wide—not that she could pace the whole eight feet, given that the slope of the roof line prohibited anyone over three feet tall to access the last few feet.

She sat on the little cot, the room's only furnishing, and sighed. She was glad for the privacy she'd been afforded so far. She'd been terribly ill when she'd woken up. She much preferred panicking alone than in the company of her captors.

Now that she felt better, she could take stock of the situation. It was probably an intended side effect of the drug that one couldn't think clearly for quite some time after waking up.

Once her head had cleared, her first thought had been for Paine. He was alive. She knew that much. Oswalt had spared him for that purpose. That worried her.

Oswalt *wanted* Paine to find her. That meant Paine knew where she'd be even though he'd been unconscious and unable to follow them. She wondered if they'd gone to Richmond. Paine had mentioned Richmond as the site of his first encounter with Oswalt.

Paine would come. Oswalt would use her to trap him. How convenient it must be for Oswalt to play two games at once—the game with the Lockharts and whatever lingering end play he thought he had with Paine over the old quarrel.

Maybe he wouldn't come, her devil-side argued. Why would he? Perhaps right now, he was cursing her for bringing him into such a mess. Sex was one thing. Dying for it was quite another. He'd promised her pleasure. He'd promised nothing else. He might decide he'd done enough for her. And he'd be right in that conclusion. He'd rescued her from Oswalt once already. He knew how Oswalt thought. He would know this was a trap simply because Oswalt had left him alive. He would know Oswalt wanted him to come. Paine was a stubborn man. He wouldn't come just because someone wanted him to.

Julia stood up and resumed pacing. There it was—for all his manipulations, Paine was the one person Oswalt couldn't manipulate. He could not ensure Paine would come, only that he had all the information to come if he chose to. She smiled at that. It would gall Oswalt no end if Paine didn't come. She would remember to take comfort in that little prod when the time came.

At least that was settled. He wouldn't come. Paine was too smart. She'd better stop counting on him to join in her rescue and start thinking of how best to rescue herself.

Unfortunately, she had none of the traditional escape routes at her disposal. All the captured heroines in the Minerva Press novels had secret passageways hidden in their fireplaces or bedsheets for ropes. Hah! That made her snort. Bedsheets were the least of her worries, not that she had any on the bare cot. She needed a window to start with

For good measure, Julia went to the wood door and tried the handle. It was locked and a guard shouted back at her. Well, that was to be expected. Oswalt knew she wouldn't sit by passively and let her fate play out on its own.

The handle turned and Julia retreated to the cot. She should have spent her time looking for something to craft into a weapon. She recognised the guard as one of the men from her uncle's house.

'Good, you're up and around. The boss will be glad to know it.' He held out the long box he carried. 'The boss says for you to put this on.'

Julia didn't move to take the box. 'What is it?'

The man sneered. 'It's a wedding gown. You have a half-hour to dress. Boss wants the ceremony to take place at sunset.'

'And if I don't?' She gave a haughty toss of her head. This man would know that she was not cowed by his bulk or brashness.

'Then you can attend your wedding naked.' He threw the box on the cot next to her.

'Get out. The clock is running,' Julia ordered in a last attempt at bravado.

He snorted. 'You can be high and mighty now—it won't last much longer.'

The door shut and Julia sighed. She might have done better to probe for more information instead of antagonising the guard. Why sunset? At least she had confirmation of what was going to happen to her. She was going to be moved to another place. Sunset wouldn't matter in this windowless room.

Compliance was her best option at present. She'd learned through unfortunate consequences the foolishness of her resistance at the house. If she'd gone willingly, she would have kept her consciousness. Perhaps she could even have attracted attention or called out for help. Unconscious, she made things easy for Oswalt.

Anxiously, she lifted the box lid. The gown was more of a robe than it was a dress: a sleeveless, shapeless robe of white silk. In the bottom of the box was a girdle of twisted gold set with gems every few links and two large gold arm bracelets set with turquoise. The ensemble looked like something a Druid priestess might wear, like something she'd seen a history book before regarding early Britons.

The notion sparked something. Druids. Midsummer. The solstice. She frantically tried to recall the date. Oswalt's idea of a wedding was becoming clear. She was certain today was June 21. It explained the odd gown and the desire to perform the wedding at sunset.

'Fifteen minutes!' the guard shouted through the door.

She needed to hurry. She didn't doubt the guard would make good on his threat to haul her downstairs naked or that anyone would mind terribly much.

Julia dressed swiftly, trying to push her thoughts away from the impending events and what they meant. The horror was too overwhelming. If she dwelled on them, she'd be paralysed with fear. She needed to stay alert, she needed to look for any opportunity to run or to defend herself. She bit her lip. She hoped she had the courage to do whatever needed to be done and, if there was a chance to kill Oswalt and free herself, she hoped she had the courage to take it.

The guard came for her as she was fastening on the last of the bracelets. He brought friends. Two of them. She was sandwiched between them as he led the way to a room two flights of stairs down from the attic.

'Where's Oswalt?' Julia asked, quietly looking about her during the walk, remembering corners and turns, anything that might prove useful in the future, but the house was unhelpfully blank. She wondered if Oswalt had done that on purpose. No pictures or colours on the walls that might provide a visual memory—what was it Paine had called it? An *aide-mémoire*? 'No, don't think of him,' she cautioned herself. Thoughts of Paine would only bring tears.

'It's bad luck to see the bride before the wedding.' The guards laughed at their joke. 'You'll be seeing him soon enough.'

They led her into a bedroom done in stark white. The large poster bed was white, the coverlet on it was white satin. The curtains were white. *Ah, good*, Julia thought. *A window and bed sheets*. Things were looking up.

One of the guards seized her hands. 'What you are doing?' Julia cried, shocked by the swift movement.

'It's orders. You're not to be trusted.' He looped tight cords of twine about her hands and bound them to the bed post.

'Please…' Julia protested against the indignity. But the protest was merely for form's sake. These men would not be swayed by any gentleman's code of honour.

One guard jerked his head towards the window. 'You've got nothing to complain about. You've got a view of the ceremonies. You can watch them set up for the wedding. The physician will be here shortly to keep you company.'

The horror was real. Julia fought despair. Being left alone was a certain torture of its own. Too much time to let her imagination run riot. But Oswalt was a master at this. He knew exactly what he was doing. She couldn't give in to the terror. He couldn't make Paine come and he couldn't make her be frightened.

The sky became her enemy as the sun inched closer to the horizon. Nature's hour glass. Someone came to set out lanterns in the yard below. It wouldn't be long. A half-hour, maybe a few minutes more.

The door opened. Julia couldn't turn to see who was there. An ancient crone older than Oswalt himself came into her line of vision, crabbed and wrinkled. 'Hello, dearie, I'm the physician. I'm here to check, shall we say, on the status of things?' Julia fought the urge to cringe. Oswalt must be mad to call this forest witch by such a title.

A movement caught Julia's eye out on the lawn. It was slight and then gone, but she could have sworn a man with raven hair had looked up at her window, studying it before blending back into the lengthening shadows. Paine had come—maybe. It was the only scrap of hope she had at the moment and so she clung to it. If Paine was down there, looking for her, she could endure a little while longer.

# Chapter Eighteen

Paine drew back into the shadows of the lawn. He was certain he'd seen Julia in the upstairs window. Crispin confirmed it, tossing him a robe and hood as he returned from his short reconnaissance mission. 'I overheard some of the guards talking. The location sounds right. Put these on.'

'Druid robes?' Paine asked, shaking out the garment.

'For the ceremony. We'll blend in,' Peyton said, slipping into another set.

'How did you get these?' Paine asked, slipping on the robe.

'Let's just say three men have a little less to wear than they did a few minutes ago, but I doubt they'll be missing their clothes for a while,' Crispin said with relish.

Paine grimaced. 'How many people will be here? We'll stand out if it's only a handful. Oswalt expects us. He'll be on the lookout for anything out of place.' He didn't like the idea of waiting that long, not only because of the torture of watching Julia engage in this ritual and being unable to help her, but also because they would be enacting their rescue surrounded by many people who would have other interests to support.

He glanced at the sky, streaked pink from the setting sun, and made a decision. 'I am going up after her now. We haven't the same odds of success if we wait.'

'We're coming with you,' Crispin put in.

Paine shook his head. He couldn't risk his brothers. 'No. You stay hidden here and proceed with our plan if I don't succeed, and get Julia away from here.'

'Better hurry, then.' Peyton nodded to the lawn where people dressed as they were in robes started to mill about.

The sight made Paine's skin crawl. He put on his hood to obscure his identity and set off in the direction of the house. *Julia, I am coming.*

His plan had certain merits. The house was busy with last-minute preparations. Guards were distracted, checking in guests and stabling horses, even though it looked to be no more than fifty men were expected. Better yet, everyone looked the same in their robes and hoods. Paine fully understood why no one would want to be openly associated with such an event. Most were on the lawn, however, making his movements more obvious and suspect the closer he got to the house.

Paine used the back entrance and went up a servants' stairwell, counting landings as he went and trying to outguess Oswalt. What did he think the plan would be? Would he be anticipating an attempt before the ceremony or during? He gained the landing and stepped out. The hall was deserted. Had this been too easy or just natural since Oswalt didn't want his guests prowling the house? Either was a viable option. Paine surreptitiously checked the pistol and knife beneath his robe. It was comforting to know the weapons were there. He only hoped he'd be able to get to them fast enough.

The window he glimpsed her in had been towards the middle on the right. Paine began trying door handles. One of them gave. Warning shivered down his spine. This was too easy. While he had the chance, Paine slipped the pistol into his hand and eased the door open slowly, not sure what he'd find.

'Julia?' He dared a whisper, but there was no doubt it was her. Even in the fading light, her auburn hair was unmistakable, hanging loose down her back in thick waves.

She struggled to turn, a little screech escaping her when she saw the hooded figure. 'It's me, Paine,' he assured her, finally seeing the reason she hadn't turned fully on his entrance. 'The bastard bound you.' Paine pulled his knife free and sliced the ropes. 'Are you all right?' He took a precious second to hold her once the ropes fell away.

'I am more scared than hurt,' Julia confessed, sinking into the safety of his embrace. 'Paine, Oswalt expects you to come. He'll be looking for you. We have to hurry.'

She no sooner spoke when the door handle turned. 'Hide, Paine,' she whispered fiercely.

The idea was distasteful to him, but he ducked swiftly down on the far side of the bed, tense and waiting for the time to strike.

'I see the crone left you untied. Unwise of her.' That was Oswalt. Paine tightened his grip around both of his weapons. If Oswalt was alone, he wouldn't get a better chance to strike.

'My man is here to take you down, my little virago. But first we have things to talk about.'

Paine could practically hear Julia flinch. He imagined Oswalt's hand with its yellow nails stroking her cheek.

'I am no good to you, Oswalt. I've been with Ramsden. You need a virgin,' Julia argued defiantly.

'I know, but since I have assurances you are not with child, you can be purified. Do you see everything out there? You have an excellent view. The high priest will do the ceremony in front of that altar block. Afterwards, you'll mount the block for an old purification ritual. It can only be done on midsummer. Would you like to hear about it, my dear? I think it will go quite far in restoring you to a more biddable nature. Perhaps you would prefer to be surprised? You look lovely.'

'Don't touch me,' Julia snapped. Paine quietly cheered her bravado. Julia had confessed how much the proceedings had unnerved her, but still she found courage to fight back.

'I am surprised that your gallant lover has not ridden to your rescue. He's leaving it rather late, isn't he?' Oswalt mused cruelly.

'He's not coming. It was never more than business between us,' Julia said staunchly. 'Why should he risk so much for me?'

Oswalt chortled. 'Firstly, because you're a lovely bit

of baggage, enough to muddle any man's mind, especially a rutter like Ramsden who thinks primarily with his cock. Secondly, aside from his feelings for you, he detests me and blames me for his exile. This would be a grand opportunity to strike back for all those wasted years.'

'They weren't wasted. He became a man of self-made wealth,' Julia retorted. 'Perhaps he's outgrown the need for revenge. Certainly that should be a relief to you. You won't have to fight him a second time. You've had your victory.'

Paine wanted to applaud. His Julia was turning out to be a fine interrogator. Even under pressure, her bold manner had Oswalt's hackles up and the man couldn't resist the urge to brag.

'My dear wife, I've decided exile isn't good enough for Ramsden. He must die. I can't afford to have him live with all that he knows. And since I am to be married to you, I would find it deuced uncomfortable to have him lurking around, insane with jealousy over my good fortune.'

'You can hardly call this wedding legal. The church will never recognise it,' Julia pointed out.

'We'll have the small ceremony I promised your uncle in a few days once the shock starts to settle regarding Gray's ship. Just think of all the good you'll be able to do your family in their time of crisis.'

There was a length of silence, a squirming sound from Julia that caused Paine to grit his teeth and then a resounding crack. 'I told you to take your hands off me!'

That was his cue. Paine leaped from behind the bed, thankful the light was behind him. 'Let her go!' He levelled the pistol at Oswalt and hefted his knife with the other. There were just the two of them—Oswalt and the guard. The guard he recognised from the club, the one who had bribed Gaylord Beaton. The man held a pistol like his own.

Oswalt grabbed Julia as a shield. 'I doubt your aim is that good in the dubious light,' Oswalt sneered, 'None the less, I am delighted that you came.'

'Sam, bring our guest downstairs. I want him to have a front row scat for my nuptials. Then afterwards, take him out and shoot him. That is, unless you'd prefer to be shot beforehand.'

Paine shifted his pistol's focus to Sam Brown. He could shoot the man accurately at this distance. If he could shoot, then so could Oswalt's guard. He doubted he could dodge the bullet at such close range. And the pistol fire would bring too many people to Oswalt's aid.

He gave Julia a look, hoping to convey to her his choice. If he could bring the big man closer, he could deal with him more effectively, perhaps be able to use his knife. Paine made a show of lifting his arms in surrender and placing the weapons on the ground.

Oswalt ordered the man to pick up the weapons. 'We don't want him getting them back.'

The big man moved forwards, stuffing his own pistol back into his belt, clearly confident in his bulk to sustain him in a fight should Paine choose to play the hero.

Paine chose his moment carefully. When the big man bent over, Paine landed a hard kick to the man's nose, sending blood spurting everywhere. The man writhed on the ground, clutching his broken nose.

'Now, Julia!' Paine cried, lunging for her before Oswalt could recover the situation.

Julia brought her foot down on Oswalt's instep. It was enough to cause the older man to release her. Oswalt drew a knife and Paine threw Julia behind him, careful to keep the door at his back. If nothing else, he had to secure Julia's escape.

'Do you know what's on this blade, boyo?' Oswalt advanced. 'A little equaliser—after all, you have years of youth on me. I can't possibly match physical strength with you.' Oswalt waved the knife blade.

'This isn't a drug. This afternoon, you were lucky. This will kill you. It's made from cobra venom among other deadly things and cost me plenty for an ounce. It won't take that much to kill you. All I have to do is throw it.' Oswalt weighed the blade. 'I've been practising.'

Paine flexed his shoulders, covertly assessing his height. Julia would be safe. He was too tall for Oswalt to accidentally hit her instead. He could charge Oswalt and hope the poison acted slowly enough that he'd be able to take the feebler man to the ground before the poison claimed him. Pinned beneath his strong form, Oswalt would be unable to go after Julia. It would give her a slight head start, enough time to get to Peyton and Crispin. She didn't know they were there, but they'd be watching for her.

'No, Paine, you won't die for me,' Julia said behind him as if she'd read his mind.

'Oh, this is so touching,' Oswalt mocked. He lifted the knife and Paine sprang into motion. This would be resolved once and for all. Paine leaped for Oswalt, making a sprawling target as he flew for the man's throat.

Several things happened at once and the world slowed. Julia screamed.

The knife sailed through the air. Paine braced himself for the jarring impact. There was no way the knife would miss him at this range. But miraculously it did, falling to the ground. An explosive sound rang out and Oswalt fell to the ground beneath Paine's weight, but he was dead already, a bullet through the back.

The door crashed open and the world sped up again, revealing Peyton and Crispin, pistols drawn and hoods off.

'Paine, are you all right?' Julia rushed forwards as he gained his feet, quickly taking in the events.

'I'm fine.' He gestured to the knife. 'Don't touch it. It's loaded with poison.' He was alive. The thought rocketed through him like liquid lightning. Then he saw the reason. Sam Brown's one hand held a smoking pistol Paine recognised as the one he'd laid down earlier. The other hand still clutched his nose.

'You fired the shot?' It made sense. Peyton and Crispin had arrived too late and from the wrong direction. In his arms, Julia trembled, quickly reaching the last of her reserves. 'I am grateful.' *Not to mention perplexed.* 'Why did you do it?'

Sam Brown got to his feet awkwardly. 'He was a bad man. I've worked for bad men before, but he was the worst. I didn't understand just how corrupt he was until recently. What he planned to do to your young lady and what he planned to do to her family wasn't right. They'd done nothing wrong, they were just vulnerable, and I don't hold any truck with preying on the weak. It was different before when it was those who deserved to be swindled out of a few pounds.'

Paine wasn't sure he completely agreed with Sam Brown's entire code of ethics, but he was grateful the man had seen fit to act on his behalf.

'All I ask is that I be allowed to disappear, go make another life somewhere, an honest life. I've tired of this one,' Sam Brown asked humbly.

'Absolutely, after one more duty,' Paine agreed. 'We still need to get out of the house. We have horses waiting. Ensure our safety.'

Dressed once more in their hoods, and with Julia between them, Sam Brown escorted the Ramsden brothers to the edge of the property without mishap, stopping only once to explain to guards that they were escorting the long-awaited bride.

They mounted up on their horses, Julia riding in front of Paine. 'What will you do now?' Paine asked Sam Brown.

'I'll go back to the house and tell the guards to disperse the crowd, that Oswalt has died.'

Paine threw the man a leather purse. 'This is to thank you for your silence.' He wouldn't suggest this was to buy the man's silence, that was too risky. He didn't want the man to think he could set up a lucrative blackmail scheme in the future, no matter how reformed he thought he was. But he did realise the man could tell everyone that the bride had escaped, rescued by the Ramsden brothers. That would cause a riot of scandal if it ever got out. It would only take one brash braggart admitting to being there for everything to become well known.

Peyton seemed to realise it as well. 'There's a ship I know of leaving for America. A man who works hard can make a good life there. I'll arrange for your passage. It sails at dawn with the tide.'

Negotiations were complete. There was just one more negotiation Paine had to manage and that was with Julia. It took all his will power not to blurt out his proposal and rush her off to a vicar immediately before further time passed. He would wait until her mind was at ease. She'd endured too much in one day to fully appreciate his proposal. The last thing he needed was for her to feel he was offering out of a sense of obligation or pity. When he proposed, he wanted her to know it was out of the only thing that mattered—his love.

# Chapter Nineteen

The family held their collective breath for the next three days. Sam Brown had boarded the boat to America and they waited to see if any hint of scandal regarding the odd doings in Richmond circulated the *ton*. In spite of Julia's ordeal, Aunt Lily insisted the family make a showing at one fashionable gathering each night. She argued that nothing would set tongues wagging faster than being absent from events three nights in a row during the height of the Season.

It was a compelling argument, especially since they'd made such a showing once the Season had hit full stride. They couldn't let those newly established inroads go to waste. Paine admired Julia's strength. Each night, she donned a new gown, looking more beautiful every time. She smiled and she danced, keeping up a happy front. If anyone inquired about the Lockhart ship, she simply said, 'We have no confirmation that the ship sank or that there were no survivors. Until we do, I prefer not to believe the worst.'

She told the truth, as best as they knew it. The day after their return from Richmond, Paine had paid a visit to the viscount, encouraging him not to announce the loss of the ship until it was a certainty.

He wasn't afraid to admit he had sound reasons and selfish reasons for it. He'd sent Flaherty to search out any truth to Oswalt's announcement. Flaherty had found nothing substantially reliable to bolster the rumour. There had been some trouble off the coast of Spain. Other sailors reported a heavy storm, but no one could agree on whether or not the *Bluehawk* had been affected.

Selfishly, Paine didn't want another obstacle put in his path when it came to marrying Julia. A mourning period would have to follow if Gray was announced dead. That could very likely come to pass, but he wanted Julia firmly wedded to him before that happened. He'd gladly spend six months quietly living outside of Society's eye tucked away with Julia. But he doubted he'd survive another six months unable to claim her. The viscount had been happy to follow Paine's lead. Recent events had upended him completely and destroyed his desire to take any action.

Aunt Lily's insistence bore better results than anticipated. Not only was the *ton* pleased to welcome back Dursley's brother, but requests for business assistance came flooding in in response to many of the letters Paine had sent out a few weeks prior and through the connections he'd established at the gatherings. There was even talk of Paine heading up an investment group at the Bank of London. As a third son, dabbling in commerce was highly acceptable.

There only remained wooing Julia to complete Paine's happiness. He knew she was inwardly worried over her cousin Gray, and that mentally she was grappling with the horrors of her brief captivity, but he could wait no longer.

Paine patted his pockets for the fifth time in as many minutes, waiting for Julia to come downstairs. The weather was brilliant and he was taking her driving. Yes, all three items were there just as they were a few minutes ago and a few minutes before that.

'I'm ready,' Julia called from the top of the stairs, a bit breathless from rushing. 'I couldn't find my parasol right away.' She waved the pale green parasol to illustrate her point.

'You'd be beautiful without it.' Paine smiled up at her, enjoying the sway of her hips beneath the thin summer muslin gown as she came downstairs. The mint colour of the gown and the forest green grosgrain trim complemented her colouring splendidly.

'You're too kind,' Julia teased, putting her hand on his sleeve. 'Where are we off to?'

She sounded like his Julia, but when she looked up at him, her eyes were still haunted. They didn't sparkle like he knew they could. Not yet. They would again, though, he vowed. He'd spend his whole life devoted to seeing that they did.

'Someplace wonderful,' Paine said mysteriously.

They drove through Hyde Park, Paine cheerfully

nodding to passers-by and stopping to talk with new acquaintances. Julia sat patiently beside him, acting the part of a banker's wife perfectly, offering intelligent conversation when needed. A banker's wife! The thought filled Paine with schoolboy giddiness. Who would have thought twelve years ago, or even a year ago, that he would find his inner peace with a wife and a career, with being restored to family and to society—things he'd thought he could live without?

Paine turned out of the park on to a quiet tree-lined street. The street was wide, clean and empty, untroubled by the traffic from the park. A few, large town houses dominated the area. It was clearly a wealthy and exclusive neighbourhood, perhaps not for peers, but for a different type of wealth and power—new wealth and power, the kind that would matter more as England grew into its age of industry, an age that Paine could see already on the horizon and heading towards its zenith.

'Where are we?' Julia asked, looking about at the impressive buildings.

Paine brought the carriage over to the kerb and jumped down. 'Come and see this place with me, Julia. I need to take a look at it.'

He helped her down and produced a key—item number one—from his pockets.

He swung the front door open and waited anxiously as Julia gazed around the wainscoted vestibule, her eye caught by the enormous brass chandelier overhead. 'It's fabulous.'

'I think you should see all of it before you decide that.' Paine chuckled.

Julia walked ahead of him, eyes wide open, taking in the rich soft tones of the walls done in creamy shades of winter wheat. She gave an audible 'aaahh' at the sight of the dining room. 'That table must seat fifteen people!'

Paine grinned at the sight of the polished mahogany table he'd ordered a week ago, anticipating such a reaction. 'Actually, it seats twenty.'

'Twenty?' Julia commented in awe. She mounted the stairs, her hand trailing on the carved banister. 'There's been such attention to detail.'

She sailed through the bedrooms, noting how large and airy they were, how well appointed the views out of the private sitting rooms were where they looked out over the gardens in the back.

When they reached the last bedroom, Paine blocked the way, an arm across the shut door. 'I have to ask you something before you go in there.'

Julia eyed him suspiciously. He pressed on. 'Would you like to live here?'

Julia's eyes went wide with confusion instead of the surprise he'd hoped for. 'You want to buy me a house?'

'Actually, I *bought* you a house, this house if you like it. The moment I saw it, I could see you in it. I could see you at the table presiding over dinners, I could see you walking in the garden, picking lavender. When I saw you in the vestibule, I knew I was right.'

Julia was nonplussed. 'I don't need a house. I don't need one this big. It's awfully large for one person and

I certainly won't ever have twenty people over for dinner at one time.'

She was rambling. Maybe that was a good sign. She was usually so logical. 'Well, I'd probably have twenty people over for dinner on occasion and you wouldn't have to live here alone. I'd like to live here, too, with you.' Now he was rambling and probably making a muck of things. Paine drew out the second item from his pockets, this one a legal document in a slim leather case. He gave it to her.

'What's this?' Julia said slowly.

'It's the deed to the house. It goes with the key.' Good lord, that sounded dumb. Of course it went with the key.

He'd better get on with it before all his faculties fled. Paine took her hands, gripping them firmly. 'I want to marry you, Julia. I want to marry you and live in this house and raise children with you. Would you consider having me?'

'Marry me? When did you decide this?' Julia stammered, unsure how to respond.

'I think I decided it weeks ago when I first met you. I never believed in love at first sight, or really even believed in love until you, Julia. You've reformed me. I don't think I can afford to lose you.'

'You were always going to lose me. Keeping me was not part of the deal, Paine. I don't expect for it to be part of the deal now. I've overstayed my welcome and you needn't feel obliged. I admit I am at sea over what to do now.' Julia disengaged her hands and began walking down the hallway.

'I didn't think everything would turn out so well. I thought I'd be publicly ruined and shunned, sent off to the country. I had planned for that in my own way. I rather thought it would all be simpler. I didn't bargain on all the, um…shall we say "adventure"? Perhaps for you, these past weeks have been quite ordinary, but for me… Well, I've got nothing to compare them to in my heretofore very common life. You've done well by me and you don't need to feel obligated to save me.' She turned her sad green eyes to him.

It occurred to him that she'd been contemplating this all week. While he had been contemplating how to propose, she'd been contemplating how to say goodbye, how to free him.

He went to her, putting his hands on her shoulders, ostensibly to steady her, but perhaps to also steady himself. He was not going to lose her. 'This is not about obligation, it's not about passion, although we have quite a lot of that, too. This is about love.

'I have fallen thoroughly in love with you, Julia. You have brought me peace for the first time in my life. I need you and I want you and, at last, I have something to offer you in return. I've got a desk at the bank now, a home that's not my brother's, a fortune for you to spend.' He laughed a little at that. 'I even have a title.' Paine pulled out the third item from the inner pocket of his jacket. He gave Julia the folded piece of paper. 'Read it, it's a letter from the king.'

Julia scanned it. 'Oh my, Paine, you're to be knighted. Sir Paine Ramsden.' She read further. 'For invaluable service to the crown. Whatever did you do?'

'The crown needed to be aware of Oswalt's treachery against members of the peerage. There were many people, his Majesty included, who were glad to have certain issues, as it were, resolved. You'll be Lady Julia Ramsden. I am worthy of you now.'

Julia's eyes watered. Damn it. He hadn't meant to make her cry. She was supposed to jump with joy, preferably right into his arms.

'You were always worthy of me, Paine,' she whispered. 'When I started this, I was looking for the most dishonourable man in London. I never thought he'd turn out to be the most honourable.' She bit her lip and smiled through her tears. 'I don't suppose you have a ring in those pockets, do you? You seem to have everything else.'

Paine laughed. 'I most certainly do.' He pulled out the fourth item, a small velvet box from one of London's finest jewellers. He went swiftly down on one knee and flipped open the box lid. 'Marry me, Julia.'

Julia feigned contemplation, tapping a finger against her chin. 'If I do, will I get to see what's behind the door?'

'Vixen!' Paine slipped the ring on her finger, a brilliant emerald surrounded by a band of tiny diamonds. 'It's from my own collection. I had it set especially for you.' Paine rose and reached for the door.

Julia laughed when she saw the room. 'You've been busy.'

Paine swept her up into his arms and carried her to the low bed. It had been restored, along with the cabinet. It would take time to fix this room up to his expectations, but he couldn't imagine him and Julia sleeping in any other bed. The need to have her was suddenly swift and urgent as it coursed through him.

She read his need and reached her arms up to draw him down to her, kissing him deeply. 'Did you bring a sheath?' Julia murmured, lifting against him.

'I brought something better,' Paine said next to her ear, nibbling and sucking at her earlobe.

'What could be better?' Julia said, on the brink of losing all reasoning.

'A special licence.'

She laughed softly, her breath warm against his neck. She shifted her body to accommodate him, taking him between her thighs. 'You once said I was like the Sleeping Beauty—come awaken me with love's first kiss.'

He didn't have to be asked twice. Julia Prentiss was his happy ever after.

# *Epilogue*

Champagne flowed freely in sparkling crystal glasses at the Ramsden wedding breakfast a month later. Surrounded by the Ramsden clan, Julia thought the wait had been worth it. True, Paine had a licence that could have enabled them to marry sooner, but Aunt Lily had argued again on the platform of good form. In the end the argument had made sense. After working so hard to erase the questions of Paine's past, it made little sense to scotch those efforts with a rushed wedding and all the speculation that would ensue.

Beside her at the head table, Paine drank yet another toast to their happiness, one hand surreptitiously under the table on her leg. Watching him recite his vows at St George's this morning, one would never have guessed that a mere three months ago he'd been a confirmed bachelor with no thoughts towards being redeemed. Today, he was a man resolutely in love with his wife.

Julia knew the look on his face well because it was

the same reflection she saw in the mirror when she looked at her own. She had never guessed such happiness was possible. It seemed a far cry from the darkness of Oswalt's proposal.

The only minor crimp in her bliss was that her aunt and uncle were not here to share it with her. Although Paine had taken charge of her uncle's finances and seen the family through the financial aspect of their crisis, no amount of money could compensate them for the loss of Gray. While there was still no confirmation of a body, the Lockharts had given up hope that Gray was still alive at this late date and had retreated to the country to mourn in private.

Still, looking around her, Julia felt she had a new family now in Aunt Lily, Peyton and Crispin, men who Gray would have liked immensely as brothers-in-law.

They were talking with Lily and Beth when Crispin tapped Paine on the shoulder. 'Excuse me, but there's someone at the door. I need you and Julia to come with me.'

Paine and Julia followed Crispin to the door where Peyton already stood waiting. 'Julia, this man says he knows you.' Peyton stepped aside to reveal the late-come guest.

He was dressed in worn clothes hardly befitting the heir of a viscount, but Julia recognised him immediately. A hand flew to her mouth and she clutched Paine's arm to steady herself, hardly daring to believe the sight before her.

'Gray! You're alive. How?' The shock of seeing

him was so overwhelming she couldn't organise her thoughts into any coherent pattern.

Paine laughed softly at her surprise and urged her forwards. 'Go to him, Julia. See for yourself that he's not an apparition.'

Julia needed no further prodding. She flung herself into Gray's arms. 'I can't believe you're safe after all this time.' She stepped back to look at him and then hugged him again, unable to decide if she wanted to hug him or look at him, to see that he was all right.

'You're here, you're really here. You're not dead!'

Gray hugged her tightly. 'I am really alive, although it was close. Thanks to Ramsden and Dursley here, I have returned home.'

'Oh my goodness, your parents, your brothers are going to be so thrilled. You don't know what this will mean to them!' Julia's happiness over seeing Gray ebbed a bit and she lowered her voice. 'They aren't here, you know. They're in the country, mourning you.'

The look on Gray's face was grim, too. 'I rather suspect they will mourn me when I get done with them. I can't believe what they attempted to force you into, my dear cousin.'

Julia cast a glance back at Paine. 'It's all in the past, Gray, and it's brought me this wonderful man. He's taken care of me and the family.' She motioned to Paine. 'Paine, come and meet my cousin, and, Cousin Gray, meet my husband. Then we must talk. You must have so much to tell.' She was still giddy with the surprise of seeing him.

'There is, but I have it on good authority that the most exciting tale to tell is yours and I want to hear all of it. I came to celebrate with you the moment I stepped foot in London. My story can wait.'

'All tales can wait until you've had a chance to change. Come with me,' Peyton offered, 'I am sure there's some clothing upstairs that you can make do with.'

Peyton hurried Gray off to clean up, leaving Julia and Paine alone in the entry. 'Did you do this, Paine?' Julia inquired, studying her new husband thoughtfully.

Paine had the good grace to look sheepish. 'I have some connections in the shipping industry and I put them to work. I was suspicious that nothing had turned up, especially since the coast of Spain is notorious for bodies washing ashore. Sure enough, someone recalled a man of Gray's description when he passed through a remote sea village. I sent Flaherty after him.'

'It's the best wedding gift ever. I could not have asked for more,' Julia said, tears in her eyes. 'I was going to wait, Paine, but I have a gift for you, too.'

Paine protested. 'I have everything I want, Julia.' He moved to pull her into his arms.

Julia twined her arms around his neck and pulled him close to whisper in his ear.

'I stand corrected,' Paine said, his voice trembling slightly. 'I only *thought* I had everything I wanted. When, my dear, do you think the gift will arrive?'

'Around February, in time for Valentine's Day,' Julia said softly.

'And to think this all started because you needed to

be ruined and I needed to be redeemed. I think this has ended rather well.'

'Ended?' Julia laughed up at him. 'This is only the beginning. Happy ever after is only for fairy tales.'

\* \* \* \* \*

**THOROUGHBRED LEGACY**
*The stakes are high when it comes to love,
horse racing, family secrets
and broken promises.*

*A new exciting Harlequin continuity
series coming soon!
Led by* New York Times
*bestselling author Elizabeth Bevarly*
*FLIRTING WITH TROUBLE*

*Here's a preview!*

THE DOOR CLOSED behind them, throwing them into darkness and leaving them utterly alone. And the next thing Daniel knew, he heard himself saying, "Marnie, I'm sorry about the way things turned out in Del Mar."

She said nothing at first, only strode across the room and stared out the window beside him. Although he couldn't see her well in the darkness—he still hadn't switched on a light...but then, neither had she—he imagined her expression was a little preoccupied, a little anxious, a little confused.

Finally, very softly, she said, "Are you?"

He nodded, then, worried she wouldn't be able to see the gesture, added, "Yeah. I am. I should have said goodbye to you."

"Yes, you should have."

Actually, he thought, there were a lot of things he should have done in Del Mar. He'd had *a lot* riding on the Pacific Classic, and even more on his entry, Little Joe, but after meeting Marnie, the Pacific Classic had been the last thing on Daniel's mind. His loss at Del Mar had pretty much ended his career before it had even begun, and he'd had to start all over again, rebuilding from nothing.

He simply had not then and did not now have room in his life for a woman as potent as Marnie Roberts. He was a horseman first and foremost. From the time he was a schoolboy, he'd known what he wanted to do with his life—be the best possible trainer he could be.

He had to make sure Marnie understood—and he understood, too—why things had ended the way they had eight years ago. He just wished he could find the words to do that. Hell, he wished he could find the *thoughts* to do that.

"You made me forget things, Marnie, things that I really needed to remember. And that scared the hell out of me. Little Joe should have won the Classic. He was by far the best horse entered in that race. But I didn't give him the attention he needed and deserved that week, because all I could think about was you. Hell, when I woke up that morning all I wanted to do was lie there and look at you, and then wake you up and make love to you again. If I hadn't left when I did—the way I did—I might still be lying there in that bed with you, thinking about nothing else."

"And would that be so terrible?" she asked.

"Of course not," he told her. "But that wasn't why I was in Del Mar," he repeated. "I was in Del Mar to win a race. That was my job. And my work was the most important thing to me."

She said nothing for a moment, only studied his face in the darkness as if looking for the answer to a very important question. Finally she asked, "And what's the most important thing to you now, Daniel?"

Wasn't the answer to that obvious? "My work," he answered automatically.

She nodded slowly. "Of course," she said softly. "That is, after all, what you do best."

Her comment, too, puzzled him. She made it sound as if being good at what he did was a bad thing.

She bit her lip thoughtfully, her eyes fixed on his, glimmering in the scant moonlight that was filtering through the window. And damned if Daniel didn't find himself wanting to pull her into his arms and kiss her. But as much as it might have felt as if no time had passed since Del Mar, there were eight years between now and then. And eight years was a long time in the best of circumstances. For Daniel and Marnie, it was virtually a lifetime.

So Daniel turned and started for the door, then halted. He couldn't just walk away and leave things as they were, unsettled. He'd done that eight years ago and regretted it.

"It *was* good to see you again, Marnie," he said softly. And since he was being honest, he added, "I hope we see each other again."

She didn't say anything in response, only stood silhouetted against the window with her arms wrapped around her in a way that made him wonder whether she was doing it because she was cold, or if she just needed something—someone—to hold on to. In either case, Daniel understood. There was an emptiness clinging to him that he suspected would be there for a long time.

* * * * *


# THOROUGHBRED LEGACY
*coming soon wherever books are sold!*

*Thoroughbred Legacy*

## Launching in June 2008

### A dramatic new 12-book continuity that embodies the American Dream.

Meet the Prestons, owners of Quest Stables, a successful horse-racing and breeding empire. But the lives, loves and reputations of this hardworking family are put at risk when a breeding scandal unfolds.

*Flirting with Trouble*

*by New York Times bestselling author*

# ELIZABETH BEVARLY

Eight years ago, publicist Marnie Roberts spent seven days of bliss with Australian horse trainer Daniel Whittleson. But just as quickly, he disappeared. Now Marnie is heading to Australia to finally confront the man she's never been able to forget.

*The stakes are high when it comes to love, horse racing, family secrets and broken promises.*

*A new exciting Harlequin continuity series coming soon!*

# REQUEST YOUR
# FREE BOOKS!

### Harlequin® Historical
### Historical Romantic Adventure!

™

## 2 FREE NOVELS PLUS 2 FREE GIFTS!

**YES!** Please send me 2 FREE Harlequin® Historical novels and my 2 FREE gifts (gifts are worth about $10). After receiving them, if I don't wish to receive any more books, I can return the shipping statement marked "cancel". If I don't cancel, I will receive 6 brand-new novels every month and be billed just $4.94 per book in the U.S. or $5.49 per book in Canada, plus 25¢ shipping and handling per book and applicable taxes, if any*. That's a savings of 20% off the cover price! I understand that accepting the 2 free books and gifts places me under no obligation to buy anything. I can always return a shipment and cancel at any time. Even if I never buy another book, the two free books and gifts are mine to keep forever.

246 HDN ERUM   349 HDN ERUA

| | |
|---|---|
| Name | (PLEASE PRINT) |

| | |
|---|---|
| Address | Apt. # |

| | | |
|---|---|---|
| City | State/Prov. | Zip/Postal Code |

Signature (if under 18, a parent or guardian must sign)

### Mail to the **Harlequin Reader Service**:
**IN U.S.A.:** P.O. Box 1867, Buffalo, NY 14240-1867
**IN CANADA:** P.O. Box 609, Fort Erie, Ontario L2A 5X3

Not valid to current subscribers of Harlequin Historical books.

**Want to try two free books from another line?**
**Call 1-800-873-8635 or visit www.morefreebooks.com.**

\* Terms and prices subject to change without notice. N.Y. residents add applicable sales tax. Canadian residents will be charged applicable provincial taxes and GST. This offer is limited to one order per household. All orders subject to approval. Credit or debit balances in a customer's account(s) may be offset by any other outstanding balance owed by or to the customer. Please allow 4 to 6 weeks for delivery. Offer available while quantities last.

**Your Privacy:** Harlequin Books is committed to protecting your privacy. Our Privacy Policy is available online at www.eHarlequin.com or upon request from the Reader Service. From time to time we make our lists of customers available to reputable third parties who may have a product or service of interest to you. If you would prefer we not share your name and address, please check here. ☐

HH08

### Cole's Red-Hot Pursuit

Cole Westmoreland is a man who gets what he
wants. And he wants independent and sultry
Patrina Forman! She resists him—until a Montana
blizzard traps them together. For three delicious
nights, Cole indulges Patrina with his brand of
seduction. When the sun comes out, Cole and
Patrina are left to wonder—will this be the end of
the passion that storms between them?

## Look for

# COLE'S RED-HOT PURSUIT

### by *USA TODAY* bestselling author

# BRENDA JACKSON

*Available in June 2008 wherever you buy books.*

**Always Powerful, Passionate and Provocative.**

## Romantic
# SUSPENSE

**Sparked by Danger,
Fueled by Passion.**

Seduction Summer:
Seduction in the sand...and a killer on the beach.

*Silhouette Romantic Suspense invites you to the hottest
summer yet with three connected stories from some
of our steamiest storytellers! Get ready for...*

### *Killer Temptation*
#### by **Nina Bruhns**;
a millionaire this tempting is worth a little danger.

### *Killer Passion*
#### by **Sheri WhiteFeather**;
an FBI profiler's forbidden passion incites a
killer's rage,

and

### *Killer Affair*
#### by **Cindy Dees**;
this affair with a mystery man is to die for.

### Look for

KILLER TEMPTATION by Nina Bruhns in June 2008
KILLER PASSION by Sheri WhiteFeather in July 2008
and
KILLER AFFAIR by Cindy Dees in August 2008.

**Available wherever you buy books!**

Visit Silhouette Books at www.eHarlequin.com          SRS27586

# COMING NEXT MONTH FROM

# HARLEQUIN®
# HISTORICAL

- **THE LAST RAKE IN LONDON**
  by **Nicola Cornick**
  **(Edwardian)**
  Dangerous Jack Kestrel was the most sinfully sensual rogue she'd
  ever met, and the wicked glint in his eyes promised he'd take care of
  satisfying Sally's every need....
  *Watch as the last rake in London meets his match!*

- **AN IMPETUOUS ABDUCTION**
  by **Patricia Frances Rowell**
  **(Regency)**
  Persephone had stumbled into danger, and the only way to protect her
  was to abduct her! But what would Leo's beautiful prisoner do when he
  revealed his true identity?
  *Don't miss Patricia Frances Rowell's unique blend of passion spiced
  with danger!*

- **KIDNAPPED BY THE COWBOY**
  by **Pam Crooks**
  **(Western)**
  TJ Grier was determined to clear his name, even if his actions might
  cost him the woman he loved!
  *Fall in love with Pam Crooks's honorable cowboy!*

- **INNOCENCE UNVEILED**
  by **Blythe Gifford**
  **(Medieval)**
  With her flaming red hair, Katrine knew no man would be tempted
  by her. But Renard, a man of secrets, intended to break through her
  defenses....
  *Innocence and passion are an intoxicating mix in this emotional
  medieval tale.*